Sherlock Holmes and John Watson:

The Day They Met

(50 New Ways the World's Most Legendary Partnership Might Have Begun)

By

Wendy C. Fries

Paperback ISBN 978-1-78092-720-6
ePub ISBN 978-1-78092-721-3
PDF ISBN 978-1-78092-722-0

Published in the UK by MX Publishing
335 Princess Park Manor, Royal Drive,
London, N11 3GX
www.mxpublishing.co.uk Cover design by www.staunch.com

Because of Arthur Conan Doyle

For Amity…
…Who inspired this book by asking,
"Well, how else *could* they have met?"

For Bob, Bobby, Diane, and Tony;
and Joseph Merrick
…Who always inspire *me*

And for Isabelle and Verity
…Who I owe, big time

Table of Contents

Preface

This is a work of fiction about a work of fiction.

After devouring Arthur Conan Doyle's nineteenth-century Sherlock Holmes stories, after watching every series of the BBC's twenty-first century *Sherlock,* after going giddy for Basil Rathbone's war-time Holmes, and Robert Stephens' melancholy turn as great detective, I formed a conceit:

There is no time and no place in which John Watson and Sherlock Holmes would not have met. If it hadn't been St. Bartholomew's Hospital in the nineteenth century, it would have been Russell Square in the twenty-first. If not there, then Dartmoor in 2009, Kabul in 1879, or a Wandsworth jail in 2012.

In a world of 7,276,066,802, I thought that the chances of John Watson meeting Sherlock Holmes weren't 1 in seven-some odd billion, they were exactly 1 in 1. Fate would see to that.

Then my friend Amity Who said, "Yes, but can you give me a for instance? Tell me of another way they could have met."

Far more than fifty stories later I'm still writing about *The Day They Met.* I think maybe I always will.

Shag

Montague Street, London — 1881

Sherlock Holmes will blame it on the shag.

He smokes best when he smokes much. Which is to say that when there's a knotty problem to solve and an ounce of tobacco in the pouch, Sherlock Holmes relishes few things more than thinking deep thoughts and turning the air smoke-blue.

The current knotty problem, however, was the profound lack of knotty problems. There was not one case calling for his attention, not one errant clue popping up to complete an old puzzle, there wasn't a difficulty to tackle, a plea to pacify, not an obstacle, a bother, a nuisance, there was not so much as a suspicious hiccough.

And it was driving Holmes batty.

Not only was there nothing to occupy the detective's ever-whirring mind, but by the time Holmes reached the end of his boredom tether, he'd also reached the end of his shag.

This would not do.

Drumming fingers restlessly, gaze darting around a sitting room that was small, crowded, and even by his own standards, utterly absurd—really, why stack the post in a little wooden box, who could possibly remember it *there?* He had to talk to Mr. Wallace about his tidying again—Sherlock Holmes said those few words aloud, as if in summation to a diatribe both detailed and decisive.

"This will not do."

Holmes upended his tobacco pouch. He shook his tobacco pouch. A shred of tobacco drifted to his lap. "This will not for one minute *do.* "

Sherlock Holmes placed the tobacco leaf onto his tongue and with a firm nod stood up. And with a groan sat right down. He stood again. And again sat unceremoniously down.

Frowning into air neither smoky nor blue, Holmes felt a sudden misplaced resentment for his physician.

Yes Dr. Kitmer was competent, yes he was patient with Holmes' sometimes-endless questions—quite helpful on the congealing properties of blood and the preservative attributes of hundred-year-old egg albumen—yet he was also deaf in one ear, partially blind in an eye, and had foolishly insisted that Holmes stay off his feet.

The reason for *that* was the state of Holmes' feet.

And that state was appalling.

And currently so was Sherlock Holmes.

"Mr. Wallace!"

Holmes is generally a good tenant. Though the man has been known to burn an astonishing array of fetid things, things whose odour not only rises, but sinks, and seems also to spread side-to-side, Aloysius Wallace has found that the man pays his rent on time *and* is tall enough to hang the next in his ever-expanding series of tintypes of favourite actresses.

But Mr. Aloysius Wallace had had it up to the proverbial here with this morning's shouting. He'd twice climbed the two flights to Mr. Holmes' rooms, only to find both times that his tenant needed little more than a person at whom to vent his spleen. Holmes might be a fine tenant, but he was a terrible convalescent.

Which meant Aloysius Wallace had decamped three hours ago to the Lyceum, to moon over his latest crush, Miss Violet, and as such did not hear his tenant's shout.

So Sherlock Holmes decided that to forestall stark raving madness *and* to get a good ounce of decent shag, there were only two things left to him.

Deduction.

And destruction.

*

Dr. John Watson rarely enjoys London's charms. There are dozens of museums, many times that many galleries, there are theatres, parks, and city vistas, and yet the good doctor has hardly made time for any of these.

With a polished walking stick, a bowl of good shag, and a jaunty step, John Watson was about to rectify this unforgivable omission.

He increased his pace. The British Museum was in sight.

*

It took Holmes less than a minute to formulate his plan: He'd get someone in the park across the road to fetch him a bit of Grosvenor or Cavendish. However, perched precariously in his sitting room window and ten minutes after putting that plan into play, Holmes was still emphatically without his shag.

Mostly that was because no matter how careful he was in choosing his potential rescuers, each one at whom he lobbed his attention-seeking missiles—a broken telescope, a dog collar, the ferrule of an umbrella, a fireplace bellows, two candle stubs, eighteen buttons joined together on a pipe cleaner, and a sugar bowl—simply ignored them as they promenaded about the park or toward the infernal museum.

In a fit of uncharacteristic frustration, Holmes snatched up the only thing left within reach—a glass decanter of brandy. He never would know if he'd truly have thrown the weighty thing because it was right then he overbalanced entirely, shouted, dropped the decanter to the pavement below.

And fell off the window ledge.

John Watson would later say he heard the shout before the twin crashes, which Holmes would tell him was impossible, which Watson would argue was perfectly possible if Holmes shouted *before* he dropped the decanter *or* fell, and though they'd never agree on the order of those three things, the end result was that John Watson looked up in time to see a shouting man disappear from view, just before a crystal decanter containing a good three fingers of fine brandy shattered at his feet.

*

"Good god man are you all right!"

Watson was through the flat's door and in the middle of a tiny, cluttered, sitting room before he realised his impropriety. And then ignored it as he bustled toward a man supine beneath an open window.

Sherlock Holmes lifted his head from the floor. "Ah, hello!"

Holmes reached for the stranger's reaching hands, rose to his knees. Shortly he'd knee-walked to the nearest chair. Once seated he reached out. "Very kind, very kind. Sherlock, Sherlock Holmes."

"Dr. John Watson."

Holmes shook his Samaritan's hand, squinted at a smudged cuff, then sniffed the general environment. "Arcadia long-cut?"

Instead of answering or sitting in the chair to which Holmes gestured, Watson nodded at bandages on big, bare feet. "What happened?"

Holmes wiggled aching toes. "I walked across hot coals. Poorly."

Holmes waited for the inevitable, *What sane person would do that?* But this oft-heard mockery did not come. What came instead was a pouch of Arcadia long-cut shag. Holmes caught it mid-air.

"So you can tell what sort of tobacco I favour by its ash?" Watson brushed the lingering soot from his cuff. "That's impressive."

Holmes grinned at the praise, rolled a pair of cigarettes. "Can't you?"

Again, instead of saying the expected, Watson said something else, "Could you do that for any tobacco?" The good doctor accepted a cigarette. Holmes accepted the offer of a light.

"What an interesting question."

Two weeks. That was how long Dr. Kitmer had told him to stay off his scorched feet. Two now potentially-interesting weeks.

"Dr. Watson?"

John Watson inhaled, peered into a shadow-box of beetles, "Yes, Mr. Holmes?"

"I see that you're between employments at the moment, live alone, and are, if possible, more bored than even I. Would

11

you mind picking up a few more pouches of tobacco to tide me over during my convalescence?" The great detective was already toying with titles for his monograph. *The Deduction of Ash.* No, no, not informative enough. *Tobacco, Ash, and the Art of—* "What?"

"I said," said Watson, "how many pouches would you like?"

Sherlock Holmes grinned. Yes, the next two weeks had a great deal of potential. "One hundred and forty should be about enough. How would you like to join me in a little experiment?"

Dr. John Watson would get to the British Museum eventually. As a matter of fact he'd visit exactly six weeks from this day. He'd be dragging Holmes to safety behind a man-sized Ming vase, just as the certainly-fatal stroke of an assassin's blade fell, but at least he'd be able to say he'd finally been.

SH

Violin Concerto in Black

Southwark Bridge Pedestrian Tunnel, London — 2007

London's lights went out for one minute and twelve seconds.

From Tower Bridge to Brixton, the Heath to Hammersmith, the only illumination anywhere came from cars in motion.

For John Watson those seventy-two seconds were some of the longest of his life.

Before being invalided home two months previous, John had served as a trauma surgeon in three London boroughs, then on Afghan battlefields. He has seen close-up how people hurt people, how quick it can happen, how deep the damage.

So when the city went black at ten minutes after midnight on a winter Monday, John stopped right where he was on the riverside path and started breathing deep and fast, on a tenterhook and listening for screams.

What John Watson got was a lullaby.

The high, high song of a plaintive violin, notes soaring, then going deep and low and long, and right away John knew he knew the tune, but the title wouldn't come to him.

So he went to it. Moving before he thought to do it, he made his way by the glow of far-away boroughs, distant light that left London orange-black at its edges, a dark city ringed in fire.

Ten seconds after the lights went out John was there, in the pitch-black pedestrian tunnel beneath Southwark Bridge, listening, listening to…ah, he knew now, it was Brahms' lullaby.

Twenty seconds after it went dark, John felt someone push against him and his hands went to fists again, but it was just someone making room for someone else who'd come quick to the sweet sounds of the unseen Pied Piper.

Forty seconds passed, then fifty, and later, when John learned the blackout lasted only seventy-two seconds, he'd say again and again, "No it didn't. It was five minutes, it was at *least* five minutes."

Yet it was only one minute and twelve seconds of chin resting on chest, of hands unfurled, and an unexpected peace instead of the feared war. When the lights came back on John only knew because spontaneous cheers opened his eyes.

He squinted against what already seemed alien-bright lights, and then, grinning, he cheered like everyone else.

The joy morphed quickly from celebration, to applause for the violinist.

Who wasn't there.

An empty case lay on the ground, a violin bow dropped willy-nilly across it, and that seemed enough for the giddy crowd. Most rained coins or notes into the case's red-silk interior and simply went on their way.

John frowned. Didn't anyone wonder about the person who'd made the music? Didn't anyone care if they were okay?

John started breathing deep and fast again, and in the sudden quiet passage, with its pretty friezes of old river frost fairs, John wondered which way to go, how he could find someone he never saw, how he could help someone who wasn't there.

In the end John did the only thing he could: He guarded that case and that bow because sure, he didn't know a concerto from a sonata, but he knew a violinist needed bow and case and so *those* things he would protect.

John Watson stayed because he wanted to give for what he'd so recently got, he wanted to help. But eventually John would realise something else: He stayed there because, over the course of one minute and twelve seconds, he'd started to fall in love, head over heels for the sweetness that could be coaxed from a small hollow box with strings and pegs and a horsehair bow.

*

Sherlock Holmes has his demons.

He grows bored and restive, lonely and hungry for purpose. Unlike most, Sherlock chases back his demons by solving puzzles, by looking in dark places for the who, what, why, and when of a thing, and most especially the *how*.

So Sherlock was patient that night, whiling away the early evening at a bright and busy riverside pub, waiting for an informant who promised to give him a suspect's where, in exchange for understanding the why.

Except the informant never showed. No matter how patient Sherlock was, no matter how slowly he drank his pint or how much he fiddled with the handle on his violin case—"I'll sit by the window, with a violin"—the man didn't show.

Yes indeed, Sherlock Holmes has many demons, and too many of them are partial to petulant over-reaction. These darker of Sherlock's devils manifest as rage focused inward, as chaotic disregard for the sanctity of his own body. So it was even odds that as his frustration mounted Sherlock would express it in ways both self-indulgent and self-damaging.

Except...

Except eventually even a drama queen grows tired of the same old performance. So despite a part of him that wanted to leave that pub and indulge in the cathartic theatrics of tilting at windmills, this time Sherlock decided to battle his demons with something in the key of G.

He knew Southwark Bridge was near, he'd a dozen times a dozen been through its *No buskers allowed* tunnel, he'd even once looked at the great stone slabs celebrating long-gone winter festivals, but this time Sherlock did something he'd never done before: He went there to play his violin, and instead of playing for his demons, this time he played for himself.

Except the moment Sherlock tucked the instrument under his chin, the lights went out.

Well, so what? Sherlock wasn't six-years-old any more, he didn't need to stick his tongue out and stare at the fingerboard, he could play perfectly fine in the pitch black, and so that's exactly what he did.

It was better than he'd thought it would be, it was, it was...a cleaner battle than those he'd fought before. In the dark he could hear-feel-almost-see people moving, coming as if called, and it was a new sensation that, speaking to strangers and not *driving them away.*

It was gorgeous.

In the dark, time moved treacle-slow, each note lingered, the song went on forever. Then in the dark someone touched him. Whispered against his ear. And Sherlock dropped his bow and followed that voice just seconds before the lights came back on.

Now, twenty minutes later, Sherlock was giddy and full with even more gorgeous, only this time it was data, clues, case-closing *intel,* if you want to be a drama queen. Now he could show how a woman no one suspected not only could, but *did,* take a two million pound manuscript right from under a dozen noses, *and* he could lead the police to where that woman was.

So caught up in the pleasure of it all, in closing a case no one thought possible to close, Sherlock didn't even realise he was heading back to the tunnel until he was there, and then so was a man, just one lone man, sitting on the ground next to Sherlock's things, the bow tucked neat in the case, the still-open case tucked safe underneath the man's hand.

And chin to chest the man was sound asleep.

Sherlock Holmes tilted his head, studied what he saw and, flick-flick-flick, he saw so many things: A healer and a helper, a soldier and a man hungry for purpose, he saw in front of him a man with demons.

Sherlock sat down on the other side of the violin case. He drew out his bow, tucked the violin—which he'd clutched close even as he ran with the informant in the dark—beneath his chin, and Sherlock started to play.

Though he woke with a start, for a long second John Watson didn't move. Then cold adrenaline dissipated, hard muscles went soft, and he lifted his head and for quite awhile he watched the violinist play.

17

It was late on a winter Monday when the lights went out in London, and on winter days years later John would still bring it up, marveling that no one was hurt that night.

"Everything grows and changes John, from bees to biomes. Maybe people are changing, too."

A soldier, a doctor, a man who has seen too much, John Watson will never be sure about that. He *is* sure that some things don't change. Centuries-old melodies. Friendships founded on shared purpose.

So on the nights when John wonders about humankind, one human is kind and plays songs for him on an old violin. Sherlock plays lullabies mostly, with the occasional waltz, concerto, or sonata.

John knows the difference now.

SH

The Diogenes Diversion

The Diogenes Club Stranger's Room — 1880

"There's another child at home. An infant."

"Ah yes, the rattle. That would make four charges to care for, no wonder she drinks so much tea."

"Coffee, I think."

Sherlock Holmes' gaze darted over the woman, rested briefly on her shoes. "I see. Unusual she would hide the habit."

"Some doctors say it's bad for you," replied Mycroft Holmes.

The brothers watched the high-strung nanny chase her small brood toward the Duke of York steps, each man easily imagining the quick, thick brews she surreptitiously took between the children's lessons, always leaning over the hot cup in her hurry, often spilling a bit of coffee on, and darkly staining, her old boots.

"The same doctors who warn against snuff and cocaine, I suppose?"

"Indeed."

The brothers call it the Diogenes Diversion, this little game. It has the comfort of habit, and has become their way of saying hello after an absence.

Today Sherlock began by taking a seat at a Stranger's Room window and remarking on passersby a half-dozen feet distant, "A number of military men on Pall Mall today."

Mycroft took a pinch of snuff. "I'm not sure three is 'a number of' but yes."

"You and your over-fondness for figures. What you observe in the reflection of that mirror isn't all that's at this window."

Mycroft Holmes did not reply. Instead he grunted himself from his fire-side armchair, settled with a sigh into a chair at the window. The two geniuses then proceeded to divert one another.

"Near the corner, a cabbie."

"The pale brow?"

"Of course. And the gentleman passing our window? Watchmaker. You can always tell by the pinching grasp."

"And the fact that this one recently repaired your watch?"

Mycroft chuckled. "Indeed. More sherry?"

Sherlock nodded. At Mycroft's glance a dark-liveried man stepped away from the wall, filled small glasses. "Thank you, Bertram."

"What would you say about this brave chap just to the left, the one who didn't so much as flinch when that hansom veered?"

Mycroft glanced up from his sherry. "The one with the old shoulder wound?"

"Just so."

Mycroft leaned toward the window. "I would say he needs to sharpen his straight razor."

"You think he shaves himself? Ah, yes, a bit of soap along the jaw. Perhaps I should borrow your glasses. That straight spine makes him seem rather intriguingly formidable, though the good doctor's come on hard times."

"Indeed."

Each man observed the precisely repaired tear in the leg of the doctor's trousers, perfect corner stitches applied with a suture needle and placed with a physician's careful hand.

Mycroft Holmes went quiet for several seconds. Sherlock glanced at him. "What's distracting you?"

"The doctor," said Mycroft truthfully, and then Mycroft lied. "I'm thinking First Lancashire Fusiliers, judging by the ammunition boots."

Sherlock frowned. "Certainly not. Fifth Northumberland. Those boots are brown."

"Burnished black."

"Mycroft."

"There's one way to settle this."

"Indeed."

Sherlock began to open the window. His brother hissed. "Good heavens you can't *call out,* Sherlock. The other members will hear."

Though most believed the Diogenes was named after Diogenes the Cynic, it was not. That loud-mouthed show-off heckled his betters, slept in a jar, and publically mocked everything he didn't like. The idea that a brace of men who craved companionable anonymity and silence would christen their refuge after such a creature boggled the mind.

No, instead, their peaceful Pall Mall haven was named after Diogenes Laërtius, a biographer about whom was known an almost blessed nothing.

"Bertram," murmured Mycroft, "If you'd be so kind."

The servant vanished, Sherlock peered out the window, interest keen. Mycroft Holmes hid his smile.

Because here's something Mycroft Holmes knows for certain: It's difficult to lie to a man who sees everything. Mycroft should know, for he sees everything.

Except it's *easy* to lie to a man who has only known you to be a liar.

Well, liar is a strong word.

Because Mycroft doesn't lie to his little brother, no. Mycroft...protects him.

From things dire when needed, but mostly from being a one, an other, an only; from being both too little and too much.

Since he was nine and his toddling brother two, Mycroft's known Sherlock was like him. He wouldn't have wished that on anyone, but neither could he wish it away. So instead Mycroft created for the two of them a way of being. He crafted rituals, systems, he fashioned a cocoon that allowed his little brother to avoid some of the slings and arrows he himself had already survived.

And somewhere along the way, somehow in creating their customs, Mycroft fashioned a few protective lies, lies told long before Sherlock could understand them as such, and so lies Sherlock came to believe as truths.

That Mycroft was lazy, was one. That he was over-fond of exactness, another. And once, when Sherlock was barely four and it seemed important he be right about something—Mycroft thinks it was about apples—Mycroft began to pretend he was a bit colour-blind.

Which was why, just now, he had lied and said a man's brown boots were black. A man Sherlock had thrice admired in as many minutes.

That brave chap…
That straight spine…
Rather intriguingly formidable…

"Ah, thank you Bertram. Please do come in, Doctor…?"

John Watson removed his hat, held out his hand, "John Watson, how do you do?"

Mycroft glanced at his brother, "Indeed, brown." Mycroft shook the doctor's hand. "I'm fine, thank you. This is my brother Sherlock, we were just enjoying a bit of sherry and wondered about your top hat. I need a new one and prefer silk plush, but my brother believes yours is beaver. We thought we'd ask. Oh my, look at the time, if you'll excuse me. Sherlock, you'll take down the name of his hat maker, yes?"

With that Mycroft Holmes glanced at Bertram, who fell into step behind him, and both men left the room.

John Watson and Sherlock Holmes blinked at one another, then laughed. Sherlock gestured to Mycroft's empty chair. "My brother is a terrible liar, Dr. Watson. Do please sit down, have some sherry. You see, what we were actually doing was wondering about your regiment and your shaving razor and your mending though that really is a rather fine hat. Where did you get it?"

John Watson accepted the small glass with another laugh. "I think I understood every third thing you just said, but thank you. As for the hat, what an interesting coincidence. I was just on my way to Mr. Jeremy's shop. In thanks for this excellent sherry I'd be happy to take you there personally."

Sherlock Holmes held out his glass, John Watson touched it with the rim of his own.

"Wonderful! Now tell me doctor, what do you notice about that dowager lady just to the right, the one with the feather-plumed hat and a history of tax fraud?"

SH

Half-Caf Cappuccino With Whip, No Sprinkles

Andromeda Cafe, Holborn, London — 2013

John Watson was busy checking the bottom of his shoe for the stupid hole he still can't find, when the first little occurrence occurred. Something moved very quickly past his peripheral vision.

John looked up. The thing was gone.

Sitting solo at his little table outside a dead-empty cafe, John went back to examining his shoe. He knew there was a hole in there somewhere because his left sock got wet when it rained. Even when it didn't rain, actually, but that was a mystery for another day. Maybe the day *after* the day he finds the hole in the bottom of—

There it was again, only this time John saw the thing that was moving fast at the edge of his vision, because this time it was moving slow.

It was a spare-built man of thirty-something, carrying a silver tray on which steamed four cups of coffee. With that much java in tow, John reflexively looked behind the man for other men. Or women. Or possibly children. In London who knew?

Having exhausted the diversion of his shoe, John kept looking at the man. This was because John was trying not to think about the dental surgery he had in two hours. The surgery for which he'd taken the afternoon off work, only why he did that he didn't know because the tension of waiting was half-killing him.

So John diverted himself by watching the man settle alone at the table next to his. The man then proceeded to be exceedingly diverting.

*

Sherlock Holmes blinked wide-eyed at his second batch of coffees. After a moment he removed them from the silver tray, lining each on the table one beside the other. He did this so quickly his hand blurred. After a fussy few moments tidying his little coffee contingent, Sherlock dropped a fat, messy folder onto the table in front of him. He blinked quickly at bits of A4 sticking out, then poked them back in with a twitchy finger. He nodded, pulled a crumpled, logo-emblazoned napkin out of his pocket, and smoothed it on top of the folder. Plucking a pen from behind his ear Sherlock Holmes proceeded to take his first sip of coffee.

At that initial swallow he closed his eyes. At the second sip he drew down his brows. The third he bowed his head over the coffee and deeply inhaled the steam. At the fourth he jumped a few inches when a voice piped up next to him.

"You must really like coffee."

Sherlock blinked at the smiling man at the table beside his. The man was strongly-built, shorter than he, and by his slightly swollen thumb and the twitch of his left eye it was clear he was also a doctor, had a toothache, and had spent the morning giving booster jabs to unhappy children.

"IT'S FOR AN EXPERIMENT."

John Watson's eyes flew wide. Though the man at the next table over was not quite one body length away, he shouted as if he was on the other side of a cricket pitch.

26

"I'M FINDING THIS EXPERIMENT MUCH EASIER THAN SMOKING ONE HUNDRED AND FORTY TYPES OF TOBACCO."

"What?"

Sherlock shook his head so fast John was pretty sure he heard the man's spine subluxate.

"IT'S FOR FUTURE CASES ACTUALLY. YOU'D BE SURPRISED HOW OFTEN YOU FIND A DISCARDED CUP OF COFFEE AT A CRIME SCENE."

John and Sherlock blinked at one another. Sherlock got an idea.

"I HAVE AN IDEA." Sherlock picked up a still-steaming paper cup. "I THINK I'M A LITTLE OVER-CAFFEINATED—am I shouting?—I COULD USE SOME HELP."

John had one hour and fifty-two minutes until he had to get a root canal. It was either sit here and nervously await his doom, or help a hyper-caffeinated stranger do something concerning coffee.

"Sure."

One hour, two introductions, and six cups of coffee on John's part and four on Sherlock's later, one man was so over-caffeinated he was shouting at nearly sub-sonic volume, the other was kind of rat-arsed, sleepy, and whispering.

"Had noooo idea drinking s'much coffee could make y'drunk." John murmured, beaming at his new best friend. In reply John's new best friend vibrated so quickly he a little bit went back in time. John kept meaning to tell his new best friend that he had a foamy-milky-chocolate moustache, but John kept forgetting.

What John didn't forget was the coffee in his hand. This one was a…it was a…ah yes, it was his favourite so far: A strong, half-caf cappuccino with a whole lot of whipped cream. He'd told them no chocolate sprinkles, but they forgot and put on the chocolate sprinkles.

John realised he'd forgotten why they were doing this.

"Why are we doing this?" he whispered. "I forgot."

Sherlock's favourite so far had been the extra hot, full-fat flat white. This was chirpily served to them by Lauren, who was an English Lit major with a fondness for Shakespeare, a boyfriend who wore eyeliner, and the eye-widening ability to make six specialty coffees whilst listening to two over-caffeinated men talk about three different things.

Sherlock leant close to John. "WE'RE DOING THIS BECAUSE COFFEE PREFERENCES CAN NARROW DOWN A SUSPECT LIST QUITE QUICKLY. SO I'M LEARNING WHAT EVERY KIND OF COFFEE TASTES LIKE."

John blinked. His blinks were now so slow he appeared asleep for seconds at a time. Sherlock's blinks were so speedy John got a pleasant little breeze from the man's eyelashes.

"Yeah, but why am *I* drinking the coffee?" John asked, sipping at his seventh cup. This one was a skinny macchiato, two sugars. John frowned at it, unimpressed. Next he thought they should try the espresso con panna. At this point Sherlock had completely given over to him the selection of which coffees they'd drink next, so John kept getting ones with whipped cream.

Sherlock replied with the honesty of an inebriated man. "I WAS LONELY DON'T YOU HAVE DENTAL SURGERY IN FIVE MINUTES?"

John knew there was something there to think about but he was now partially deaf in his right ear from all the shouting, so he thought he misheard what Sherlock just said. He swung his legs over the cafe bench so he faced wrong way round and could aim his *left* ear at Sherlock. The problem with this was that once he was wrong way round John drunkenly thought to himself, *well I'm wrong way round,* and swung back and aimed his half-deaf right ear at Sherlock again.

"I SAID—"

John shook his head as his brain parsed what it had already heard. Blearily he checked his watch and shook his head in the other direction. "Kind of lonely too to be honest I'm gonna be so late you don't happen to know where Cock Lane is do you?" John closed his eyes. He fell asleep for three seconds, woke with a start. "Also, stop shouting!"

Sherlock Holmes had drunk ten cups of coffee and was now so loud he could project to the rear seats of a theatre half a mile away, so wound up he could probably hover three inches off the ground, and completely certain he could get his new best friend to the dentist on time.

Sherlock thought very hard about not shouting, then very carefully whispered, "That's just across the street from St. Bartholomew's Hospital. I live there." Sherlock narrowed his eyes owlishly. "No I don't. I do something there. Experiments I think. The hole in your shoe is in the tread near the toe."

John Watson looked at his shoe. Then at Sherlock Holmes. They shook hands for no particular reason. Seven minutes later they had run half a mile, dashed in front of eight taxis, and John Watson was passed out in a dentist's chair somewhere along Cock Lane. He proceeded to sleep through his entire root canal.

When he emerged a couple hours later Sherlock Holmes was loitering on the pavement outside.

John smiled. "You waited."

Sherlock grinned back. "I'd be lost without my...barista." Sherlock waved his coffee folder in the air, "Suggestions?"

John thought. "Hmm. Let's start with double mocha lattes. Extra hot. With whip."

SH

Blood Will Tell

Peshawar Police Station, India — 1879

"Yelling'll do you no good."

John Watson continued yelling. The Irish man in the cell across from him continued providing unwanted counsel.

"They won't listen. Never do."

John Watson did not stop yelling.

"Cause we're all as innocent as pretty little lilies here in the nick."

John Watson stopped yelling long enough to give his neighbour the side eye. The man shrugged. Watson went back to yelling.

"To be fair," said the Irishman, "they don't listen at home neither. And the food's better in a Peshawar prison than the one up my street in Frobbing, I'll tell you that much right now."

*

"He just yells a lot. I think he's trying to say he didn't do anything," said Inspector Verit Burns.

Hands clasped behind his back, Sherlock Holmes, consulting detective, temporary British diplomat in his brother Mycroft's stead, and exceptionally bored tourist in India, matched the inspector's stride across the dusty station courtyard.

"Then again that's what they all say," said Burns, "Whether they're from Indore or Islington."

Sherlock Holmes smiled politely, then reflexively checked his pocket watch. As usual this did not make the

31

fortnight ahead—or the arrival of his boat back to London—hasten along any sooner. "Don't worry inspector, we'll soon reach the bottom of your mystery."

Burns, recently of the West Hackney police force and now attached to Her Majesty's embassy in Peshawar, nodded. "Of course Mr. Holmes, grateful as always for your help these last months."

In his years dealing with cranky English nationals, many who came to India with the mistaken belief they could here be more malcontent than at home, Burns had become slightly blasé. The yelling gentleman inside the station was a case in point. Burns had given up trying to get one word of sense from the man, everything he said sounded like gibberish, or like drunk granddad Kume.

As Holmes reached for the station's door, Burns laid a hand on his arm. "You do realise this is not a murder investigation, Mr. Holmes?"

The detective looked surprised. "I'm sure you said he was found covered in blood, clutching a pair of eyeballs. I fear I presumed."

"With respect, sir, this week alone you've come by the station twice a day to see if we need you. Though we appreciated your help with that dreadful business last month, things have calmed since then and, in the absence of a complete corpse, I thought I'd bring you in on a partial, so to speak."

Burns ushered Holmes inside, then gestured in the general vicinity of cell B. "The shouting man's all we can offer, and I for one think he'll be a challenge. We haven't got a lick of sense since we brought him in, all bloody and clutching an eye in each hand, as I told you. Funny-looking things, eyes."

Burns frowned through a few thoughts, then leaned conspiratorially close and dropped his voice. "I for one think the gent's an *opium* eater."

Holmes narrowed his eyes. It was true that being his brother's temporary equivalent at the British embassy was stupefying. It was correct he'd already plundered every one of Peshawar's charms in his six weeks here. And it was exceedingly accurate to say that, at this point, Holmes would happily deduce the provenance of a stolen parakeet. So this little puzzle? It was beginning to sound quite promising.

"Right, let me talk to your mystery man."

*

The mystery man was not talking. Nor was he any longer yelling. As a matter of fact the man appeared to be sleeping the sleep of the good, the just, and the deeply drugged.

Holmes didn't wonder Burns thought the stranger under an opiate influence. The signs seemed clear enough, from flushed skin and trembling limbs, to half-lidded eyes and the thrum of a fast pulse.

Yet, kneeling beside the prisoner's prone body, Holmes knew this was not a man on morphine and so, flick-blink quick, he saw *and* he observed.

Blood...

Sherlock Holmes knows blood spatter, has seen its gruesome elegance spit across walls, hands, the faces of the guilty. This was not that, this blood was...applied. Holmes peered close. This blood appeared *scooped* and spread up the man's linen shirt, from belly to breast bone.

Flick-blink...

33

The blood was new, just over one hour old, still more red than brown. Burns had said that the man had been found wandering Peshawar's streets less than one hour previous, and as yet no crime, no victim, no bodies had been reported. This was not human blood.

Eyes...

Holmes called for the eyeballs the man had been carrying, then used his own to study them as they floated in a small, clear bottle.

Flick-blink...

Indeed, they were 'funny-looking' as Burns had said, because they, like the blood, were not human. Again Holmes employed his own eyes, this time to roll them. Surely even Burns should have noticed these were calf's eyes, and had not only been removed recently, but with care.

And then...

Over the stranger's bloody and too-large shirt and themselves untouched by the blood: an over-large waistcoat and overcoat, each once fine examples of the tailor's art and evidence of a man of decent means.

Flick-blink...

This fact was of less interest than what Holmes found in the overcoat's pocket: A half dozen newspaper clippings. These were highly informative, as was the fact that the man wore the coat and the rest despite Peshawar summer temperatures of nearly fifty degrees.

And yet...

The wearing of all of this was more than explained by the tiny cloth tags secreted into coat, waistcoat, and shirt, each bearing the name of—

"Ah, hello Watson, J.H." Politely tucking the clippings back into Watson's coat pocket, Holmes smiled. "My name is Sherlock Holmes, and I'm very glad you sent for me."

John Watson tried to answer Holmes, but his words now and for some days yet would be a garbled mix of Pashto and fever-delirious gibberish.

It didn't matter. What mattered was what Sherlock Holmes said, and these words Watson understood. "Don't worry Watson, we'll get you home."

Watson, J.H., closed his eyes, from one a tear fell slow and warm into the shell of a fever-hot ear.

*

Later Watson would say he'd decided, right after a Jezail bullet nearly took his life, that he might as well get all his bad luck done at once.

This bright fancy was why, he later told Holmes, he allowed his wounded shoulder to become infected. It was also why, after being transferred from Maiwand to Peshawar, he permitted the robbery of the truck transporting him from the train station to hospital.

Then, not quite content with such a sterling string of misfortunes, Dr. Watson, J.H., who was ill with as-yet undiagnosed enteric fever, let himself become separated from the orderly caring for him.

Because Watson had no clue what came after all of this, Holmes deduced the rest. This he did after they'd settled into 221B Baker Street's homey comforts, sharing his thoughts in that rapid-fire way he had, with words that made it all sound positively self-evident.

Words like 'wandered pain-blind in Peshawar until you saw a British flag in an English butcher's shop window. The proprietor took you in, cared for you and, once the delirium of fever took your reason, he no doubt saved your life.'

In return, during those moments when he was well, Watson boosted the butcher's livelihood, his surgeon's expertise suiting not only the medical career for which he'd trained, but apparently also that of apprentice butcher.

"Both your care with cutting out those calf eyes and your lack of squeamishness with the blood—and yet your hesitancy to get the gore on your other clothes—spoke of a man with a career slightly more elevated than that of meat seller, perhaps doctor. Your clothing also made clear another career, as it's only military men who label their attire with a capitalised surname, then initials.

"So, military doctor. That you came from London was obvious by the tailor's labels in your clothes. Oh, and it was a stroke of genius to wear them all once you, in a moment of lucidity, put your plan into play. Though they were ill-fitting due to illness, that clearly marked them as yours.

"And then there was the little matter of me." Here Holmes paused to light a pipe.

"Those newspaper clippings in your pocket. Each contained light-hearted news on one side, but all were folded in the other direction, to protect the information there." Holmes opened a creased clipping at random, its headline clear despite a smudge of blood:

Murder & Mayhem In Peshawar: London Detective
Sherlock Holmes Solves Terrible Mystery of Missing
British Diplomats

"And here's where we explain why you covered yourself in so much gore."

Holmes tapped out the ash from his pipe, refilled it slowly, his motions not at *all* designed to magnify the drama of the moment.

"Journalists are forever making melodrama out of my simple science, and though I may have mentioned blood in some fashion during my newspaper interviews about those diplomats, I certainly said nothing as lyrical as 'Blood my man! Every time, blood will tell.' *That* purple prose came straight from the fevered imagination of the *Daily Reporter's* Mr. Scott."

Holmes puffed placidly on his pipe awhile, as Watson scratched away at a notepad on his knee.

"I deplore the florid phrase, it so rarely *clarifies,* don't you find? Watson? What on earth are you doing?"

When he received no other answer than the scritch-scritch of his flatmate's pen, Holmes rose to stand behind the man's chair, peered down at a hasty scrawl.

"*The Adventure of the Doctor and the Detective.* Good lord Watson, what in the world are you writing?"

SH

Hot Seat

King's College Lecture Hall, Central London — 2012

"We start in five minutes! Sit wherever you like! Enjoy the talk!"

Sherlock ignored the perky constable, took his seminar ticket, glanced at it. *Homicide in the Capital: London as Battlefield,* was done up in a festive, gory red.

Sherlock pushed in to the auditorium. Frowned. People milling everywhere. Almost all the seats taken. And people were *talking* to each other.

Uncaring that the incoming crowd had to sluice around him, Sherlock Holmes stood in that doorway and *flick-flick-flicked* his gaze over the audience.

His foot hurts. He's going to tell me about it.
She's already chatting up the man two seats over.
He's been stood up by his boyfriend again and wants a shoulder to cry on.

That sharp gaze scudded fast over faces, deducing, judging—*too much, too much, too much...ah.*
There.

Compact. Arms and legs held close. Flyer folded neatly on his lap. Not fidgeting, not looking around, not doing anything but sitting quiet, focused, inward.

Pushing through the crowd, then past a dozen sets of knees, Sherlock at last arrived beside his seat mate.

And didn't sit.

No, in that narrow aisle Sherlock did what Sherlock does: Exactly what he wanted. And what he wanted was to stare down at his silent seat mate and flick-flick-flick past the obvious—doctor, military, injured—to observe the less obvious: This quiet man thrived under fire. Under metaphorical fire, under literal fire, under battlefield conditions that threatened soul and safety.

Oh how interesting.

With a dramatic flourish, Sherlock sat beside the intriguing stranger and said, "Of course they think they know."

John Watson heard but did not listen. He didn't know a soul at this seminar. No one could possibly be talking to him.

"But they really don't."

John glanced at the tall man next to him. Then at the man beside *him.* Nope, it didn't look as if the tall guy was talking to *that* guy. That guy was texting like a tweener.

Finally John looked up. "Beg pardon?"

Sherlock sighed, as if at the end of an exhaustive lecture. "They put together profiles, perform case studies, but of course they don't know because they don't see."

For some reason John checked the other guy again but he was still texting, so clearly this chatty stranger was addressing *him.* "I'm sorry, have we m—"

"See? There?" Sherlock pointed. "The lecturer. His posture, that chin-down gaze, the hands clenched tight behind his back? He's recently entered into a sexually satisfying relationship. Finally getting all those submissive tendencies tended to. But he's worried his ex-partner will find out...she's the director over there, trying to figure out what's different about him."

John Watson glanced at the woman on his other side, crossed his legs, stared straight ahead.

"Pressure's her thing. Dom, sub, oh that's for confused children. But a deadline, a ticking clock, the need to hurry, to do it now or not do it? That's what gets her going."

John Watson stopped facing forward, looked at Mr. Chatterbox. "Why are you—"

"All of them, they look for clues where there are none, and so look right past the clues already there. No wonder they can't catch criminals. *Or* have satisfactory sex."

John leaned away, to make room for his incredulity, and said, "Who the hell *are* you?"

Sherlock grinned. "I'm Sherlock Holmes. I'm the man who's about to make your life a lot more interesting."

John Watson tilted his head. Then slowly tilted it in the other direction. He said precisely nothing. But his smile? Oh that said exactly this: *I dare you.*

Sherlock smiled right back. Accepting that wordless challenge, he stood, stepped up onto his own seat, then armrest-walked a dozen rows down, until he at last jumped onto the raised stage.

This behaviour, of course, drew most eyes. When Sherlock began shouting about evidence—the phrases diamond-embedded false eye, conjunctiva, and *youthoughtnoonewouldnotice* featured prominently—even the texting man looked up.

When Sherlock pointed right at John, intoning, "—and my colleague can prove it," John *almost* turned in his seat to look behind him. Then, completely understanding that the parameters of his life had irrevocably changed, John Watson stood and, with nineteenth century manners, murmured his *excuse mes* all the way to the end of the aisle, then the good doctor joined Sherlock on the stage before he'd even asked himself why.

Three hours and four times that many laughing fits later, John said, "—and you're just lucky I backed you up when it was the man's *other* eye that popped out!"

Sherlock grinned down into his plum wine. He was pretty sure plum wine intrigued him. Plum wine fascinated him. Plum wine was so very, very *interesting*.

"I want some," John Watson laughed, tilting toward Sherlock a small, empty glass.

Sherlock grinned wider. He poured his tablemate some very good plum wine. And flick-flick-flick, his gaze meeting the gaze of a man who reflected back at him *let's do that again*...well Sherlock Holmes understood that the parameters of his life, they had irrevocably changed.

Follow That Cab!

The Edgeware Road, London — 1883

"Pardon me, this cab is taken."

"Yes sir, by me."

Dr. John Watson, sitting snug in the back of the hansom, frowned at the pushy old man tugging at the cab's closed door. "I sir, was *in* this cab before you were. Therefore it is *my* cab."

"I'm on my way to Scotland Yard," insisted the grizzled old fellow. "There I will save a life, protect a fortune, and foil a blackmailer. At the same time. I assure you my need of this cab is sharper than yours. Therefore this is my cab."

John Watson took off his hat and stuffed his gloves into it so as to give his clenching hands something to do. *"I* am about to deliver my first baby you insistent old—"

The 'insistent old' wrested the cab door open, jabbed at the step with his walking stick, and clambered in. "You're not married."

Watson wedged his glove-filled hat on the seat between himself and the old man, as if this would somehow remove the old man. "I didn't say it was *my* child."

"I assure you, you did. Now—"

"Listen Mister whatever-your-name—"

The driver opened the trap, peered down at his passengers. "'Scuse sirs, you haven't said where you're going."

The sudden courteous quiet within was so *loud* the driver actually winced. He was about to suggest hailing another cab when the old man stole some of Watson's lap blanket and gestured magnanimously, "Oh all right, you first."

John Watson is a polite English gentleman and so instead of muttering, "Suit yourself you ancient git," he took a deep breath, another to slow his heart, and said carefully to the cabbie, "Royal Free Hospital, please." He then sat back, arms crossed for exactly two seconds.

Only two because the decrepit piece of work next to him was suddenly going *grrrrr*. The actual sound *grrrr,* like some sort of cartoon dog, and so Watson turned in his seat and said, "Excuse me?"

"That's three point three miles in the *wrong* direction, I thought you'd be going to St. Mary's which is only zero point six."

"If it were St. Mary's I'd have walked the brief distance—"

"Which means the delivery of 'your' child is not quite so urgent as—"

"—*however,* since it is at the Royal Free in Hampstead, I have elected to take a cab. And the urgency of the child is none of your concern."

Urgency was really beside the point no matter *whose* cab it was, being as they were currently stuck behind three other cabs who were in turn stalled behind two men in the road, who seemed to be employing themselves in the *preparation* to employ fisticuffs. Thus far not one fist had landed nor one finger been laid, instead they danced around each other in shirtsleeves, doing a great deal of nothing much.

The elderly gent made that growling sound again and John Watson thought very impolite thoughts such as *Well it serves you right, you old madman.*

Watson was just about to check his watch, when the old madman ceased growling, bounded from the cab, and stormed away. And then came right back again. He snatched up his stick and disappeared.

Certain he'd seen the last of the creature, Watson contemplated abandoning the cab and walking to Park Lane for another, when the driver spoke. Moments later over-eager horses gave the hansom a jerk and the old man jumped back inside.

"That'll get us going!"

As if whipped with the words, the horses cantered off, the surprisingly-agile old man started laughing and, despite himself, Watson joined him.

Holding out an ungloved hand, the man said, "Sherlock Holmes."

Watson shook, found the oldster's grip more firm than infirm. He was beginning to have suspicions.

"Dr. John Watson. And I'm beginning to have suspicions about you."

Holmes laughed louder, his voice not at all the papery rasp with which he'd first spoken. "Well you're more observant than the blackmailer I met this morning. What gave me away?"

Watson narrowed his eyes. "Aside from the fact that you now move and speak like a man not yet forty? Or the fact that the driver, who could see what was going on, told me you pulled a sword from your walking stick and stopped the fight? Aside from these facts, which are quite enough, I've had the

44

unreasonable desire to throttle you since you climbed aboard and started *fussing.*" John Watson cleared his throat and straightened his coat. "And, sir, I've never once had such an inclination toward a man of genuine advanced years."

The following silence was both pregnant and prolonged. And then it became raucous with their laughter.

"What a fantastic disguise!"

"I could have accounted for all those variables but that last!"

As they laughed, Watson removed from between them the wedge of his hat and gloves. Acknowledging this largesse, Holmes firmly reseated the rug over both their laps.

And then Sherlock Holmes proceeded to metamorphose.

First came the removal of the grey wig, wild eyebrows, then side-whiskers. The jowls and wrinkles at neck and mouth resisted, and Holmes winced as they peeled away. "I always forget the glue sets firmly." Finally he took the entire mess and stuffed it inside the wig, then handed the wig to Watson. "Here's the old man!"

A youngish one with dark hair, a high forehead, and alert eyes looked back at Watson, who grinned as if given a treasure, not the remnants of a trick. "You rogue! Why did you do this?"

"Give people what they're looking for and they'll stop looking," said Holmes.

Watson would become used to Holmes making statements that left out all the explanatory bits, just as he'd grow used to fishing for those necessary bits when writing up their adventures. Here was the first cast of his line into that water.

"Explain."

Holmes took out his handkerchief and scrubbed at the back of a hand that had been made to appear both wrinkled and age-spotted. Watson noticed that a great many of the spots didn't scrub off, and was so diverted he missed part of his cab-mate's reply. Holmes noticed his distraction.

"Sometimes seconds matter in an experiment, so I can be rather careless with mild acids and the occasional fire. Nothing too damaging." Holmes wiggled long fingers. "So long as these stay dexterous their attractiveness isn't important."

Holmes scrubbed the makeup from his other hand. "What I meant is that, if you learn a suspect will be meeting his new accomplice at the train station, and is on the look out for a hatless old man in striped trousers, with a walking stick, and a yellow flower in his lapel, the moment that suspect sees such a man I promise you he'll stop looking, despite there being—and I counted—three other such gentlemen loitering at Paddington."

"So I gather this suspect was attempting to blackmail someone out of a fortune and you stopped him?"

"Just so! Though I've only *almost* stopped him. I have to get to Scotland Yard with my evidence before the case can be concluded."

"Ah!" Watson gestured as the cab pulled up to the hospital. "Then that'll be shortly as I've arrived at my destination."

No sooner had the good doctor alighted from the cab than Holmes cried, "My word, I've just spotted the lead suspect in a brace of arson attempts!" Clapping his hands gleefully Holmes shouted, "Driver, follow that cab!"

With Watson's laughter sending the *young* madman off, the hansom disappeared into the night.

*

For the good doctor the evening was long, but rewarding, as it ended in the somewhat tardy birth of a healthy little boy.

Tired but triumphant, Watson elected to walk the four miles home but, instead of going to his own lodgings, he on a whim diverted the half mile to Scotland Yard. As he was going in, Sherlock Holmes was coming out.

"Holmes! How go your cases?"

"Ah, I hoped I'd see you again! The cases are closed. A fortune has been found, an arsonist apprehended, and a blackmailer soon behind bars! And how is your baby?"

"'My' baby is quite fine." Watson grinned and the two men fell into step, heading toward the river. "He's healthy, happy, and very well-named."

"Excellent, a celebratory drink at Simpson's?"

"Excellent."

Settled a short time later in one of the venerable old restaurant's booths, Holmes asked, "So what have the proud parents named their babe?"

Watson beamed. "As you'd guessed, the baby decided on a leisurely arrival, so the prospective parents and I had time to talk. When I told the young couple about who had shared my cab, and our various adventures, they were saucer-eyed and open-mouthed. It seems they knew your name from newspaper articles and kept exclaiming, 'And then?' to the point that I had to promise I'd finish the story *after* their infant arrived.

"And arrive he did not a half hour later. I'm pleased to announce that young master John Sherlock Andrew Marsden has a crop of dark hair, is of medium size, and cried so lustily for so long, I could still hear him as I left the hospital."

The waiter placed down two whisky and sodas. Holmes snatched up his glass and raised it. Watson did the same.

"To John Sherlock Andrew Marsden," grinned the consulting detective.

"To John Sherlock Andrew Marsden," agreed his soon-to-be Boswell.

SH

You and What Army?

Near Victoria Street, London — 1996

The likelihood that Sherlock Holmes would join the army was…can you have odds that are negative-never-in-a-million-years? How about minus-the-military-is-for-the-feeble-minded?

Outside a pipette's measures Sherlock's not good with maths, so he doesn't know what the odds would be but never mind, it doesn't matter. What matters is that Sherlock's as likely to join the army, the navy, or the secret society of ninja assassins as he is to stop burning things in the name of *I wonder what would happen if...*

However.

Sherlock's twenty years old and it feels like every time he opens his mouth *heat* comes from it. The heat of words bunched up and burning on the edge of his tongue, the heat of *almost* knowing what he wants to say but not quite, the heat of genius trapped behind will and want and confusion and—

Sherlock shook his head. Never mind. *It didn't matter.* What mattered was that Sherlock looked at the glistening black exterior of the army recruitment centre and he wanted to go in.

This would surprise everyone. His parents, his tutors, his brother. Oh especially his brother who thought he understood everything, who thought he'd paved the way for Sherlock because he too could speak of heat on the tip of the tongue, but it was different. Somehow for Sherlock it was different.

So when Mycroft suggested that god-forsaken university in Switzerland, the one to which he himself had gone, the one he said was for 'the special,' the one that would 'help focus your talents, rein in your excesses, give you goals,' well Sherlock had stood up from the table in the Diogenes' smoking lounge, pocketed a brace of imported cigarettes, a pouch of tobacco, gold-lined rolling papers and a lighter, knocked back his own and his brother's imported scotch, grabbed both monogrammed serviettes for good measure, and said in the sweetest of voices, "Negative, nada, nay. Forever times eternity multiplied by infinity *no,"* and, amidst a frankly *fierce* cadre of frowns, Sherlock had decamped from the building.

And ended up not so very far away, standing in front of a small, nondescript office, a tiny office that said on the glass door: Army Careers. He'd meant to walk along the Thames shore and catalogue river sand, or smoke the Diogenes' cigarettes and study their ash, but there was no reason to do those things really, no purpose in everything that interested him, except if he didn't do something the heat in him would continue to burn and so…

…Sherlock Holmes opened the door that said *Army: Be The Best,* and walked in.

*

"—I've just always wanted to be a soldier I guess."

Captain Herrig smiled at the young man in front of him. A lot of kids wanted to join the army but couldn't—or wouldn't—say why. Usually it was to get out of a rut, make or follow friends, maybe find a career.

This kid didn't feel like any of those. In some ways he was too distracted *and* too focused. It wasn't Herrig's job to discourage, but it wasn't his job to *encourage* either, not if they ended up with a soldier who didn't belong where he was.

"I understand, that's pretty much what you said before Mr. Watson, but—"

"Call me John, please."

"Right, John, that's not exactly a reason, you know? It'd really help me to help you if you could tell me *why.*"

John opened his mouth but Herrig held up a staying hand. "I really want to talk some more, but give me a minute to help this other gentleman, all right? Think about what I'm asking, enjoy your tea, and remember there are biscuits right behind on that desk."

Herrig straightened his tie, crossed the room, extended his hand. "Hello, I'm—"

"—disabled."

Herrig stopped so quickly he grunted. He dropped his hand, stood tall. "Excuse me?"

Oh god oh god oh god this was *it,* this was what he did, this was what he always did—spoke instead of thought, thought instead of slept, slept instead of get out of bed and do it all again and the *it* at the root of it all was *this*—seeing too much and then saying what he saw at exactly the wrong time and in exactly the wrong way.

Sherlock stepped back from the straight-backed soldier, as if someone else had dropped the faux pas between them.

He started to stutter, then hiss, then close his eyes, and if he wasn't careful he'd start talking again, a stream of facts, the sort of facts that no one else—except Mycroft—saw. Things like a soldier with two metal rods either side of his spine, a soldier invalided out of active service not for wounds sustained in battle, but for late-onset scoliosis that had cut short the military career which had helped him focus his talents, rein in his excesses, given him goals.

Then given him new goals: To help young men and women who needed the same thing, but needed it *this* way.

This was not one of them, Herrig knew that, but he raised his hand again and smiled. "My name is Captain Robert Herrig, and you are?"

Sherlock's used to that, to people pushing past the words that come from his mouth, used to people pretending to be deaf. He mumbled "Sherlock Holmes," and looked at his shoes.

"Well, Sherlock, I've got someone before you who—oh, John."

John Watson was there now, nodding toward Sherlock. "It's okay, I'll just...you know, I don't mind waiting."

Sherlock looked up and into serious eyes. "Why?"

John shrugged. "'Cause I'm not in a hurry. And the biscuits are good."

Herrig and John grinned at each other and Sherlock wished he could do that. Say simple things that made people smile instead of pretend-deaf. Instead he opened his mouth and let the heat out. He *always* did.

"He doesn't really want to join the army, he wants to pay for college. Can't you see the white thread in the black button on his cuff? The navy blue sock and the brown one? The spectacularly bad haircut he did with a pair of bandage scissors? Mr. Watson here is broke, making do, mending things. He can't pay for those books in his rucksack." Sherlock tilted his head, read aloud. *"Essential Clinical Anatomy, Wheater's Functional Histology,* and everyone's favourite hundred quid text *CWB's Organic Chemistry."*

Sherlock clapped his mouth shut, stepped back, to make room for his own shame, for the pending *deafness,* for—

"That was fucking fantastic."

Startled, Herrig and Sherlock looked at John. "Sorry. Um, wow, that was right. All of it." John looked at Herrig. "Which is a shame because I don't think I'm supposed to join the army for money, am I?"

Captain Robert Herrig doesn't operate on instinct, no, but he does let it play a part when the feeling's strong, so in the prevailing spirit of just opening your mouth and letting the words fall out, he looked at John, "There are much, much worse reasons John. Let's talk about the reserves." Herrig looked at Sherlock and said, "And you, you don't want to be in the army for any reason, do you?"

Sherlock looked at his shoes. He shook his head.

"What do you want to do?"

Sherlock's toes fitfully bunched up in his shoes. He shrugged.

"Oh! You could be a spy. Or a *detective."* Sherlock and Herrig looked at John. John looked at his shoes. "Sorry."

Here's where instinct shut Herrig up because he saw something in Sherlock's face just then, a spark in the eye, heat in the cheeks, a fire trying to catch.

It was a long, long minute of silence then, of two young men, and one not so old, listening to things changing.

Then rain started outside. Three Englishmen did what the English always do: They noticed. Eventually Herrig insisted on tea and biscuits for the duration. And so for twenty minutes or so two young men and one not so old talked about quite a lot of things.

*

It would be a bit more than a dozen years before John and Sherlock met again, but they would be aware of each other that entire time.

John began noticing small articles about Metropolitan Police cases where a Sherlock Holmes, 'consulting detective,' provided a vital clue. Over time those articles got longer and instead of the occasional assistance, it was a case closed *because* of Sherlock Holmes.

Sherlock began noticing letters to the editor, praising the small articles that mentioned him. Over time the letters got a little longer and the titles appended to the writer's name changed from John Watson, to Dr. John Watson, to Lieutenant John Watson.

It would be just a bit more than a dozen years before they met again, Stamford walking John Watson into a hospital lab and introducing him to Sherlock Holmes.

And it would take only that many seconds more before two men would recognise each other, laugh themselves silly, then make plans to go see a flat together.

℘ℋ

The Impossible Man

221B Baker Street — 1880

Nanny needed for nine boys, to start next November, near Narringwell. Apply in alliterative verse, Narringwell PO Box 9.

Lady's silver hat pin lost on the Edgeware Rd. Required for occult purposes. If found, contact Mrs. L. Wilson, Quakers Court.

Botanist keenly in need of lizard orchids. Will pay premium. Deliver by night to 666 Grey's Mews, Hackney.

"Curiouser and curiouser," murmured John Watson. Settling in more comfortably beside the pub fire, he sipped his pint, then said, "All right Watson. Focus."

Pencil poised, brow furrowed, Watson focused.

Gentleman's hostel seeks respectable men for long-term lodging. No smoking. No late nights. Temperance and attendance at Sunday services encouraged. References essential. Reply Box 2, Westminster Post Office.

Watson scowled, crossed the advert out with a paper-slashing flourish.

Poodle breeder requires lodger for small home east of the city. Prefer handy man with advanced carpentry skills. Need animal lover who will walk dogs when owner is away. Ability to cook a plus. Apply in person 9K Poe Lane, Bethnal Green.

"Phhffft," said Watson succinctly. "Sounds more like you want a bondservant." Another fortifying sip of his pint, another pencil slash, and Watson read on.

Impossible man seeks same for shared accommodation. Helpful if potential flatmate partial to violin, strong tobacco, chemical experiments, and unusual hours. Knowledge of poisons a plus. Interested parties reply by post to S. Holmes, 221B Baker Street.

Watson sat up so quickly he dropped his pencil and nearly knocked over his pint.
"Oh how very curious."
He began his reply immediately.

*

Dear Mr. Holmes,
I am a doctor recently returned from service in Afghanistan. I am tidy of habit, quiet of nature, and prone to insomnia. I have detailed knowledge of anatomy, vegetable alkaloids, and antiserums. I enjoy a well-played violin, whisky, and 'ship's' tobacco. Perhaps it's possible you find me impossible enough? — John Watson, 8, The Strand.

Dear Dr. Watson,

Delighted to hear from you. Yours is the first and only reply I've had to my advertisement. You sound rather ideal, and your knowledge of antiserums is a positive boon.

That said, I did say 'impossible' for a reason, so I should come clean with all my shortcomings before we go further. Let's see. I can be morose at times and may go silent for long patches, but with a bit of work I'm soon right. I travel occasionally for my work, and sometimes have the odd client or two drop by. I've just taken these rooms and so my papers and other collections are all about the place, though I'll confess I hate tidying. Let me know if all of this is suitable. Now, what have you to confess? — Sherlock Holmes

Dear Mr. Holmes,

Well, you still don't seem all that impossible to me, or perhaps we share impossibilities. That's for you to judge once you hear my 'confessions' I suppose. They are as follows:

I was wounded in the war and fell ill soon after, so I am still recovering from these effects and seek a steady, tranquil life. My insomnia means I roam about looking for reading or other diversions at all hours. I write the occasional bit of doggerel on scraps of paper but it always comes to nothing as I'm extremely lazy. I confess I'll have other things to confess when I'm well again, but those are my principal faults at present. — John Watson

Dear Dr. Watson,

Fantastic! What you call faults I list as virtues. I myself am the most incurably lazy devil that ever stood in shoe leather, together we will slouch away the winter.

As for doggerel, I'm intrigued. I write the occasional monograph, and am keen to create a precise and scientific record of the criminal cases in which I sometimes lend a deductive hand. Perhaps you could help in this endeavour? If you've no interest in my hobby, fear not, I don't expect you to be my Boswell. SH

Dear Mr. Holmes,

Criminal cases? Now it's I who am intrigued. I don't know of what real use I could be in the writing-up department, but I'm happy to listen, learn, and see what I can do.

You know, we seem of such like mind that I really have no need to see the apartments. If you're willing to take the risk of living with me sight-unseen, I can move into Baker Street at any time. I own little and can make the transition with two cases and one cab. Awaiting your reply. — John Watson

Dear Dr. Watson,

Myself and Mrs. Hudson, our landlady, have spruced up your rooms, all they want for is your arrival. Though we've yet to discuss rent, I'm sure you'll find your share far more reasonable than what you pay at that private hotel on the Strand. Pardon the brevity of this note, I'm in the middle of a case. SH

John Watson arrived at Baker Street just as the winter sun was setting. He'd later reflect that the pleasant little block that contained 221B showed to its best advantage in such light, and through the years he'd come to pause often on the kerb opposite, enjoying the slant of the sun on black iron and stately gas lamps.

His new landlady proved chatty, polite, and quickly scarce. Before she vanished she had a few words.

"This morning Mr. Holmes asked me to tell he will be home before nightfall. He's very keen to meet you, has chattered on about it all day. Don't tell him I told you. I'll be bringing up breakfast at seven sharp. Do you like kippers? Oh, that's grand. G'night doctor."

Once left alone, Watson roamed from room to room. He liked what he saw. The place was well-furnished, snug, and pleasantly crowded with Holmes' possessions—a box of retorts, a brace of test tubes, and stacks of files rested on the dining table. Yes, this place would suit, thought Watson, it would suit well indeed.

Weary with the exertions, Watson settled with a sigh into an armchair by the fire Mrs. Hudson had well-stoked.

There was a knock on the door. The good doctor answered.

"Telegram, sir," said a slim boy, handing over a thin slip of paper with a click of his heel. Tipping the lad and closing the door, Watson unfolded the note.

TELEGRAM
TO: J. H. WATSON
FROM: S. HOLMES

CALLED TO SWANSEA UNEXPECTEDLY. RETURN
TOMORROW MORNING. PLEASE MAKE YOURSELF AT
HOME. TOBACCO IN PERSIAN SLIPPER BY FIREPLACE.
WINE IN ERLENMEYER FLASK BESIDE SOFA. DON'T
OPEN DECANTER ON MANTEL. IS NOT WHISKY. SH

Watson grinned. What an interesting man. He was
looking forward to meeting his new flatmate, learning a bit
about his business, then enjoying peace and quiet so that he
could recuperate.

Watson put the telegram in his breast pocket, went
looking for then found the wine. That just left a hunt for wine
glasses or—

Another knock.

Watson opened the door again to find a second telegram,
held by different boy, who deposited it with the same curt heel
click. Watson tipped the child, closed the door, and read:

TELEGRAM
TO: J. H. WATSON
FROM: S. HOLMES
DO NOT UNDER ANY CIRCUMSTANCES EAT THE
KIPPERS MRS. HUDSON MAKES FOR BREAKFAST.
ALSO IGNORE HER STORY ABOUT THE SEVERED
FINGERS CASE, SHE NEVER GETS THE DETAILS
CORRECT. WATER THE BLACK SLIME BESIDE THE
SINK AND IT WILL STOP SMELLING. WINE GLASSES
UNDER SOFA. CASE HERE SOLVED. BACK SOON. SH

"Curiouser and curiouser," murmured the good doctor.

Within a few minutes Watson had tucked away this second telegram, poured a glass of wine, and was enjoying one of Holmes' old briar pipes and a bit of excellent tobacco, when there was yet *another* knock.

Was it possible it could be a *third* telegram?

Watson opened the door and looked down for a small boy.

He stepped back from the door and looked up at a large man.

A pleasant gaze met his, a heel clicked, and the tall, grinning man handed him a card. "Hello, Dr. Watson."

John Watson looked at the card. Then back into mischievous eyes. His own grin grew, then morphed into a bright laugh. "Hello, Mr. Holmes."

Oh yes, thought the good doctor, this was going to suit him. This was going to suit him down to the ground.

SH

The Hounds of Dartmoor

Dartmoor National Park, Devon — 2009

Sherlock Holmes didn't mind the shaggy Highland cattle.

As a matter of fact, he'd have kissed on the mouth the half-ton cow who stood, unbudged, in front of their idling holiday coach. That precious ten minute delay as the placid creature gazed toward the tumble of Black Tor, gave Sherlock time to ask fellow coach passenger Harvest Rainne ("That's really my name!") two questions. Her answers, as well as the fact that she favoured button-fly jeans, allowed him to deduce that the perky American wasn't the jewel thief for whom he was searching.

Sherlock also didn't mind the sheep.

As a matter of fact, Sherlock would have knit nice jumpers for the three who, eight miles later, could be found lying in the road, looking so very dead that half the holiday makers *on* the coach got *off* the coach to make sure the sheep were fine. As the surprised ruminants gazed sleep-bleary at the gathered saviours, Sherlock employed that extra time to question another passenger. The old man's answers, as well as the *I Love Mummy* tattoo on his inside wrist, told Sherlock this was not his jewel thief.

Sherlock positively loved the pornographic ponies.

It was equus mating season in Dartmoor National Park, and apparently the sturdy lot of them favoured the stability of the park's winding roads for committing their carnal acts. And commit them they did, with such orgiastic fervour that both coach driver and tour guide said they had not seen the like in a dozen years. Sherlock would've personally delivered each future foal in thanks for the nearly two hours the libidinous activities tacked on to their trip. With that extra time he was able to discount four CEOs, the man in leopard print, the tomato farmer, the twins, their significant others, and the professional whistler, which just left—oh! *Oh of course!*

*

"Can't this thing go faster?"

The coach driver ignored him.

Now that Sherlock had identified the jewel thief he had the self-restraint of a sugar-addled toddler in a sweetshop. So he bulled up and down the coach aisle as if the propulsion of his pacing would make the thing go faster.

The tour leader watched him.

"We've seen three tors and a nice stream—tra la la la very pretty—now can we just get back to somewhere *anywhere* that has a mobile signal?"

To make the complaining and pacing just that teensy bit more annoying, Sherlock held his mobile aloft as he went from one end of the slow-moving coach (this time stymied by three cows and a small herd of goats) to the other, grousing about 'primitive conditions,' 'frankly awful coverage,' and finishing with 'I find it hard to believe *no one* else brought their mobile.'

"We could drive around the cows you know. I could walk back faster than this."

It was John Watson who stopped him.

Sort of.

"Look mate, you can't keep hounding people like this. They'll set you out on the road if you don't stop."

'Mate' stopped all right. Right in front of John Watson. "Hound? Hound? I'm not *hou*—"

"Off."

John and Sherlock turned. The tour leader was suddenly there, looming in the narrow aisle, huffing and puffing so hotly it was only by some misfortune of genetics that she wasn't actually breathing fire.

"What?"

The tour leader looked at John. "Don't you get involved in this, Watson, I'm not talking to you." A small woman, swollen right on up with righteous indignation, can appear a great deal larger than she is. "I *am* talking to you, Mister Mobile Reception. Get. Off. This. Coach."

"Look you can't just abandon him—"

Sherlock Holmes pursed prim lips. He abstemiously narrowed his already slim frame so as to slip by the tiny giant. The tiny giant glared at him as if she would burn down his village. Sherlock collected his one small bag—case notes and blurry photos he'd frustratedly stared at so long his left eye still had an intermittent twitch—and Sherlock Holmes decamped from the Dartmoor National Park holiday coach and into a herd of Highland cattle.

They did not notice.

Sherlock began walking down the road. He got a good half mile before the coach made it through the recalcitrant cows. The coach stopped beside him.

John Watson got out.

"Your gloves. You left them on the—"

"Thank you."

"Yeah, uh, sorry about—"

"Thank you."

"Well, see you back at the inn."

"She's eating the evidence."

"Beg pardon?"

"There's a jewel thief on that coach. She's *eating* three million pounds of black opals. Some have quite ornate and priceless settings."

"I...what now?"

Sherlock huffed and puffed but unlike a tiny tour guide he did not manage to conjure a dragon-like essence. "The evidence," long fingers, bunched and shoved toward a still-talking mouth, "she's eating it so that when I can at last call the police—if I ever again have mobile coverage—she won't appear to have any of the stolen—"

The coach driver honked. John turned and growled. Slightly terrified, the driver did an elaborate *you've got one minute* gesture. John smiled ingratiatingly, showing teeth, then turned back to Sherlock.

"So you're telling me someone in there—"

"The woman who's invisible."

"Eh?"

"The one who has no distinctive hair colour, clothing, face, voice...the one you actually almost don't see."

John thought about this a moment. "You mean that nice young one, Becca?"

Sherlock actually recoiled in his shock. "You know her name? You—"

"She's *eating* opa—"

"I...it's..." Sherlock batted at the air to dispel his confusion. "Yes, she's eating gems and—"

—and John Watson was gone.

The driver opened the coach door, John boarded, and twenty-eight holiday makers, a coach driver, and a tour guide watched Sherlock Holmes recede into the distance. The one who did *not* watch was busy stomping down a narrow aisle, then standing in front of a woman with a very large packet of...crisps.

"I once had a patient who swallowed six of her grandmother's heirloom silver teaspoons. Another swallowed a rubber duck. A third enjoyed the mellow flavour of some rare Tibetan shag. *When it was still in the pouch.* Do you know what each of these people had in common other than being the beneficiary of a twenty minute lecture from me? They all needed surgery due to life-threatening obstructions in their GI tract."

The jewel thief did three things in reply to this. She pretended she was deaf. She looked out the window. And she reached into her crisp packet for another...crisp.

"Give over."

Fingers groping for the priceless ring she was still trying to get herself to swallow, Rebecca Helen Hanilar did not—

"—Give. Over."

"Mr. Watson."

John ignored the tour guide.

"Don't make me ask again Becca."

"John."

"I am going to count to three and you are—you did *not* just swallow what I think you swallowed."

66

Whilst Hanilar gulped an unset gem and continued to work herself up to downing a thirty carat black opal in its fussy platinum setting, the tour guide said at volume, "You can't keep hounding people John, now you're acting like—"

John whirled. He leaned close and barked into the tour guide's face, "Hound? Hound? Did you say *hou*—"

*

Sherlock raised his mobile into the air again. No signal. "Damn it."

Sherlock walked around a cow in the road. Stopped. Returned to the cow in the road and pressed his mobile to her massive, shaggy, perhaps-conductive side. No signal.

"Damn it."

Sherlock walked another quarter mile, his arm in the air. No signal.

"Damn. It."

Sherlock stuffed his mobile into his pocket, and stomped the long and winding road back toward Dartington. He mumbled dark and mumbley things. He wondered how he could have handled this case better. He passed a herd of sheep. Briefly wondered if wool improved phone reception. Didn't feel like trying. He walked around a bend in the road...and found John Watson sitting on a tiny tor.

Sherlock Holmes blinked, frowned, looked behind him for reasons unknown, and then walked up to John.

After a moment John smiled. He hoisted his rucksack and stood. After another moment both men began walking toward town. For about eight seconds Sherlock flew through a dozen deductions. He was about to share his conclusions when

John, as would become his habit over many years, surprised Sherlock.

"She'd only eaten three unset opals by the time I got back on the bus. She should be fine excreting those."

Sherlock was about to be strident about *evidence* and *not-at-all-fine,* but John opened his rucksack and withdrew a crisps packet.

He handed it to Sherlock, whose mouth hung open in a gratifyingly silent fashion.

"I told her we wouldn't raise a ruckus back at the inn if she gave me the rest of the gems. I may have implied I was an undercover police officer and you were a Russian secret agent who'd been put on her trail by Canadian mafia. I might have slightly over-played the international intrigue, but she seemed to believe me."

Sherlock peered into the crisps packet. About two million, eight hundred thousand pounds of salty, greasy black opals glittered merrily back at him.

"I might have also said something about ninjas, too. It all got a little confusing. Anyway, act all mysterious when we get back to the inn, and for the love of god keep your mouth closed and let *me* talk to the police."

Sherlock, as would become his habit over many years, totally didn't do even half of the smart things John suggested once they got back to the inn.

It ended up just fine anyway. Sherlock got most of the invaluable valuables back to their well-paying owner and got another case. John got a flatmate and a new job running down alleys after the flatmate.

For their part, the jewel thief and the tour guide got off the holiday bus together, not quite a dozen miles after John and Sherlock. Last seen dashing by foot across the moors, they were never heard from again.

Though on quiet autumn nights, quite near Devil's tor, it's said you can sometimes hear a small, but quite fierce dragon-like roaring.

SH

Vegetable Alkaloid

St. Thomas' Hospital, South London — 1882

It was Saturday night. It was snowing. The snow was not sticking, though John Watson saw a horse slip on fast-forming ice down by London Bridge.

"Ah there you are Watson, give this to nurse Edleman would you?" Dr. Morgan handed patient notes to St. Thomas' newest doctor, who glanced at the file in his hand: *Holmes, Sherlock.*

"Looks like his larder disagreed with him is all. Gave him a purgative, he'll be right in a tick." Morgan put on his heavy coat, headed to the door, and forgot about Mr. Sherlock Holmes.

*

It was Thursday night. Snowing heavily. The snow had begun to stick. Watson attended a woman and a man who came to the hospital with sprains after slipping on ice on Westminster Bridge.

Dr. Morgan, paused in a winter-dark hallway scratching out a note, looked up as Watson passed. "Ah there you are. I'd appreciate it if you'd file this for me. Same lad, ate the wrong food again. Gave him a purgative, told him to stay away from shellfish. I'll be late again tomorrow, Watson, hope you don't mind. G'night," said the old doctor, forgetting about St. Thomas' Hospital and his final patient of the evening, Mr. Sherlock Holmes.

John Watson did indeed mind, but so far never had the chance to say. With a resigned shrug he glanced at Morgan's notes on Holmes, then placed them on a stack of others waiting to be filed. Though he didn't quite forget about it.

The next day and the next were quiet. The storm had come on with an icy viciousness, keeping much of St. Thomas' staff away. Drs. Morgan, Roberts, and Alyxpoe had not made it in by afternoon, and half the nursing staff had yet to appear. Because Watson lived not a mile from St. Thomas' he braved his way in.

So Watson saw Morgan's patients, Roberts', and Alyxpoe's, too. The workload was not great, as a storm that keeps away carers tends to keep away those for whom they care. By evening the only patients Watson had seen were a Miss Michaelas Vixis and Mrs. Zelie Courage, the most interesting thing about each had been not their nearly-identical flu symptoms but unusual names. Watson wondered if the theme would continue and *Holmes, Sherlock* would be in next.

Watson grinned to himself. He'd known a Sherlock once. Miss Katharine Ann Sherlock had been slim as a reed and tall, taciturn and regal. Bright, too, with a stillness that would turn to quick motion without warning. He'd been a bit mad about her, but then he'd come to London for medical school and they'd—

John Watson dropped his files and his tea as Sherlock Holmes dropped to the floor at his feet.

*

Barely fitting on the small sofa in the chilly staff room, Holmes wasn't quite the 'lad' referred to by Morgan, but that doctor was well into his sixties, so the thirty-something

71

Holmes—a reedy man with an ascetic's deep-set eyes—would likely seem rather youthful.

About the time Watson finished counting the fast pulse in his patient's neck, his patient woke.

"Hello there Mr. Holmes, I'm sorry we're seeing you again."

Holmes glowered at Watson, peevish. He sat up quickly, his movements jerky, breathing rapid.

"Mr. Holmes," said Dr. Watson, "this is the fourth time in less than a fortnight you've presented with similar symptoms, I think this time however—"

"Weather keeping Dr. Morgan away I presume. No matter," said Holmes, fingers twining. "I simply need the medicine he's offered in the past."

"And if that's what will help that's what I'll offer. But first I'll need to examine you." Watson gestured to the sofa. "Now if you'll kindly relax, I'll—"

Holmes stilled his agitated fidgeting. "Thank you sir." He stood. "I'll be on my way."

Helping is hard when people don't let you help. Dr. John Watson knew that to help sometimes you had to *make people let you.*

"Mr. Holmes."

"If I could...just something to—" It was clear Holmes was in pain and attempting to hide that pain by addressing the rest of his words to his hands he couldn't seem to still. "—something to induce vomiting, I'd be in your debt."

Every doctor has patients who demand purgatives. Many believe ill humours must be expelled, after all, and no doubt an

72

emetic or laxative could relieve pains brought on by excess or bad food, but Watson had a suspicion.

"Yes, I understand Dr. Morgan has offered emetics on previous occasions. Just give me a moment for a brief exam and a question or two."

There was no way for Watson to enforce his request and so he offered something he had no right to offer. "In exchange I'll give you enough medicine to take home should symptoms recur."

Holmes was still a long moment, then, clearly miserable and desperate to be less so, nodded once.

Then Sherlock Holmes proceeded to vomit all over John Watson's shoes.

*

A steady stream of patients appeared almost immediately after Watson admitted Holmes, so it was well over three hours before he revisited him. When he did, the good doctor was nonplussed to find the man fully dressed, standing beside his bed, a scattering of papers across its rumpled surface.

He looked up as Watson entered, clapped his hands together. "Ah, thank you doctor for your excellent care. I'm feeling far better and was just writing down some thoughts." Holmes gathered his papers primly, then sat on the bed, Watson on a nearby chair. The doctor then proceeded to first berate, then trick his patient.

"You're clearly feeling better. No more panting or racing pulse, and your agitation's been replaced by alertness which is good. Now I'd like you to know that patients who frequently self-diagnose frequently become *expired*-patients. Next time leave the doctoring to doctors. It's for this reason I've decided I can't give you that promised bit of antimony oxysulfate."

They'd later laugh at how easily Holmes fell for Watson's trap, but fall he did, reflexively correcting the doctor. "Tartrate of antimony and potassium is, I believe, what you mean."

"Ah yes, how silly of me."

Watson didn't tell his patient he had no business knowing the chemical composition of such a preparation, nor the fact that knowing it was all the evidence he needed to become convinced of one thing. Looking steadily at his patient, the good doctor said simply, "Tell me, Mr. Holmes, why are you repeatedly poisoning yourself?"

*

Even a genius of deduction can't deduce why one man will trust another, or why friendships form. Not that Sherlock Holmes ever tried to explain this particular inexplicable. No, instead Holmes simply answered Watson's question, trusting that the man would help.

"Two street children are dead and the police haven't the time nor propensity to find out why. I'm a…call me a consulting detective. I believed the children were poisoned with a vegetable alkaloid. I'm sure you know many are undetectable, so I set about detecting by ingesting likely culprits myself. I knew once I discovered what, I'd know who."

"And nicotine was your latest poison of choice?"

At Holmes' clear surprise Watson smiled. "I may not be a detective, but I am a doctor. When you were unconscious I saw small chemical burns in your mouth, they were similar to ones I saw in a soldier in Afghanistan. You think it was nicotine then?"

A bloodhound on scent and now certain he had a companion in the hunt, Holmes just about vibrated. "I know that it was! And now I know it was the tobacconist on St. James' Street who did it."

"He poisoned children? For the love of god, why?"

"It's a pitiable fact, but such children live by stealing. He often fell prey to their light fingers."

Watson stood, "Well he's got to be stopped!"

Holmes rose as well. "Exactly so. You'll help?"

Watson's answer was to show Holmes his back, "Get a move on man, you seemed spry enough when I came in."

With an entirely inappropriate hoot of glee, Holmes grabbed his notes and his coat, catching up to Watson at the door. "I've had a few plans for helping some of these poor street boys. Many simply want for solid employment. I've an idea on that. Now, my plan may be slightly *irregular...*"

The Dancing Man

The London Eye — 2010

Sherlock Holmes has twice enjoyed the high-flying pleasures of the London Eye.

From the outside.

And if you stand still barely long enough, Sherlock will tell you about it, starting with the fact that it's no easy feat spidering along the exterior rigging, yet Sherlock has done it. Twice.

That he broke into the wrong capsule that first time doesn't matter, because he caught the arsonist that second time and, if the man in the capsule next to his would just stop flapping around distractingly, Sherlock would catch his criminal *this* time, too.

In some year or other. Because honestly, this giant wheel could not possibly move slower. Sherlock had asked the uniformed attendant in the capsule with him if they couldn't just make the whole contraption go round more quickly, so he could *some* day get to the top where the actual *views* were, but the huge, unsmiling creature had looked at him as if he'd asked for the Queen's purse.

Clearly it didn't matter that a woman's alibi was on the line, it was minus eight degrees outside, *and* the entire achingly-slow wheel had on it five entire people including themselves, the dancing man one capsule over, and two chatting attendants in the capsule with him.

Sherlock glanced at that capsule again. The gathering fog made it difficult to see, but if he wiped away condensation with his arm, cupped his hands, then *peered* he could just make out the man. He was still gesturing wildly to the attendants, both of whom kept looking over at the capsule containing Sherlock and Mr. Colossal.

Sherlock peered harder but—never mind. *Never mind.*

What was going on in the next capsule didn't matter, what mattered was blackmail, an iffy alibi, and using his favourite pair of opera glasses to see what he could see across the Thames.

If they ever got anywhere. Good god they were still at least five minutes from perihelion. Sherlock could crawl the rigging to the top faster than this, and he knew that for absolute fact.

Fine. *Fine.* It didn't matter. What mattered was that Mark Mithen, MP, London Eye habitué, said he saw Lady Sakura having sex with another lady—the Senior Shadow Deputy Minister for something or other—on the deputy minister's desk.

That he was in the London Eye at the time and the minister's desk was across the river and in one of the spiky towers of Whitehall Court…well despite this he claimed *he* very clearly saw Lady Sakura steal the deputy minister's confidential papers. This whilst deputy whatsit was in the loo getting Sakura's engagement ring out of her hair, where it had snarled during a particularly vigorous desktop tête-à-tête.

Sherlock didn't believe Mithen, and it had nothing to do with—what on earth? Sherlock put down his opera glasses and peered at the man in the next capsule over. The man was tapping on the capsule's glass, clearly trying to say something using a few broad, emphatic gestures.

I...am...choking.

Sherlock Holmes was about to gesture back *what?*, but the man had stopped semaphoring and was again talking to the two attendants. Sherlock glanced at the attendant in the capsule with him, but Mr. Mammoth was otherwise occupied with his cuticles. Sherlock went back to seeing if he could actually see into a fourth floor office across the river.

He suspected he could if this fog would ever clear, but that wasn't going to happen in this lifetime, just like he was never getting to the top of this creeping wheel. Honestly he had no idea why this thing was usually crammed with tourists. You could take a lift up the Oxo tower and see about as much.

As if seeking corroboration, Sherlock glanced at Mr. Massive. Like the Eye, it seemed Mr. Massive hadn't moved an inch.

Sherlock frowned, glanced at the other capsule. He was pretty sure he could hear the dancing man yelling at the attendants.

Whilst all of these distractions were distracting indeed, they were almost *at the top.* A few more minutes, just a few...

Sherlock grinned over at Mr. Prodigious. Mr. Prodigious was standing a bit closer, though his cuticles continued to fascinate.

Sherlock grinned over at the other capsule. The dancing man wasn't. Now he seemed to be on his knees and fighting off the two attendants with him.

Well indeed all of this was somewhat peculiar but...almost...almost...and there it was: The summit!

Sherlock lifted his opera glasses. He wiped away condensation with his sleeve. He peered. He leaned hard against the curved glass. He wiped with the other sleeve. And the world's only consulting detective, a man who can see what no one else does, that man saw…not one thing. The fog was impenetrable.

Fine. Right. This wasn't going to answer the question at all. Though it had been colder and foggier this winter, there was no doubt Mithen would claim a clearing at just the right time. Sherlock growled and leaned against capsule glass, the button on his coat sleeve tapping…

…like the dancing man had been tapping.

Why did that hover at the edge of his mind, like Mr. Immense hovering closer?

Oh!

Sherlock grinned and looked over at the dancing man. He could no longer see the man in the capsule beside, but that didn't stop Sherlock from feeling quite fond of him. Because now Sherlock had it, he *had it.*

And it was this: Mithen was a liar and, like so many liars, he was fond of adding *details.* Yes indeed, oh my yes, the devil really was in the details.

For some reason this thought made Sherlock look over at Mr. Mountainous. Mr. Mountainous, no longer curious about his cuticles was right next to Sherlock. He smiled down at him with a mouthful of shiny teeth.

Suddenly Sherlock knew what the dancing man had been trying to tell him.

*

John Watson is not afraid of snakes or spiders. He's not afraid of enclosed spaces or wide open ones. He's not particularly afraid of public speaking, dogs, cats, or carp (he had a girlfriend who couldn't stand koi).

However, John Watson is afraid of falling from a great height and dying quite dead and, right now, inching his way along the rigging of the London Eye, he believes that this fear is really very reasonable.

"Oh god, oh god, oh god."

Another thing John Watson is not is overly religious, but the only thing that kept him from looking down as he inched slowly to the next capsule over was the chanting. The chanting was keeping his mind busy as his hands and feet crept him across fog-slick surfaces, and the chanting also kept him from chanting the stuff he was chanting previous, which was along the lines of, "You're an idiot, you're an idiot, normal people don't do dangerous stuff like this John, you're an idiot," which, though true, hadn't really helped him not have the panic attack for which he didn't currently have time.

So.

Praying. Sort of.

"Oh god."

John was more than halfway toward the next capsule over. The capsule whose interior he could no longer see, but whose exterior had just begun swaying in an alarming fashion.

John frowned, gritted his teeth, and changed his prayer.

"Oh *hell* no you don't mister, not on my watch."

John Watson moved faster.

*

80

It took Sherlock and Mr. Immense a few seconds to understand that someone was knocking. Then a few more for Sherlock to gain the upper hand. Then just a teensy bit more to open the capsule's fire escape door once Mr. Over-Large fell unconscious on top of it.

A bit of grunting and Sherlock managed to heave the heavy man off, open the door, and peer down at a wide-eyed man peering up.

"You're the dancing man," said Sherlock.

John made a noise. Sherlock understood that noise to say *I'm out here on the rigging of the London Eye and it's wet and slippery and I could die at any moment so if you'd help me up and let me in I'd be pretty grateful. Oh god, oh god, oh god.*

Sherlock helped John up and in. As John lay flat on his back belatedly having a panic attack—one that manifest with a great deal of hysterical giggling—Sherlock closed the capsule door, sat down on the capsule floor, and said a very obvious thing.

"Well that was incredibly dangerous."

John Watson stopped giggling. Still spread-eagled and pretty much trembling in every limb, he looked up. It wasn't the man's words that drew his attention, it was the unmitigated admiration in them.

John grinned. Sherlock grinned back. John remembered why he'd just done the incredibly dangerous thing. He sat up and looked at a frankly enormous man lying unconscious on the floor. He pointed.

"That's the Golders Green Garrotter. He strangles people. I tried to tell you."

"Yes, I eventually gathered. Thank you."

"What did you do to him?"

The garrotter groaned. Sherlock moved closer to the dancing man. Sherlock is brave, not stupid. Safety in numbers.

"Mostly tried to wind him by running around the capsule. Then you knocked, he got distracted, and I jumped on his back. I kind of strangled him until he passed out."

At this John frowned, crawled over to the giant man and checked his pulse. Even that was big. It hammered.

"He's fine."

"Good."

After a few long, silent seconds Sherlock said, as if asked, "I solved the case."

John stopped taking his own pulse. "Case?"

"Blackmail. You see Mithen forgot that the shadow minister didn't propose to Lady Sakura until the week *after* Mithen said he saw them, so Lady Sakura wasn't wearing her frankly enormous engagement ring—the one she keeps *tapping* against thing so people notice it—that night he said he saw them having sex on the minister's desk. So, that frankly enormous engagement ring couldn't have tangled in the minister deputy's hair, so obviously Mithen was lying and he took the papers himself."

John did then what John would do often in the coming years: He nodded as if he understood, then he mentally reinterpreted what Sherlock said into something he could understand. This tendency was going to lead to a lot of arguments in the future but that was for another time.

Right now was for John saying, "So do you do this a lot?" John gestured at Mr. Monumental, the Thames, the Eye, pretty much everything.

"All the time."

"Seems dangerous."

"Yes."

John scooted closer to Sherlock, dropped his voice as if they'd be overheard by enemy agents.

"So, like, how dangerous exactly?"

SH

Nursery Rhyme

Denmark Street, London — 1881

"Which violin piece would you pick for a young lady just learning?"

Sherlock Holmes looked away from a sheaf of Lassus and to the moustachioed man across the shop aisle.

The man smiled widely beneath his bristles. "You look as if you're a violin-playing sort of fellow, so on behalf of the lady I thought I'd ask."

Taking the simple question seriously indeed, Holmes thought a few long seconds, then plucked up blue-bound sheet music, "Beethoven's Für Elise, a song I learned when I myself was quite young." Holmes gestured further to the right. "Or there's Brahms' Wiegenlied: Guten Abend, gute Nacht. Both can be tamed by small fingers." Holmes held up a long one. "However, if your young charge would enjoy a challenge, perhaps she'd favour Bach's Minuet in G?"

John Watson noticed but did not remark on the man's presumption that the lady in question was a youth. "Would those suit one of 'thpritely' temperament?"

"Ah, there are better pieces for little lion hearts. To be honest I liked best playing Vivaldi's spritely 'Spring.' I played it so often as a boy I think my parents may have come to dread spring."

With a flourish Holmes lifted a pretend violin, tucked it snuggly under a pointed chin, and began to 'play' as he hummed the lively tune.

Watson watched as the lean man swayed about the small store, and before he knew it, he was tra-la-la'ing along with the stranger, and before both knew it Madam Vilranda, the proprietor, had joined them, her contralto clear and firm.

At the end of the impromptu concert the trio clapped each for the other and everyone took a bow.

"How can I do anything now but buy the young lady all four of Vivaldi's seasons?" said Watson.

That, however, was not to be.

Plucking up the sheet music before Watson could, Holmes said, "Allow me to make 'Spring' my gift to her."

After a moment's prideful hesitation, Watson agreed, with a proviso. "I'll need to tell her the name of her benefactor."

"Easily done!"

Once both men had paid, Holmes plucked up Vilranda's pencil, scrawled a moment, then handed the loose sheets to Watson, who read:

Play well for your god-father, he is very proud of you.

Your humble servant,
Mr. Sherlock Holmes

Watson tipped his hat. "John Watson and young Leigh thank you, Mr. Holmes."

Holmes returned the gesture and the man's smile. Watson tucked the music under his arm, headed to the door, and that would have been the end of that.

But that wasn't to be, either.

The bell chimed over the door as Watson opened it. He paused. A raw winter wind whipped at his coat. He closed the door and opened his mouth, and he said something interesting.

"How did you know Leigh was little? I always call her young lady, even to herself, though she's only four."

Holmes looked at Madam Vilranda, his expression one of surprise, as if the question could not possibly be serious. The lady shrugged.

"Well, to be honest it was many things. When you talked of the girl you twice imitated her lisp, which tells me she's still quite young. As you looked through the sheet music, you were humming—but only scraps of nursery songs. Your expression as you browsed was, quite simply, besotted. Usually it's the fresh and innocent that bring out in us such tender emotions as pride, devotion, self-sacrifice."

Watson wandered back to where Holmes stood near the till. "You say pride and devotion and I can feel them on my face when I think of her, but that you see it amazes me. And the self-sacrifice?"

Holmes again glanced at the proprietor, as if she would say the indelicate thing. "Forgive me for noticing, sir, but your shoes need shining and your hat a brushing, yet you've spent a pretty penny on a bit of music." Holmes gestured, "But the most telling are the scratches on the back of your hand."

Watson looked at his own ungloved hands, then laughed long and loud. "Ah yes, Leigh has a kitten, as tiny, bold, and brave as she is. If two very different creatures can bond, those two have. The little cat also happens to be rather fierce of tooth and claw. But they're small wounds, easy to bear." Watson might have left it at that, he even took a single step away…but there was one more thing.

"God-daughter. How?"

Holmes would grow quite familiar with the mixture of astonishment and pride with which Watson would in the future ask such things.

"You wear no wedding band and, as has been mentioned, your attire is a bit…roguish. You've the bearing of a military man and wear a ring on your right hand that marks you as such. I'm aware that military men are inclined to sentimentality about certain things. It was therefore a natural assumption that a fellow soldier made you god-father to his wee babe."

Watson's laugh filled the small, dusty store and could even be heard out on a street that would eventually become famous for the music made on it. "Oh that's genius, well done, bravo."

Madam Vilranda watched with delight as Sherlock Holmes' pale cheeks flushed a bit. She almost clapped when Holmes instinctively and perhaps somewhat coyly returned the compliment, though she was sure Watson wouldn't realise the quality of praise offered. "I'll say it was quite well-done, your picking me as a violinist. How did you deduce it?"

Watson shrugged. "I suppose I just presumed. Your leanness makes you seem quite tall and your fingers are of a complimentary length. You're wearing a black frock coat, reminiscent of those one can frequently see on musicians. All that combined creates a traditional portrait I suppose, but one that spoke violinist to me."

Holmes smiled, ran his thumb over fingertips, "I'd have said the calluses on my fingers, the unconscious bowing I caught myself at twice whilst looking at music, my slightly stooped posture as well as my request of Madam Vilranda as to whether she'd got in Viotti's 22nd Violin Concerto in A Minor." Holmes clapped a firm hand on Watson's shoulder. "Yet our two methods would get us to the same place in the end. Well done!"

John Watson was right and Madam Vilranda wrong. Though Watson was quite correct in judging his deductions pedestrian, there was a much sharper, wiser part of him that was well-able to deduce the rarity and the sincerity of Holmes' praise.

"Let me buy you a coffee, Mr. Holmes, and you can tell me more about how best to instruct a young and spritely lady in the art of violin playing."

Holmes smiled, then gestured at the door. "After you."

Madame Vilranda was right about something she later said to her own god-daughter: If two very different creatures could bond, those two had.

SH

PTSD

St. Pancras International Railway Station, London — 2008

The big man touched Sherlock Holmes only once. During the three hours he kept them both locked in the restaurant's freezer, he barely talked, just muttered and rocked and then finally asked Sherlock a single, soft-voiced question.

He did not like Sherlock's answer. So the big, big man— a gentle giant his colleagues later said—raised a butcher's knife to Sherlock's throat and asked the question again. This time Sherlock changed his reply. Then changed it again. And again. Finally the man accepted the answer, brought the knife to his own throat. He cut deep and true. The blood was everywhere.

Sherlock Holmes has seen worse. Dead bodies a week in the Thames, dead bodies after a broken-bottle bar fight, dead bodies hung, poisoned, beaten.

The problem is, for the entirety of Sherlock Holmes' career as the world's only consulting detective, he's only been there for the after, never the now, never the moment when the madness leads a woman or a man to take life.

Still, Sherlock didn't see that there was a problem with that, which was why he waved away counseling afterward and why he didn't see any of the signs of his post-trauma stress. Not until he was posing as a homeless man at St. Pancras station, rag-dressed and foul-smelling, and the tannoy, the damn tannoy, the *never ceasing wretched tannoy* announced another, another, *another* meaningless message.

89

Without knowing he was doing it, Sherlock responded to that relentless brain-numbing noise by holding his head and rocking on an empty bench in the middle of the train station. Eyes closed and humming, he never saw a man approaching until that man was near, murmuring something, something, *something*.

Sherlock opened his eyes, saw the man's perfectly polished shoes. He tried to ground himself without knowing that's what he was doing, so began reciting the ingredients of shoe polish. As he muttered, Sherlock looked up at the man, a big man, he was so, so big.

"Naptha, turpentine, gum arabic," Sherlock said, and the man nodded as if he knew what that meant, and then he held out his hand.

There was a bag in it, a paper bag with a pretty red star on it and little white handles and a sandwich peaking from the top and hot soup warming the bottom and *oh!* The man thought Sherlock really was homeless, he was giving him take-away food and okay, that was good, that meant his disguise was perfect, so maybe just one more day or two and Sherlock would spot the *other* false vagabond preying on the traveling lonely except that *tannoy*...

At the thought of that incessant noise Sherlock rocked harder and still didn't know he was doing it. He closed his eyes just for a second, then opened them when that voice was back, the soft and gentle murmur of the kind man, the very big man who was now holding out a serviette, one tightly-wrapped around a red plastic spoon.

And a red plastic knife.

Sherlock howled.

It was a wall of sound to put up a wall around himself, to get the knife away because it would cut, it would cut, the man would cut him and—

—one hundred yards distant John Watson heard shouting. He turned, looked toward the sound because John Watson *always* goes toward shouting, has done since he was a boy. It's not prurient interest, never has been, but until he was a man John couldn't have told you why such sounds draw him, then he learned it wasn't just any shout, it was only shouts of distress or pain that brought him like a moth to fire.

John Watson needs to be needed and so, when there's a scream in the dark John's usually halfway there before he even knows he's turned.

The crowd was small and they stood far away from the dirty man on his knees on the station's cold tiles. Just as well as the man was waving his arms in every direction, ready to strike anyone who came near. Not that anyone would, for he smelled like a rubbish tip and his clawed fingers were grey with city dirt.

It wasn't until John got just at the edge of the reach of those flailing arms that he heard the words between the shouts.

"Naptha! Turpentine! Pine resin! Gum...gum..."

On his knees Sherlock rocked and shouted and swung and John Watson got on his knees in front of him and listening, listening close, he guessed what would help, because John's good at that and always has been. So John looked around at the small crowd and lifted his hand, "Lipstick?" he said until someone put one in his hand, then John Watson started to draw. And talk.

"This is your hypothalamus," he said, sketching a peach lipstick brain and brain stem on the station's chilly floor. "The

91

medial zone constrains the circuitry and is responsible for defensive behaviour just like the behaviour you're showing. Now the hypothalamus produces corticotropin-releasing hormones and though there's debate about a relationship between elevated corticotropin-releasing hormone and stress disorder, there's—"

John kept talking chemicals until he got to the point where he was making some of the names up, but the man wasn't shouting any more, the man wasn't rocking any more, then, then, then the man was…complaining.

"Did you say deccinose? What on earth is *deccinose?*"

The entire time Sherlock Holmes was being cleaned up and hydrated and talked to by too many healthcare professionals hours later, he didn't shut the hell *up* about the deccinose. Then he remembered John had also said something about kiwis and really, by the time John got the man to just *stop talking about it*—which would actually be approximately *never*, though now Sherlock brings it up only every June and October—well anyway, by then Sherlock was somehow promising to meet John the next day, even though he knew the doctor would want to *talk* about things, things like *stress* and *therapy*, but Sherlock figured it was the least he could do and if it made the doctor happy, *fine*, and if, in the twenty-four intervening hours, Sherlock remembered John bringing up hot cross buns when they were in the station, it wasn't *his* fault being reminded of that would make John sigh his first sigh of long-suffering in Sherlock's presence.

But very, very, *very* much not his last.

SH

The Cold Shoulder

The Brazen Head Pub, Dublin — 1880

"You have such lovely eyes."

John Watson would not call himself an especially observant man, but then again he's not precisely *blind.* He sees obvious things, such as what the tall man two tables over just did. *That* was obvious. And now, watching through the mirror behind the bar, Watson couldn't take his eyes off the man, even as the woman behind the bar couldn't take her eyes off him.

"They've got bits of brown round the edges." Ticopi Smith placed Watson's Guinness on the bar top, followed it with her elbows, and peered dreamily into the doctor's dreamy depths. "It's like they have constellations in them."

Dr. Watson smiled at Miss Ticopi—"People just call me Tee"—with his mouth and cheeks and all the rest that gets involved in smiling. He left out his eyes though, because those were skewed left, watching the man two tables over. Watson could not have taken his gaze off that man if promised the Queen's hand in marriage.

Well *that* actually got Watson's gaze off the tall man because *that* was just a very strange thought.

So Watson brought his eyes into the smile directed at the tavern owner. He dabbed at his red nose with a pocket square and said, "That may be the nicest thing anyone's ever said to me."

Ticopi Smith is not a shy woman. When your sainted father leaves you a tavern and you've run it single-handed since

93

you were nineteen, you do not truck with timid. Still, Smith felt her cheeks turn pink, so she beamed at Watson and his constellation-containing eyes. "It's true, doctor, and you ought to be told more often."

Watson used the peripheral vision of his lovely eyes to notice that the man two tables over was now pacing in tiny, tight circles in front of his tablemates. One seated tablemate wore a police constable's uniform and was consuming a plate of chips as if famished. The other seated gentleman, a corpulent individual in plain clothes, held a notepad that loudly proclaimed itself a detective-style notepad. Largely because *Inspector Kavanagh's Notepad, Dublin Police* was written on the back of it in a bold hand.

"I'd be happy to tell you more often, if you like," said Smith who, after fifteen years of tending a tavern, was not only far from timid, but also very good at snap judgments.

Though she'd chatted with Dr. Watson only four times since he'd been in her fair city, she knew he wasn't quite like most of the men that came through the Brazen Head. He was quiet and chatty both, gentle and fierce, she knew he would protect as well as follow. And Smith knew something else: John Watson was lonely. That last bit didn't take much in the way of judgments, snap or otherwise, for most men in a pub alone are lonely. Maybe too, are most tavern keepers.

"And I won't mind, because true things just ought to be said."

"There's a *terrible* cold going around, put that down!"

The entire pub, currently containing seven people, went dead silent.

Two cabbies in a back booth each put down their pints. Inspector Kavanagh placed his notepad on the table. Constable Vamberry took a chip right out of his mouth and carefully set it back on his plate.

And Sherlock Holmes stopped pacing. But he did not put down his glass.

Well that was it, that was *just* all that John Watson, army veteran, physician, and man seriously bunged up with a cold, could take.

He slid off his stool—sparing a nod for Miss Smith, because John Watson is a gentleman, even when deeply congested—and walked over to the tall, pacing man with the half-glass of Guinness in his hand, and he said, "My name is Dr. John Watson, may I ask yours?"

Holmes could see no reason not to share this information. "Sherlock Holmes, sir. Consulting detective."

Watson didn't care about any of that. At this point he was just following the formal steps of politeness. Those taken, he launched into a small diatribe.

"I am fresh back from an Afghan tour of duty in which I was soundly done in by a Jezail musket. I then saw fit to contract enteric fever. I have yet to find particularly satisfying employment back in London, I cannot afford my over-priced lodgings, even less so a rain-drenched holiday to my mother's father's native land. Therefore, sir, my nerves are shot and watching you distractedly pick up a half-empty half pint from an entirely different table as if no one saw you do it, pace restlessly with it in your hand, then *nearly* drink from that glass, into which I personally saw a hacking, cold-riddled old lady spit…well it's more than flesh and blood can stand."

The cabbies looked shocked.

Inspector Kavanagh scooted deeper into the booth, to get away from Holmes and his...drink.

Police constable Vamberry put more vinegar on his chips, as if disinfecting them.

And Sherlock Holmes said with cheer, "Ah, I'd wondered why you were so intent on our little trio." Holmes waved the contaminated glass. "I'm afraid I don't like Guinness and picked this up merely to blend in."

Watson tut-tutted and harrumphed and made other noises through his moustache. He was about to return to his own pint when Sherlock Holmes said, "I've heard your confession sir, now here is mine: I too live in London. There I am always leaving chemicals about for some experiment or other, I smoke entirely too much strong tobacco, I play the violin at every hour, and have a tendency to go haring off on wild chases—" Here Holmes made a stern eye at Inspector Kavanagh. "—sticking my substantial nose into shady doings. If none of that troubles you, I'm thinking of taking a suite in Baker Street, and could really do with someone to share the cost. Interested?"

John Watson will tell you that small decisions can have lasting impacts.

Kindly attend:

If, on a dark desert night, you veer left when the rest of your company goes right, that one, small decision can end not only your military career, but your surgeon's career as well.

Then, if you make the small decision to ignore a perfectly lovely woman because you hate cold germs possibly worse than you hate Jezail muskets, you might just gain yourself a desirable address and an exceedingly interesting flatmate.

And then, if you go ahead and live with that interesting flatmate, you may come to find that fate has brought you not only a new career and a lifelong friend, but soon you'll meet another perfectly lovely woman, and her name will be nearly as plain and simple as your own.

Yes, sometimes life is made of terribly important small decisions. Like a doctor nodding once and handing a tall man his card.

Like a tall man smiling. Taking that card. And putting down his glass.

SH

Stop! Thief!

Along the River Thames, South London — 2013

"Stop that man!"

The black woman walking down Victoria Embankment did not stop that man.

As a matter of fact the black woman, who was wearing six inch stiletto heels and every other week taught a night class in how to use them to lethal effect, *side-stepped* the short man that the tall man had demanded she stop.

The woman did not do this out of fuss for her lovely coiffure or manicure or her really very nice business suit, she did this because she was texting and wouldn't have been aware of anything short of an asteroid streaking across the face of the sun.

So the thief ran on and Sherlock Holmes—after tripping over the scooter of a scooting child—rose up and ran after him.

"Stop that man!"

The bald man walking across Hungerford Bridge did not stop that man.

As a matter of fact the man walking across the bridge, who had a jackknife in his back pocket, brass knuckles in his man purse, and a wallet attached to his waist by a heavy chain, scooped his two-year-old son from the running man's path.

The bald man didn't do this to keep his baby son safe, he did this because he was besotted by his wee one's happy giggles and so he cuddled the little boy close and they danced across the bridge, oblivious to everything but each other.

The thief ran on, and a limping Sherlock Holmes—after being viciously struck in the head by an oblivious tourist's camera—continued on after him.

"Stop that man!"

The brace of rugby players shouting along the bank of the Thames did not stop that man.

As a matter of fact the brace of rugby players, whose black-and-blue jerseys proclaimed them *The Tottenham Terrors,* as a group scrambled out of the running man's way and down the steps leading to the river.

They did this because they couldn't agree who was the best faux mezzo-soprano of their half dozen and so who should play Kate in their Christmas production of *Pirates of Penzance.* Clearly the only way to settle the issue was with a sing-off on the shore near the Oxo Tower.

The thief thought the rugby players had a grand idea, and so he flung himself down the embankment steps and onto hard-soft River Thames sand.

Sherlock Holmes stopped running after the man for three entire seconds.

Because Sherlock completely lost the man. Then Sherlock got his detective on and, because he didn't see anyone ahead of him darting out of the way of a short missile, the good detective deduced that the only place the man could have gone was down by the river.

Sherlock—limping on one leg and bleeding from his right temple—hobbled down the steps after him.

"Stop! Thief!" he yelled.

The thief ignored him.

But on that hard-soft sand John H. Watson, a cast on his foot, crutches in his hands, and a patch over one eye, looked up. And though John Watson couldn't see the man who shouted, he did see a short man coming at him like a shot.

On instinct John Watson stopped the man.

Moments later a tall, limping, bleeding one appeared hobbling round a turn in the river and John stopped him, too.

Strong arms suddenly clamped around his waist, Sherlock Holmes nearly jumped out of his skin in frustration. As a matter of fact he *did* jump. And twist. And shout.

"Let me go! I almost have him!"

But Dr. Watson's used to holding on to all manner of creatures trying to wiggle away from booster jabs, stinging ointments, or the removal of teeny, tiny plasters, so the good doctor clutched the wounded, flailing stranger until the stranger finally calmed down and heard him.

"—I said I *got* him. The guy. The short running guy. He's just the other side of the pier wall. Kind of knocked himself out when he tripped on that patch of chalk. I might have helped him trip. He'll be fine. Tide's coming up anyway, he can't get any farther."

Sherlock Holmes sagged. John Watson grunted with the weight of him. They both stumbled and sat down hard on the sand.

"Sh'lock H'lmes," said Sherlock, deciding now to catch his breath.

"John Watson," said John. A few more seconds passed and then John waved an aluminium crutch in Sherlock's face. "You sit back down mister."

Completely against his will Sherlock's body obeyed the command, planting his bum right back on the sand.

"You're bleeding all down the right side of your face and running on what I bet is a serious sprain, so just *give it a rest* would you?" John gestured behind him with the other crutch. "What's so important anyway?"

Sherlock sat up self-righteously straight and muttered darkly, "He's stolen my key to Buckingham Palace."

John thought a moment about this. Then John crawled over to Sherlock Holmes. He peered into the man's eyes. Then he reached out and peeled back a lid. Sherlock glowered but did not flinch.

"I'm just checking for concussion or insanity or alien abduction or something because it sounded like you said that guy back there—"

John and Sherlock turned. 'That guy back there' was still unconscious back there.

"—stole your key to the Queen's house."

Sherlock couldn't hear John at that moment as the blood in his eye rendered him temporarily deaf. When the good doctor had pushed groping detective hands out of the gore and cleaned the blood with a wad of gauze he happened to be carrying in his pocket, Sherlock answered.

"Yes."

John put the bloody gauze in a sterile pouch he happened to be carrying in his other pocket. "Yes you've got a concussion, you're insane, you've been mentally abducted, or yes you actually have a key that lets you walk right in and have tea with HRH?"

101

Sherlock Holmes peered at the strange doctor. The strange doctor was taking all of this remarkably well. Sherlock decided to see exactly how far *remarkably well* went.

"No, no, no, and yes somewhat. Actually," Sherlock gestured 'back there.' "I stole the key from *him.*"

John checked his watch to see if he had time for this. Yep, he had time for this. Mostly because, right now? Right now John Watson didn't have a job, a destination, or pretty much anything on other than looking for seventeenth century pipe stems along the Thames foreshore, and frankly that was dull because 1) they were a lot less rare than you'd think and 2) it was hard to see them with the eye patch.

"And now," said Sherlock, rising, "if you'll just stop doctoring I need to get my key back."

Sherlock Holmes rose but the intriguing doctor intrigued him further by tugging a solid silver key ring out of his back pocket. "I thought it looked a little above means for a guy wearing stained trainers and a torn concert t-shirt. Then again, you never know."

Sherlock pocketed the tossed key, flicked his fast gaze over the man with the cast, the crutches, and the eye patch. *Flick-flick-flick.* A bad bar fight, defending a boy, a gay boy, against three mean drunks. The boy hadn't ended up with a scratch.

On instinct Sherlock Holmes asked John Watson a question. John's answer would go on to change both their lives forever.

"How would you like to fight crime. Sort of. No pay. Except occasionally. When we have a client with money."

John peeled back his patch, squinted until his swollen eye at last focused. After a few seconds he reached for Sherlock. The detective helped the doctor to his feet.

"Where do I sign up?"

SH

Shoe Leather

Gower Place Surgery, London — 1880

Pain is not a progression, John Watson decided that long ago. It's a vine-choked maze inside which there are blind turns, double-backs, wild things with thorns.

There are also tiny, shadowy corners of stillness and peace. But somehow those spots are too small to hold a body, you can stand there a moment and breathe, you can hear a bird, perhaps see a flower, but you can't *stay*, not at first. You have to move on, back into the thorny blind.

Dr. John Watson's watched people make this journey through pain a dozen times a dozen and though some ask him "when will this be over," the good doctor has never been able to tell them at what day or hour healing finally comes, because everyone goes through the maze a different way, because the maze is—

"—infinite," said Sherlock Holmes to the doctor sitting in front of him. "The sights, the sounds, the smells, the textures. The *possibilities,* whether investigating a robbery, a murder, a disappearance or deception, oh Dr. Watson, the possibilities are infinite. But the end, the solution, there's always just the one."

The words were very pretty, no doubt, but they had not at all answered Watson's question, and so he dug deeper. "And the cocaine helps...how?"

Holmes looked down his hawkish nose at the locum doctor sitting so still and steady in the chair across from him. This was not his usual physician. Not his regular *supplier.*

Holmes' usual doctor was as familiar as a worn, velvet-lined case. He was steady like this one, but he didn't ask questions, not any more. Then again, he hadn't understood the answers so long ago, had he? Because when Holmes is asked the *why* of something, the how, or the what, he always answers in detail and at length. If Sherlock Holmes knows a thing, he knows it from each and every side.

And so Sherlock Holmes knew this: "You want me to earn my hit."

Watson was good at still. And steady. He didn't used to be. Once in a while he wished everyone could take a bullet. Because if you survived something like that, it clarified, stripped things down, settled mind and body. It made you patient. And maybe, just maybe, a little bit wise.

"I want to understand your maze Mr. Holmes. Everything I do is focused on stopping, or better yet, preventing pain. The problem is you can't *see* pain, so you have to..." Holmes watched the doctor look at nothing. "...you have to find it with words."

Holmes knew the power of words. They were his stock in trade, essentially. After he's seen, heard, smelled, well then he has to explain, so people understand that the murderer was narrow-shouldered yet stout, wore freshly-polished size four shoes, that her husband smokes Metropolitan cigars and yes, that all of this was based on a toe print, three drops of blood, the scent on the curtains.

"You insist that it's pain that brings me here but surely you're projecting. I understand that patients often do this with their physicians, do physicians do so with their patients? Or am I wrong, when you took that bullet to the shoulder, did it not shatter bone, tear flesh, heal poorly? Did you not suffer fever and lose much more than weight? Perhaps a surgical career, a purpose. Are you sure, Dr. Watson, that you aren't projecting your pain on *me?*"

There are many things that bullet taught John Watson and another was that pain rarely brought grace. When people hurt they sometimes lashed out and *hurt,* which, by some miracle, seemed to lessen pain. *This,* if anything, was John Watson's real wisdom. And so Watson went about helping his patient lessen his pain.

"Ah, and there's the proof of it, those infinite sights and sounds you talked about. Was it the way I hold my shoulders that told you about the bullet? The ill fit of my suit that said fever? Do I so clearly have a cutter's hands? You'd need to stop all that seeing sometimes wouldn't you, just to have some peace?"

For the first time since he entered the doctor's small consultation room Holmes smiled.

This man understood…nothing. He'd got it all wrong, every last bit, but oh my did he try.

Some thought Holmes didn't appreciate effort. That genius found only frustration in anyone not genius, but that was wrong. Though everyone was wrong almost all the time, Sherlock Holmes relished it when people *tried.* It was like a little bit of breath, their effort, a spark for his tinder, it was as if, for just a moment, he wasn't alone.

Yet it was funny how quickly people stopped trying, once they watched him burn.

"Seeing so much," said Watson, "must hurt."

People are shy when they talk to a doctor. Being vulnerable before a stranger is a bashful business, so another bit of Watson wisdom was this: Talk and talk, about things of no consequence if you must, and people will eventually talk about what's important.

"People think that *thinking* can't produce pain, Mr. Holmes, but of course it can. A man heavy into deep thoughts wrinkles his brow, clenches his teeth, he may fist his hands, stoop. Migraines, headaches, a sore back and so much more can be the results."

No.

No.

"No."

Holmes knows the trick of chattering the air full with wrong so that a suspect corrects with what's right. What he didn't know until this moment was how much self-righteous satisfaction comes with the correcting—no wonder people were so keen to correct *him*.

"I would never stop the seeing," said Holmes, closing his eyes. "That would bring a special madness don't you think? The kind that comes when you know there was something you used to know. What a badly-bargained peace that would be."

Holmes opened his eyes, leaned forward in his chair. "No, my frustration doesn't come from too much, Dr. Watson, it comes only and ever from too little. From a troublesome lack of shouting, a dearth of movement. The cocaine isn't to dull a perceived pain, it's to stimulate daydreams, visions, it's to turn the contemplation of the old grocer's new bruises into a puzzle worth solving, because the only other pressing problem I may have today is trying to remember whether I filed the newspaper clippings and discarded the breakfast kippers, or whether I filed the kippers and discarded the clippings."

Holmes clasped his hands, which caused him to sit straighter, which lead to a raised chin, which, he was completely unaware, made him look so holier-than-thou and full of affectation that Watson bit his cheek not to laugh.

Instead the good doctor said, "Then you must be the laziest devil that ever stood in shoe leather."

Holmes blinked, then grinned so broadly he was nearly unrecognisable from the dour-faced man who'd sloped into the consultation room fifteen minutes previous.

"You said when you first arrived that you solve mysteries. That that's your oeuvre." Watson scooped up a newspaper, tossed it to the tall man. "What of those robberies up Belsize Lane near Hampstead? A small fortune's gone missing between three completely unrelated shops."

In the last eight weeks Holmes had solved a murder, found missing minor royalty, and recovered for a politician a letter that would not only have stripped him of his power, but of something far more dear: The trust of his wife. The Yarders had pocketed the credit for all of these.

"What's all that to me?"

Holmes tossed the paper back to the doctor, who didn't catch it because he was busy standing, reaching for his coat.

"Get your hat."

Holmes widened one eye, narrowed the other. This had the interesting effect of making him look both excited and slightly mad. In other words, like Sherlock Holmes.

"You'd like me to come…where?"

"To the scenes of the crimes. If you have nothing better to do."

Holmes' reply was wordless but clear. He crossed one long leg over the other. He squinted that squinting eye harder, opened the other wider. Then he looked at the bottom of his shoe. "Yes, there seems leather to spare."

"Now," said Watson, as they stepped out onto the street, "What in the world is a consulting detective?"

SH

Bloody Charming

St. Mary's Hospital Laboratory — 2015

"Can I have your blood?"

Sherlock Holmes looked up from his swab and Petri dishes. On the other side of the lab bench stood a mild-looking man with a clipboard, a pleasant smile, and an expectant expression.

Sherlock Holmes blinked. He's been asked many slightly unusual things by many people in his thirty-something years. Why just yesterday police constable Derrida asked:

"Can you just go away now and go away fast? Don't say anything don't look back, the detective inspector is still glaring and really, really didn't appreciate you solving the case in one minute when she's been working on it for six weeks so run, run like the wind Holmes before she arrests you for wearing fancy shoes or a stopped watch or something, can you do that? Please?"

(He did.)

And, month before last an heiress, whose name Sherlock is pretty sure he wrote down somewhere, asked:

"I've lost a brace of rare silkworms, a five hundred year old book, a diamond, and my husband. If you find them for me by eight o'clock tonight there's ten thousand pounds in it for you. Double that if you find them in the exact order named. Do you think you can?"

(He did.)

And just last December that interesting chemicals salesperson called and asked:

"Why do you want these incendiary compounds again? And you can't just say what you wrote on the web form because 'an experiment vital to nation security' makes you sound like James Bond and since I'm not Q or Z or whomever it is who gives him those ridiculous—never mind okay? Just *never mind.* Right. So. What do you need the iron sulfide and the triethylaluminium for *exactly?"*

(He explained. They didn't send him the triethylaluminium.)

Even as a child he was asked unusual things, including:

"Darling, did the frozen peas really get onto the ceiling in the kitchen 'somehow?' Since peas can't levitate or locomote on their own, your father and I think they must have had *assistance,* and so we believe that perhaps you, that large bottle of cola behind your back, and the majority of those minty sweets you shoveled into your mouth, may have united to blast those peas into orbit. So tell mummy and daddy, is that what happened?"

(It was. He cried.)

So, yes, Sherlock's been asked many slightly out-of-the-ordinary things by a great many people over many of his years, so this newest question shouldn't have startled him but it did. And frankly it was a little unfair.

However, aware that a certain degree of charm had on more than one occasion retained for him the use of the hospital's electron microscope, their acids and bases, the use of their showers when he's accidentally spilled such items on his person, well, realising that being *charming* was likely what was called

111

for here, Sherlock did not say "Absolutely not." Instead he answered the question with a question.

"May I ask which parts?"

Dr. John Watson was told that this Sherlock guy wouldn't be an easy sell. However, they'd also told him Dr. Jamison over in orthopaedics would not only refuse to donate, she'd also swear at him on general principle. Within sixty seconds John had had Anne's ("May I call you Anne?") signature and a promise she'd bring both of her boyfriends to the blood drive, too.

Then there was Dr. Le Patourel in dermatology. He hadn't held out even half as long as Jamison, had asked John for a date, and when that was declined tried to set John up with his daughter Kim over in cardiothoracics.

As for what Drs. Bell, Blackwell, and Keebler in urology had laughingly said (aside from yes) when he asked them, well John's too much of a gentleman to say.

So yes, good doctor Watson has been told he can charm blood from a snake ("Valerie, I think you're mixing your metaphors"), so he felt reasonably confident he'd get this Sherlock guy ("A consulting what?") on board. Though the man's reply was slightly left of centre John felt it was promising.

Yet before he could answer with a waggle of his eyebrows and, "Whichever part you want to give," Sherlock expanded on his question.

"There are of course the erythrocytes, I've a lot of those. There's leukocytes, thrombocytes, there's also plasma or whole blood but I'm afraid I can't spare much whole blood. As a matter of fact I was told I wouldn't have to share any and, frankly, I need most of it if I'm to catch the duchess before she makes another bomb. However, if you want some of the erythrocytes I really do have a lot of those." Then Sherlock smiled in what he hoped was a charming, but go-away fashion.

John took a deep breath to say something. John exhaled the breath. John sat down on a stool opposite this Sherlock guy, laid his clipboard on the lab bench between them, and he said, "What now?"

Look, to retain lab privileges at a hospital in which he doesn't work and isn't technically supposed to be, Sherlock Holmes knows when to be winning. He knows when to be magnanimous. He knows when to *keep his mouth shut.*

That doesn't mean he actually *does* any of these things, merely that he *knows* when to do these things. So Sherlock Holmes put down his swab, his Petri dish, and said, as if at great length, "Bat's blood has a higher number of erythrocytes than human blood, which is what makes it perfect for this experiment.'" Narrowing his eyes as if he would be refuted, Sherlock added, "And they're smaller, which increases oxygen binding."

John fast-blinked at Sherlock. Then there was revelation. "Oh! You think I want that." John gestured to the Petri dishes, the swabs, the vials of gore.

Sherlock fast-blinked at John. Then there was revelation. "Oh. You want *my* blood. My actual blood."

Each man smiled charmingly at the other, at last on the same page. John sat up straight, straightened his clipboard, plucked up his pen. Sherlock unbuttoned his left shirt cuff, rolled his sleeve up past his elbow, and said, "I've got good veins." He presented his arm to John and said, "Take as much as you need." Then he went back to culturing his Petri dishes.

John put down his pen. John checked his watch.

John remembered he was still deeply pissed with the entire lot in urgent care, the whole ruddy bunch who still treated him like he was a damned student when no, no, in fact he was an army veteran who'd got *shot,* not a dogsbody meant to plague people to donate for the sodding autumn blood drive.

John tossed the pen over his shoulder, chucked the clipboard after. Sherlock looked up. John reached across the table. "John," he said. After a moment Sherlock reached back. "Sherlock."

Then with a charming grin John moved to the other side of the bench, clasped his hands behind his back, looked close at Sherlock's cultures, and said, "So what's this about a deadly duchess?"

Sherlock rubbed his hands together and said, "She's a genius actually. Using bat blood, prussic acid, a loo roll, and a few chemicals found at any well-stocked chemist, she makes very small, very deadly bombs. I'm still trying to get the measurements right."

"You know, I dated a bomb squad lieutenant when I was in the army. She told me an interesting thing once…"

❦

Shaggy Dog Story

Greenwich Gardens — 1880

"Go away!"

John Watson's granddad—in Her Majesty's service from the age of sixteen—had a saying: He who cannot obey cannot command. Interestingly, this truism is…true. So it follows that a man disinclined to obedience doesn't enter the military. Likewise, one unfond of being bossed around is unlikely to last as a medical intern.

Which is to say that, despite the entirely human tendency toward resisting authority, an ex-army physician is more familiar than most with following orders. So when a voice at the end of a shadowed Greenwich alley boomed, "Go away!" John Watson and his three-legged dog damn well went away.

This was not one bit okay with four-legged Toby.

To be sure, Toby found that getting out and about with Mr. Gentle Hands Tobacco Fast Walk was always an adventure. They'd go skulking down deliciously mucky mews, dash along the fetid shore of the Thames, and Toby would get to sniffle and snuff to his heart's delight. Most of the time he and Mr. Gentle Hands Tobacco were on the trail of something or someone far away—a creosote-besmirched man or yeast-covered baker—but sometimes Mr. Gentle Hands came along and simply took Toby on a long walk about London and those were the very best of days.

On those days Mr. Gentle would come with a walking stick and a great coat whose pockets would be full of bits of bacon and egg or buckwheat cake. In those voluminous pockets he'd have paper-wrapped mutton, scraps of jam toast or lumps of sugar.

But. Today.

Today Mr. G's pockets were boring and dull and *same.* A pipe and magnifier and flat cap in one, a great rattling of ha'pennies and tanners in the other, and in the Important Pocket, the one over his high-thrumming heart, Mr. G had *crackers.* Dry crackers, dry crackers without salt, dry crackers without a hinting of liver or *anything.*

Toby knows how to be a good dog because Toby *is* a good dog, but they had already tromp-run-walked from Hackney to Greenwich and still they hadn't found the other dog, the one they were looking for, the one with a key jangling from her collar, and whose old collar smelled of tea and curried chicken and iron.

Yes in kindness Mr. G had stopped and fed them both crackers, so many crackers that Toby even went to drink out of the Thames and he has got *some* standards, but that's not the point, the point is that the man down along the alley, Mr. Whisky Newsprint Chicken Tea, smelled good and right and Toby wanted to see *him.* He whined eagerly.

"Toby!"

But. Today. Mr. G wasn't *listening.*

So Toby talked in one of the only ways he knows how. He—now!—stopped walking. Mr. G, despite being a big person, stopped too, because even the smallest dog can summon the density of a star when need is sharp.

Sherlock Holmes turned and looked at his purloined dog (it really wasn't his fault that Sherman wasn't about when he

116

came along to borrow the mongrel). Though Toby was indeed a good dog Holmes knew that the mutt was, like himself, easily bored when his gifts were not of much use and, to be honest, they had been on this trail for nearly seven hours, with little to show for it but cracker crumbs in Holmes' pockets and an even-scruffier dog.

As such Holmes suspected Toby wanted to play with the three-legged dog he'd spotted at the end of the alley but...

Holmes sighed. No doubt they could both use something else to focus on for a bit. With a pat to Toby's neck, Holmes unleashed the mutt and murmured, "Go, boy," and so Toby went.

John Watson and Lady Amity Who sat in a sunbeam, sharing a chicken sandwich. Lady Amity wolfed, Watson nibbled, both enjoyed the warmth, the day, and one another's company.

They saw each other often, did the doctor and the dog. Mostly because each had not much else to do. Lady Amity's own Lady was old, and failed to walk the young Airedale much, whilst Watson was still himself fever frail, home from Afghanistan not yet a half year.

So the good doctor sat with old Lady Verena several times a week, and in exchange she allowed Lady Amity to spend time with John. It was an equitable arrangement. That Lady Amity, born with only three legs, sometimes grew tired on their rambles before Watson did, made the man-mutt partnership even easier. And that she told no one about his little nips of whisky to help nip away some of the boredom of being an invalid...well why do you think he brought her bits of meat and cheese and cake?

When Toby rounded the corner at a gallop, Watson grinned. When Toby trotted up to them, tail wagging, Lady growled—she would *not* be sharing her egg! Watson stroked her neck with one hand, held a bit of chicken out to Toby with the other.

"There's a good lad, would you like some?"

"He would indeed," said Sherlock Holmes, hands in pockets, Toby's leash draped over his shoulders. "I wouldn't mind a bit too, if you've enough."

A red letter day, this, not one visitor but two. Eager for conversation—Lady Verena talked about lawn bowls, grandchildren, and cake—Watson unwrapped another sandwich and handed it to his guest, who immediately shared half with his four-legged companion.

"Toby and Sherlock Holmes," Holmes withdrew then doffed his cap, "sorry for being snappish before. Now, if you'd care to share a sip from the flask in your far pocket, doctor, I'd be grateful."

An hour later the dogs had run themselves tired around the park, the whisky was gone, and Holmes had explained to Watson how it was reason, not magic that told him the doctor's profession, lodging, illness, and slight gambling habit (Watson didn't notice pressing his own hand against the racing broadsheet in his pocket).

It wasn't until that hour was up and the men had fallen to silence and the dogs fallen at their feet, that Holmes startled everyone with a shout. "Oh what a fool I've been!"

Instantly he was on his knees, petting and praising Toby—and taking Lady's leash from between Toby's paws. A small key chimed against the leash's eyehook.

"Oh Toby, I'm sorry. I see but I clearly do not observe. It wasn't the good doctor's sandwich you wanted before."

If Toby could have spoken just then he'd have corrected Mr. G's assumption, but he couldn't and so he didn't. There were many things Toby didn't share with Mr. G, including the fact that his landlady pinches his tobacco and the corner grocer is sweet on him, and that's why he always gives him a honey cake.

So no, Toby didn't let Mr. G know he was wrong. Instead what he did—what they all did—was decamp to Marton Manor, where Lady Verena learned that not only was her eldest grandchild an embezzler, but he'd been using her favourite set of lawn bowls to secret away his ill-gotten gains.

She did not take this news at all well. As a matter of fact her snit was so great she withdrew Watson's Airedale walking privileges for an entire week. Feeling quite responsible, Holmes offered the diversion of "walks with a new flatmate, if you're amenable"?

That those promised 'walks' turned out to be mad dashes down shadowy alleys should have been obvious, Holmes would later tell a complaining Watson, given the way they'd met. "Clearly you saw, but you did not ob—"

The less-than-courteous name Watson called Holmes just then is not repeatable here.

SH

The Tell-Tale Heart

Phillimore Place, West London — 2015

"Stay in the van."

A veteran of the Fifth Northumberland Fusiliers, John Watson was always a good soldier. He knew when to follow orders.

A veteran of St. Bartholomew's hospital, John Watson, however, knew three entirely different things:

This scowling sergeant was not his superior officer.

This sergeant had not made the emergency call that got him out of a warm hospital and into a minus ten degree night.

The man who *had* called—"hurry, please please please"—was very aware that seconds are sometimes all that stand between a dead hostage and a living one.

So John Watson got out of the van.

And kind of wished he hadn't.

It started with the sergeant's complaint—"You'll only be in the way!"—it continued inside and at volume.

"If a herd of buffalo had come through here you couldn't have left a worse mess!"

John couldn't tell who was yelling because, as the man outside had implied, the place was crawling with cops and John was one body among far too many.

So he did one important thing: Found someone with a detective's insignia and asked, "Has the little boy been found?"

The young detective frowned, wide-eyed. "There are six hundred self-storage companies in greater London. *Six hundred.*"

"Oh god, he put the boy in a—" John stopped talking when the detective actually looked as if he'd cry.

Instead John tucked himself into a corner of the four thousand square foot mansion as police continued pouring in, and he tried not to think that somewhere in London a very young child huddled in a small, freezing space, waiting, hoping.

No, instead John Watson looked at the blond hardwood floor at his feet, and then he went Zen and started pacing along the thin, dark inlay at its edges.

"So help me I'll be the one to cut out *your* heart if you—"

The voice cut itself off and this time John saw who'd been yelling because the tall man was clutching his own head as if trying to stop it from shaking *no, no, no.*

John looked back down when he reached a corner. He tapped his toe onto the pretty starburst inlay there, continued pacing.

"Lestrade," said the tall man, pacing now, his strides frantic.

John reached another corner. Tapped his toe onto another dark starburst. Watched a rumpled inspector tiredly usher his crime scene crew from the room.

Quiet and a couple dozen feet from the pacing man, John paced. Another corner, another tap.

And so it went for three more minutes. Then everything went to hell.

"Sherlock. *Sherlock.*" Lestrade stood still, so much more weary now than he was just minutes ago, his body already rounded with defeat.

The pacing man—Sherlock, apparently—stopped pacing. John continued.

Sherlock turned on Lestrade. John turned at a corner, but first...*tap.*

Sherlock stepped close to Lestrade. John stepped to the next corner...*tap.*

"Thirty-eight police. Thirty-eight police touching everything, papers, clothes, evidence, *the body.* You let them move the killer's corpse." Sherlock bent over, hands on knees. "I could have found the boy, but you let them touch *everything.*"

The inspector closed his eyes. "He didn't kill this one, Sherlock. The boy's still out there somewhere. We can find him."

Sherlock stumbled back, slid down the wall. "He's dead, Lestrade. Frozen to death by the time we get to him. Just..."

Pacing, tapping, pacing, tapping John hadn't noticed that the big man had shut up. John stopped pacing just short of his favourite corner. He liked this one, the corner with the crooked inlay, the strange one that didn't look like a starburst at all.

John looked up. From across the room John said, "The killer. What was his name?"

Neither the police officer nor the man on the floor heard him, so John Watson of the Fifth Northumberland Fusiliers, spoke. "What was the killer's name?"

Lestrade looked up, squinted, confused. "Who're yo—"
"Tell me."
"Who—"

"Is this the one who takes out the heart when the victim's—"

"How do you know that, the public don't know that."

"I'm an emergency responder, I *hear* things. Now tell me."

"What is it?"

The doctor looked at the man slumped on the floor, he was now no longer slumped.

"What have you noticed?"

John crossed the room, held out his hand. Sherlock reached back. John tugged the man tall and all three people in that massive, empty room walked across it and to John's special corner. He tapped a toe onto the crooked...not starburst.

"I thought it was an accident, that someone made a mistake. They didn't. They got it perfectly." John squatted, laid his fist over the inlay.

"Oh. *Oh.*"

John nodded. "There are none of the arteries or veins leading off, just the—"

"Left and right atria and—"

"—left and right ventricles."

Lestrade said softly, "There's no basement in this house."

Sherlock fell to his knees and banged at the floor with his fist. "There doesn't have to be."

*

Eighty seven minutes later the drugged child was removed from what would have been his tomb, three feet below that tell-tale heart.

Twelve hours later Dr. John Watson had finished giving his statement at New Scotland Yard.

Twelve hours and three minutes later Sherlock Holmes appeared suddenly beside him and they both walked out the Yard's double doors.

Thirteen hours later they were eating the best Indian food that has ever been, *ever.*

Two days later they were flatmates.

Two weeks later they were being hauled out of the Thames, the priceless pearls in Sherlock's hand, evidence—gloves, coat, wallet—in John's.

Three weeks after that John Watson wrote his first account of their adventures.

Three months later the little boy—his name was Amadeo—came with his dad to 221B. Sherlock gave the child an electron microscope scan of bees. John gave him one of his military medals.

Two years later John Watson published *The Adventures of Sherlock Holmes.*

And for many of the years after that, the good doctor Watson and his friend Sherlock? Well, they lived quite legendary lives.

SH

Doctor's Orders

Stamford Street, South London — 1886

"You. Here. Now."

There are some men who will resist a direct order on general principle. Sherlock Holmes is not such a man.

This was not obvious at the moment.

For Sherlock Holmes was walking quick-smart right past a short man lying in the middle of Stamford Street, and the man kneeling beside that man, barking out orders.

"Big man. Jaunty step. Here."

The clipped cadence did what the words could not. They thump, thump, thumped into Sherlock Holmes' awareness. He blinked his gaze up from a police report, and stopped in the centre of the street.

"Here, before he wakes and starts moving. Accident with a hansom, not sure how badly he's hurt. Must avoid shock. Dr. John Watson. Hold him here, thank you."

Holmes dropped his reports to the ground, followed them to his knees, took hold of the prone man's head. Watson knee-walked toward the man's legs, continued rat-tat-tatting out orders. "Keep him still. You," Watson pointed to a bowler-hatted man, "Two streets over, Westminster Surgery, go tell them we need help."

As Watson began loosening the injured man's belt and collar he woke and started talking.

"There are several things you have to do. Stop my bleeding if there is any is there any bleeding if there is press on the artery above the wound. I'll need to avoid shock so elevate my feet have you done that? Also you'll want to loosen my clothing but don't go too far as I shouldn't be too cool or warm. I just realised I can't move my head oh god that's bad that is very—"

"I'm Dr. John Watson, of St. Bartholomew's hospital and recently Afghanistan, where I served as assistant surgeon with the Fifth Northumberland Fusiliers. And you are, doctor...?"

"Stephens. Steven Mark Stephens. The first Steven is with a V and the second a PH and have you sent for medical assist—"

"Please be still Dr. Stephens we—"

"—ance? You'll need to elevate my feet. Did you elevate my feet? I can't feel my feet! Oh god I'm going to die from your incompetence."

"—and you might have mentioned it John, but you did not. Were you going to tell me that Dr. Becher invited your entire department to his Christmas party or simply keep me ignorant. Again. And please, no, 'But Sherlock...' I will not listen to one more excuse that begins with 'But Sherlock.'"

The big man holding Stephens' head had been so silent, so much like a second set of hands for Watson, that somehow the good doctor had forgotten he was there. Still, it took only a moment to realise what the man—Sherlock—was doing.

Distracting.

Shock can kill where a wound has not. Avoiding shock—a plummet in blood pressure, thready pulse, a heart beating an irregular tattoo—is therefore vital. One key is to keep a patient calm, but if they refuse to be calmed, distraction just may do. Pressing firmly on Steven Stephens' femoral artery,

John Watson picked up the ball thrown by Sherlock, he leaned across the anxious doctor's body, and he damn well *distracted.*

"Oh, no you don't Sherlock."

"That's Mr. Holmes to you, Mr. Watson."

"We will not talk about this here."

"At least I have your *attention* here."

Steven Mark Stephens stopped struggling.

"Now is not the time, *Sherlock.*"

"Now seems a perfectly good time, *John.*"

Sherlock Holmes held Steven Mark Stephens' head so firmly he'd have been secured through hurricane winds, but that did not stop Stephens' eyes from moving. Darting back and forth between each man, his gaze wide, avid, and deliciously scandalised.

"I'll need my tuxedo laundered I think. Benjamin can do it in time for the party. Perhaps it would make sense to send out yours as well, John."

"You are not coming."

"Then you are not going."

"Sherlock Gillette Harding Holmes, do I have to remind you what happened the last time you came to one of the hospital's fêtes?"

Steven Mark Stephens would not at that moment have risen up from the pavement if he'd been given his heart's truest desire. He stayed very still so that the two men above him would forget he was there, and he radiated very hard *remind him, remind him.*

Sherlock Holmes cannot read minds—despite what some will insist during his rather illustrious career—but he can read the physical tells of a gossip. As such, he gave Dr. Steven Mark Stephens something to gossip *about.*

"They never proved it was me and Dr. Becher declined to press charges John, you know that."

"I know it was you, Sherlock, and so does that poor intern. He had to move to a different hospital after what you did."

Steven Mark Stephens radiated *what? what did he do* so hard at John Watson that there were quite nearly bruises.

"I'll remind you that you've more than one time *encouraged* me to do what I did."

"But never," here Watson dropped his voice, leaned closer to Holmes, hissed, "in public."

It was very good that help arrived then, for John Watson was sure he had no more than two more extemporaneous moments in him. After that he was going to resort to speaking in Pashto just to have something to say.

It didn't come to that as an ambulance at last arrived from St. Mary's.

The hand-over was swift and included Watson's sharing with the medical personnel their patient's profession and tips on how to keep him calm.

As Stephens and ambulance receded, Watson clasped his hands behind his back and Holmes rocked on his heels.

"Sherlock Gillette Harding Holmes?"

"I was trying to think of things to say. There was a hansom right behind you, I read the maker's plaque on the carriage. Good lord that was…that was…"

"Fun?"

Watson laughed suddenly, turned toward the river path. Holmes collected his papers, and followed. "Yes! Though I've likely ruined my reputation at Bart's."

"Indeed, Dr. Stephens will have shared the particulars with the St. Mary's staff before the first stitch is put into that leg. I suspect St. Bart's will have the lurid details by nightfall."

"You insult the gossip network, Mr. Holmes. It'll be common knowledge before afternoon rounds. Yet I can't say we did *your* reputation any good."

"Ah, but here's where we differ. I've been accused of everything from committing crimes so that I can solve them, to a supernatural pact with Mephistopheles. My reputation has never been particularly sterling. Still I suppose it's all my fault, tarnishing yours so badly."

"How so?"

"I'd been reading a police report when you ordered me over, the grisly particulars of a murderous domestic. I'm afraid I got carried away on a tide of melodrama."

Watson laughed again. "You certainly lead a life more interesting than I do. So why do people accuse you of criminal activity exactly?"

Holmes stopped in front of a pub. "Shall I tell you over a whisky? I could use a doctor's opinion on that domestic I mentioned."

Holmes opened the door, then followed behind Watson. "So what would you say about a wife who insisted her husband could not stop humming? She claims he hummed even in his sleep. In response she then did a most unusually bloodthirsty thing. Shall I tell you?"

The man entering the pub behind Holmes and Watson hastened through the door, and trailed close, radiating very hard, *tell him, tell him, tell him.*

SH

The Bees'...Elbows

French Embassy, Knightsbridge, London — 2011

The two dancing men put Sherlock in mind of honeybees.

And really that should have tipped him off right then, exactly then, but it didn't. It was long seconds before the detective *detected,* and it took him so long because sometimes Sherlock Holmes takes things quite literally.

Only female honeybees dance, you see. Inside the hive they buzz and waggle, dancing to each other the location of nearby nectar, but the male drones? They do little more than mate, then die.

So when Sherlock looked at the two men dancing together at the embassy's black-tie affair, he at first didn't see what was right in front of him—because *drones don't dance.*

And then there it was, simple and sweet as honey from the comb: The dancing men were relaying information, with each step they were sending data to an unseen colleague.

When he finally saw what was right in front of him Sherlock just about buzzed, giddy, pleased, impressed. Because for all its simplicity the plan was brilliant. It was ingenious. It was...impenetrable.

Damn.

The information they were sending was the location of a drug cartel's bolt hole. Once that data was passed on, now, tonight, Sherlock would lose his one-day advantage over the criminals and the case was lost.

But there was no way to break the dancing men's code, not in the five or ten minutes he had to see and observe. Nor could he find the person to whom they were sending their message—not in that time and not in a room of three hundred and fifty people.

Damn it, damn it—*oh*. Oh, no no no no, all was not lost. Sherlock smiled. He knew *exactly* what to do.

Gaze dancing around the room, he knew what he needed to change everything.

There. Near the wall. And not dancing. A short man in a black suit and gleaming blue waistcoat.

Sherlock narrowed his eyes. Lifted his chin. Straightened his bow tie.

Making a beeline through the crowd, the good detective approached the black-tie wallflower, grinned flash-quick. Held out a hand. "Sir, may I have this dance?"

Blue Waistcoat looked up, smiled politely, said, "I'm sorry, but I—"

Sherlock stepped close, murmured, "I'm not wooing you, asking for a date, or proposing life-long cohabitation."

John Watson opened his mouth to reply but Sherlock Holmes wasn't done yet.

"I'm not done yet. No, the only thing I'm asking, please, is if you'll dance with me for five minutes. Five minutes in which we just may foil a very dangerous coterie of drug runners."

John Watson blinked at the tall man for a moment to be sure he was done.

"Are you done?"

Sherlock nodded.

"First: Are you serious about the whole criminals thing?"

Sherlock nodded.

"Second: Can you dance?"

Sherlock nodded.

"Third: You're actually really serious?"

Sherlock nodded harder.

"Fine."

As if he was often asked to cut a rug in order to scupper the plans of ruthless racketeers, John Watson finished his wine, asked his dance partner's name, proceeded to introduce himself, then the good doctor Watson stood, and held up his arms.

*

There's a trick to dancing a dance you don't know: Let go. If your partner is talented and you stop trying to guess what they'll do, it's almost easy to move across the dance floor, two minds, one motion.

So John was doing spectacularly well at this, dancing smoothly with his partner through hundreds of black-clad men and women...until his dance partner started making conversation.

"Drones, that is, male bees, die after sex. Their penis and abdominal tissues are ripped out right after they've mated."

John tripped, stepped on Sherlock's foot, then choked on his own spit. "Good god," he wheezed, after long seconds. "I'm glad you're not trying to, what was it? Woo me, because that was a terrible chat-up line."

Sherlock made a harrumphing sound, danced them across the floor. But John wasn't done yet.

"Also, I wasn't going to decline to dance with you because I thought you were hitting on me. I *was* going to wait for my date to get back from the ladies', first."

Sherlock had the decency to look briefly embarrassed. Then not embarrassed at all. "So why *didn't* you wait?"

It was John's turn to look embarrassed. "Well, the whole catching drug runners thing sounded kind of more important."

"You mean more interesting."

John frowned, then grinned, then laughed out loud, because yes, this *was* more interesting. His date—by her own admission a middle-management embassy drone (ha!)—had been gone to the ladies' so long he was pretty sure she'd scarpered with the pretty diplomat she'd eyed half the night.

That was fine. John was helping thwart crime, doing something that *felt* like something and, bonus, his partner really could dance.

"So why were you on about bee sex?"

Sherlock turned his partner. "Making conversation as we get closer to…" He turned again, "…those two men. Do you see? A tall one and a short one?"

"Ah."

Sherlock danced them closer. "They're sending a very simple message through their dance: Directions to a vital pass-through point for eighty million pounds worth of drugs."

"Can you decipher what they're saying?"

"No, but neither can they. Each knows his own dance, but not the other's, nor for whom they're dancing. It's the only way to secure such vital information."

"Do you have time to work it out?"

Briefly Sherlock looked fierce enough to sting. "No."

"And now?"

"Now we cut in."

It took a moment, but then John got it. "Oh, that's perfect."

"We confuse whomever is decoding their dance, by imitating their dance. Then *we* give directions. The wrong ones."

Sherlock danced them closer. "There are four basic moves: Turn head left, turn head right, elbows high or elbows low. Those are the directions. How long they hold each posture: distance. The rest is a typical waltz. So. Are you ready to...wing it?"

John groaned at the pun, nodded a bit breathless, felt himself gearing up.

The good doctor has done time in a very active A&E, he's triaged trauma patients in a base camp being actively targeted by insurgents, and he's faced down fifteen cranky five-year-olds in need of booster jabs: John Watson's familiar with the adrenalin rush of winging it.

John laughed, clutched Sherlock Holmes' hand more firmly, danced them closer, "Let's do it."

John let go of Sherlock, Sherlock of John, and each man asked another man to dance.

*

John never figured out how it all went so quickly from doing a stately waltz and buzz-buzzing about a dance floor, lifting his elbows, turning his head, trying not to grin giddy over the sheer ridiculous sense of being a secret-agent-international-spy to...to...to what happened.

And what happened was that Sherlock shoved another not-tall bloke his way and that not-tall guy asked John's tall guy to dance, and then *that* not-tall guy started doing the elbows thing but was getting it all wrong, and then Sherlock was right there, hissing in John's ear, "Keep dancing. Keep cutting in, only at random now. Teach each partner a move and then move on. I figured out who they're sending the message to."

And then Sherlock was gone.

That's when everything really seemed to go off the rails, and in no time the dance floor turned into a contact sport with people changing partners so quickly and elbows flapping and jabbing everywhere so pointedly, and if anyone could figure out anything at all after that it would have been a miracle.

As it turned out, Sherlock Holmes was pretty good at those.

It was the next night and over a restaurant table that he explained.

"It was obvious John. The only person who could have had an unimpeded view of those men on that crowded dance floor wasn't *on* the dance floor. The queen bee of the operation—"

John groaned.

"—wasn't a guest at the party at all. He was the security guard."

Sherlock stole three chips from beneath the remnants of John's fish. John reflected that when, earlier in the evening, they'd made a deal to share a flat, stealing food hadn't been on the list of faults Sherlock had disclosed.

"When we entered the guard's office you should have seen him. He was staring at three monitors, his mouth hanging open, one fist in his hair, the other clutched around a pencil riven by bite marks."

Sherlock grinned, as pleased as a bee buzzing over a pollen-heavy blossom. "He was so confused he didn't even notice when half of Scotland Yard just...waltzed right in."

Sherlock didn't have to steal the next chip from his new flatmate's plate. Groaning, John threw it at him.

SH

The Freaks

Islington, London — 1881

"I'll just go an' stick this freak, and then I'll stick you."

On that night-dark street John Watson shrugged, as if the big, blonde man with the knife had said, 'D'ya think it'll rain?'

That big man rocked side-to-side, his knife at a small Chinese man's throat, and Watson saw the child inside the big man's body. Really just a child clutching a homemade knife to another child's throat.

Yes, well Dr. John Watson's seen up close the evil of which even children are capable, seen in the name of Queen and country more than he ever needs to see. And though this wayward fool was two stone heavier and a half foot taller, the good doctor wasn't going to—

"You might think about throwing these little ones back."

Everyone—the big blonde man, the small Chinese one, and John Watson—turned toward a shadow standing in the shadows.

"I think," that darkness murmured, shifting, "maybe you should fight someone your own size."

A tall man with a hawk's austere face stepped into the street's pale light. Then a few things happened very fast.

The moment the shadow-man moved right, Watson threw his body left, against the boy—the one without the knife. They both stumbled hard against a brick wall. At the same time the shadow-man fell against the blonde boy and they both tumbled to rough stones.

The knife flashed silver, the shadow-man groaned, and then his shoe connected with the blonde boy's wrist. The boy moaned and the knife clattered away, loud and clear.

John Watson paid this no mind. He helped the Chinese boy to stand, was about to look at his throat in the bad light, but the man-child shook his head, pulled out of Watson's careful hands, and disappeared into the night.

That's when Watson at last registered the commotion behind him and turned in time to hear the shadow-man hissing, "The freaks are never who you think they are." The shadow-man took his booted foot off the big man's chest, stood there still and predatory as a bird of prey, and said, "No more. Do you understand? This. No more."

"You're letting him go?"

Sherlock Holmes turned toward John Watson as if seeing him for the first time. And in those initial seconds he saw everything he would ever need to know about this fellow…freak.

Here was a healer who went to war, a warrior who would plead for peace, a homebody who again and again left his small comforts to aid others. Holmes smiled and the severity of his face softened. He bowed a little toward Watson. "Of course you're right sir. We'll do this in due form of law."

The young man shifted there on the cobbles, yet it was not to rise but to close his eyes, cross arms over chest, to wait for blows as he had in his past so often waited.

"This infant has himself an infant. Two as a matter of fact, and though his is a rough justice, it's the only one he knows. Shall we teach him something kinder?" Holmes looked down to the boy, who did not look back though he listened most careful. "Taking from men weaker or smaller than you will lead to a knife in your belly before you're twenty, boy. And then who'll feed your babes?"

The boy on the dirty stones closed his eyes tighter, as if this would stop up his ears. It did not.

"There's a coarse job for you down at Queen's docks, swabbing and tarring boats. The man that needs the doing is a friend of mine, James Smoot. The wage will be...just enough."

The tall man bowed toward Watson again, "Sir, I am a British jury. This hungry man has done all the wrong things for all the right reasons. I find the prisoner not guilty. What say you, my lord?"

Both doctors and soldiers are used to triage, to assigning *degrees* to things. They understand the need for snap decisions, the necessity to judge and move on. Such men learn to trust their instincts and though John Watson's instinct was not so much to let the boy go, it *was* to trust the stranger who wanted to set him free.

"He's acquitted," said Watson to the man he'd soon call Holmes and eventually Sherlock, "and he can go." Watson bent, scooped up the boy's rough knife. "So long as he makes for himself no other victims and goes to Smoot tonight."

Holmes grinned and though the light was poor and the shadows sharp, Watson saw humour sparking there.

Holmes squatted by the boy, whose eyes were now open, though he still held himself in a protective embrace. "Tell Smoot that Sherlock Holmes will be by tomorrow to pass on his thanks. Will you go to him tonight, as judge—" Holmes paused.

"John Watson."

"—as Dr. Watson has willed it?"

140

The boy, his name was Marcus Meredydd and he was only a boy in his years, nodded his assent. Holmes offered his hand, and they both stood tall.

"Go care for your family," Holmes said, and stepped away.

Watson, however, stopped Meredydd before he could disappear into shadows. He reached, for then carefully palpated the boy's arm. "Just a bit bruised I think. Be as gentle with it as you can," he said, unobtrusively pressing a folded fiver into the boy's palm.

A few hours later a few things happened.

Meredydd fed his family. After that he met with Smoot. He had an argument with Smoot. He shut his mouth in the middle of a string of curses. Opened it again to mumble an apology. He bowed his head and clenched his hands and waited, as he was used to doing.

Smoot mumbled a string of curses too, though these were directed at the absent Holmes. Against his better judgment Smoot hired the boy, started him off right there. He did this because it would in part repay a very large debt he owed to Sherlock Holmes. In the end Smoot would be glad of the new lad, though their immediate enmity would take some time to turn to mutual respect.

And in those after-hours of that night, John Watson and Sherlock Holmes sat in Watson's small rooms, chasing the chill from bones with a bit of brandy. The doctor tended and dressed his new friend's hand, cut shallow by Meredydd's simple weapon, and eventually a companionable and extended silence fell.

In the wee hours it was broken by a question.

141

"I've just realised…how did you know I was a doctor? Back there with the boy, you—"

"—ah yes. A very good question I'll answer with a question. You mentioned looking for less pretentious quarters than these. I've just taken a place on Baker Street. Perhaps you'd like to go halves?"

Holmes' brain—which even in shadow could absorb the minute things that told him a child-man was hungry, that a wounded doctor needed purpose—had for years made him something of a freak, an easy epithet uttered by those who didn't understand the elegant simplicity of what he did.

Watson was an even rarer bird than the hawkish Holmes. A man who moved always toward peril rather than away, one who'd help despite his own frailties, he more than one time wondered at the rightness of his causes, at his—there was no other word for it—*freakish* devotion to duty.

But yes, John Watson's got good instincts and he's learning to stop questioning them. So the good doctor stood, saluted Holmes with his glass. "You'll give me a mystery to untangle then? Well, the proper study of mankind is man after all. So, let's see these digs of yours."

Sherlock Holmes grinned, "Study away my friend, study away. Now, to Baker Street."

SH

Milk Men

Tesco Extra Supermarket, Cromwell Road, London — 2015

Sherlock Holmes knows a large number of unusual things.

He knows how long it will be before a dead body goes from pliable to stiff as a stiff. He knows when retinal blood columns will fragment after death. Sherlock knows the navel is replete with scent glands, no two people have the same tongue print, and a man can be rendered unconscious after exactly nine seconds of denying blood to his brain (this inconvenient truth garnered from a slight bit of personal experience).

Not all of Sherlock Holmes' knowledge is of use only in instances of mayhem or murder. Sherlock also knows many things applicable to the supermarket environment in which he currently found himself.

For example, the good detective could tell you that sports drinks contain a chemical which also doubles as a fine flame retardant. Some of the food dye that makes lovely red jams and specialty coffee drinks comes from the dried, crushed bodies of cochineal beetles. Several kinds of mushroom glow in the dark. And cheese is the most frequently stolen food on earth.

If pressed—and you would have to press only very lightly—Sherlock could also tell you that ground human hair is a fine source of the food additive l-cysteine, and that polydimethylsiloxane is not only marvelous for creating some of the heat-resistant materials he uses in his home lab, but also for keeping fast food from forming bubbles.

However, standing in a supermarket almost half again as big as his brother's Mayfair flat, Sherlock was prepared to admit that he had no clue what—

"It's soy milk. Keeps a bit longer than regular milk."

Sherlock stopped staring at the vacuum-sealed container of…milk. He gazed intently at the man beside him. "Soy?"

For a moment John Watson was sure he was being teased, then as quickly realised he wasn't. "It's a bean. A legume. A…they get milk from it, apparently."

"Like a cow."

Again John thought he was being mocked. "Uh, not unless they crush cows. I don't think they do. To get the milk I mean. I suppose they might when they make hamburger." John took a step back from his own unnerving babbling. "What?"

Sherlock put the container of soy milk back on the shelf.

After a moment spent frowning at each other, both men started laughing.

Then John, who has always had a very strange inclination to move toward strange things, took a step toward the tall stranger and the goat's milk. He picked up the latter, and said mock-gravely, "Given the turn of our conversation maybe we ought to forget about this one."

It was then that Sherlock, who has always had a very strange inclination to share his strange knowledge, said, "Pigeons secrete a sort of milk. They regurgitate it into their offspring's mouth. Doves, flamingos, and certain penguins also produce crop milk. It looks rather like cheese." Sherlock paused, but it wasn't in deference to John's disgusted expression, mostly because John—a rock-steady doctor for more than a dozen years—wasn't making one. It was for Sherlock to recall why he could recall such an obscure fact.

"Ah! I learned that during the Barking Bakery Murder."

Now John made a face. It was a thinking face. "Barking Bakery, Barking—oh, I heard about that. Last year."

It would be true and correct to say that Sherlock Holmes politely cleared his throat and remained politely silent.

"Something about toxic buns?"

"Spotted dick."

"Pardon?"

"It was the spotted dick the bakery produced—and of which the CEO was excessively fond—that lead to her death."

Sherlock again paused in a somewhat noticeable fashion.

"Did you work on the…were you…are you a detective?"

As if he hadn't been waiting for precisely this question, Sherlock Holmes said, "Of a sort. I'm a consulting detective. And by the process of deduction, I figure out things that no one else can. Such as when a CEO is allergic to pigeons."

"Pigeons?"

"Pigeons."

"Pigeons were in the pudding?"

"Not at all."

"Wait…if…what?"

"Crop milk was in the pudding."

"The cheese stuff? *That* wasn't in the news reports."

Sherlock Holmes sighed in apparent long-suffering. "Of course not, because they'd already arrested the head baker—who was also a stripper at night—with whom she'd just broken off a long-term affair. That was the front-page news, along with an exhaustive array of photos showing the gentleman's assets."

John laughed at the joke.

It wasn't a joke.

"Sorry. Go on."

"The page eight news three weeks later concerned the baker being released upon new evidence, the discovery of crop milk in the pudding, and my unearthing of the murderer."

John Watson reads biographies, medical journals, and the occasional historical novel. He does not read mysteries. John Watson was somewhat belatedly learning he loves mysteries.

"And? Who was it?"

"Who?" Sherlock dropped his voice, glanced at the hemp milk as if it couldn't be trusted. "Who do you think?"

Instead of responding to these theatrics by rolling his eyes, grabbing Sherlock's shirt front, or swearing—as any number of police officers, clients, and crime-scene-passersby had been known to do—John Watson carefully reviewed the evidence, thought deep thoughts, and came up with the exact wrong answer.

"Her significant other."

A smile flashed fast over Sherlock's face. "Her husband of twenty-three years was in the Chinese space station at the time."

John propped an elbow on the shelving beside him. He reviewed a bit more, had more deep thoughts. "The husband or wife or significant other of the baker!"

Sherlock clapped his hands. "Well done."

"I got it right?"

"No, your conclusion's utterly predictable and completely erroneous."

"Oh."

"But you're one of the rare few who fail to genderise, even unconsciously. You'd be surprised how quickly a suspect pool expands to include the killer when you don't presume CEOs are male and wives only have husbands."

John felt an odd mixture of pleasure and annoyance. It would all-too-soon become his steady state of being.

"Come on, who do you think it was?"

John glanced at the almond milk, as if it could give him a hint. The cherubic cartoon child on the carton's cover gave him a hint. "Did she have any kids?"

"Not even a goldfish."

"So no childre—"

"Of which she was aware."

"Oh!" Well that clinched it. Thus guided, John Watson nodded sagely, and pronounced the next absolutely wrong answer. "Adoption."

Sherlock Holmes said nothing. Loudly.

"Right. No. It'd be hard for a woman to be completely unaware of the existence of a child to which she'd given birth. Well."

This was long past the point where most people would have given up on this particular conversation with Sherlock Holmes. But John Watson was not most people. And John Watson minds being wrong in inverse proportion to how much he likes a good puzzle.

John glanced at the shelf of non-dairy milks again. They'd helped once before, he might as well stay with a goer.

The hemp milk offered nothing. The rice was mum. The coconut milk was playing dumb, and the almond milk had already given all it was prepared to give. That just left the milk that had started it all.

There they were, lined up in a Neapolitan regiment. Plain soy. Vanilla soy. Strawberry soy.

Chill Chocolate Soy! Now With Tapioca Pearls!

"Human egg donation."

Sherlock stood tall, a little bit hooted. "Twenty-five years previous."

"How on *earth* did you figure that out?"

"Sometimes the evidence is right there but it's as unremarkable as a glass of milk. She still had the key ring bearing the name of the agency to which she'd donated eggs twenty-five years previous. It was worn, oft-repaired. She'd even taken it to a jeweler's to have the small gems on its face reset."

"That's not just a trinket then, that's a touchstone."

"Yes, it had great sentimental importance to her."

John unconsciously clutched a hand round a litre of chocolate soy and tapioca pearls. "What happened?"

"Misunderstandings. Two posh young girls, one young-married and keen on children, the other bent on business. A year after her marriage Katri found she was unable to have children, she begged her best friend Ariel to donate eggs. Her friend did and Katri went on to have a son, to move to America with her small family, to fall away from everything left behind in England. Katri also went on to have a tumultuous marriage, a ruinous divorce, and a dire dependence on alcohol.

"She became bitter, convinced that everyone, especially her old friend—now quite more than a millionaire—had abandoned her. She weaned her boy on that bitterness and as he grew, so did his discontent."

"He's the one," John Watson frowned at the almond milk and its cherub-faced, cartoon baby. "He came to England and murdered Ariel. Oh, and he knew how to do it because he was the bakery queen's biological child. He had the pigeon allergy, too."

Both men fell silent awhile, having their own thoughts, staring at the array of not-milk. Eventually Sherlock said, "Do you know there's something called bee milk?"

"Please tell me it's not crushed bees."

"No, worker bees secrete it."

"There's that word again. Secrete. I have one. Eliachi milk. What country do you think it comes from?"

Sherlock Holmes' geographical knowledge is about as spotty as his food knowledge. He shrugged.

"I'll give you a hint. When I was a soldier—"

"India."

"How on earth did you do that?"

Sherlock looked toward the front of the store, where he knew there was a small cafe. "Coffee?"

John grinned. "Will you tell me how you did that?"

"In exhaustive detail."

"Then sure."

They began to walk through the gargantuan supermarket. "So…do you take milk in your coffee?"

SH

149

A Regular Day, Like Any Other Day, Only More So

St. Bartholomew's Hospital, Sort Of— 1881

Momentous days can be sly as master criminals.

They can creep toward you on shadow feet, silent, unassuming, and only somewhere before midnight—when a man you've just met is asking you for the first time (though not the last), "Why are there severed fingers in my bag, Holmes? And toes! And two kinds of nose!"—yes, only then will you realise everything in your life has changed, and you just didn't see it coming.

*

For Sherlock Holmes the day had gone like so many others, only more so. There were experiments, detailed notes concerning the experiments, bored pacing trying to think up more experiments.

That progressed to pocket watch checking, token resistance, then finally giving in, pounding down the stairs from his Montague Street rooms, and walking to Scotland Yard.

There he found little as usual (solving their one small 'international incident' in thirty-seven seconds), so next he whiled away some time with his brother Mycroft then, after exhausting that diversion, proceeded to deduce tourists in Trafalgar Square.

An hour later he found himself at St. Bart's hospital, pestering the new morgue assistant for body parts, several of which he tucked away into Mycroft's satchel (sometimes he steals his brother's things; it keeps them both sharp) and, finally exhausting every weak entertainment of which he could think, Sherlock Holmes eventually perched like a glum, long-legged bird in a Bart's lunch room chair, nursing an overbrewed tea.

And then he thought the day was about to change.

Because a young Scotland Yard constable was suddenly there, handing over a large envelope, addressed to him. Yet when opened, it contained not something divertingly criminal, but a few drawings of a twenty-year-old crime scene. Trailing after as the constable went in search of pie, Holmes pressed for case particulars and, whilst he wasn't looking, *that* is when everything changed.

Holmes didn't know this at the time. All he knew was that the case details were sparse, and that the obnoxious young constable had already formed a highly unpleasant opinion of him. In a fit of ennui Holmes picked up his brother's satchel—he didn't remember bringing it along with him, but that was what boredom did to a man, it made his brain *rot*—and Holmes decamped for home.

There he ignored his morgue-pilfered body parts and the envelope, in favour of staring out his sitting room window, smoking the air blue, and reflecting that it had been yet another dull day, like every other day, only more so.

And then, at eleven thirty-eight p.m. precisely, the pounding on his door began and Sherlock Holmes learned he was absolutely wrong.

"I'm coming!" he shouted gleeful, dropping his pipe to the sill, tripping over his brother's satchel, yanking open the door with a breathless, "Has there been a murder?"

What there was was a long moment of silence whilst a regular man, with a regular moustache, and a regular hat, glowered up at him and then quite nearly barked, "Are you Sherlock Holmes?"

Holmes nodded.

"Good! I'm John Watson."

Watson pushed past, strode into the middle of Holmes' sitting room, and there he put down a brown satchel that looked exactly like Mycroft's brown satchel.

Because that is what it was.

Backing away from the thing as if it were a bomb ominously ticking, John Watson turned to Sherlock Holmes and he said carefully, as if *he* were now the bomb ominously ticking, "Why are there severed fingers in my bag, Holmes? And toes! And two kinds of nose! My satchel smells terrible!"

Sherlock Holmes is not a genius for nothing. Without answering, he stepped over the ominous satchel, picked up the one that had been knocked over one minute previous, and he handed it to John Watson. Who, though not a genius, realised almost immediately what had occurred.

"At St. Bart's?"

"In the lunch room."

"Ah, that's why you look familiar. You were talking to that skinny bloke who was making sheep's eyes at a piece of pie. I had the Sunday roast. It was dry."

"Oh."

"Well then."

"Yes."

"I'll be on my way."

"Thank you for returning my…things."

"You're welcome. You might want to put the human remains on ice."

"Certainly."

"Though I think it may be too late."

"Very likely."

"Have a good evening."

"You as well."

His hand on the door, his satchel in hand, John Watson was almost gone, and that day *quite nearly* became a regular day, like any other day, only more so. But instead John Watson paused in the doorway, he turned around, and he said, "Those drawings, did you do them?"

Again, Sherlock Holmes isn't a genius for nothing. Sensing *something,* Holmes went and opened the satchel. Indeed the stench from it now was great. Fetching the envelope on which his name, address, and the date of the crime were written, Holmes rose and laid its contents out on his small table.

By this time Watson was beside him, looking at two detailed drawings of a bedroom crime scene, furniture broken, clothing and houseplants scattered, and a drawing of a dead body, its limbs askew, gore dripping from a head wound, eyes half-mast.

"It's a cold case from Scotland Yard. I haven't studied the particulars yet."

"Did you know the victim may have had brittle bones? Or been deaf?"

Holmes' gaze swept over the drawing of the corpse. *Brittle bones? Deaf? What did such things look like? What clues did they leave?*

Holmes held the drawing close, scrutinising every corner. "What do you see?"

"His eyes."

Again Holmes peered close. In the drawing, blue irises faintly peeped from beneath half-closed lids, brown eyelashes were clumped with blood, and—

"The sclera of his eyes, it's a bit blue."

No man is infallible, not even a very bright one. But only the *very* brightest understand this. "Blue? I...I presumed the artist was sloppy."

"And smudged the blue of the iris into the white of the eye? He seems to have been precise about everything else. He even drew the exposed roots of the potted plants." Watson pointed. "When the sclera is that colour it can point to a range of conditions, some of the more prominent are brittle bones, deafness, and myopia."

Holmes sat down heavily. "They say that genius is an infinite capacity for taking pains. By this definition I am a fool."

Watson was about to say something reassuring, for that is the nature of Watsons, when Holmes bolted upright, snatched up the crime scene drawings, shouting, "Of course! He wasn't just the victim, he was the murderer!"

Holmes spun around his sitting room, dressing gown flaring. He gestured dramatically with the drawings. "The broken chair, the cracked mirror, the three plant pots shattered on the floor. He didn't hear when his own trap sprung early. He was the victim of his own crime!"

There was a long moment of silence whilst both men blinked at one another, then Watson crowed, "That's genius, sheer genius!"

Though one definition of genius may be the infinite capacity for taking pains, a definition of friendship could be the infinite capacity for seeing in a friend *gifts,* where obnoxious others see only flaws.

By this definition John Watson and Sherlock Holmes would go on, from this regular day, like any other day, only more so, to be the very best of friends.

SH

Expletive Blasphemy Obscenity

Royal London Hospital Mortuary — 2011

"Bloody fucking god damn fucking bloody buggering hell!"

A startled John Watson threw his clipboard at the wall, his pen at the 'dead' man on the body tray, and his own entire self against his nearby desk.

"Mother of a shitting dick-faced whore-headed god what the bloody mother fucking hell do you fucking think you're doing?"

Lying on the metal body tray, Sherlock Holmes squinted up at the bright morgue lighting and made a baby-animal pained noise in the back of his throat. Instantly John Watson stopped swearing.

"Oh no, I'm so sorry. Did someone lock you in the fridge? Are you okay? God you must be freezing."

Sherlock's tearing eyes took their time adjusting to the blazing brightness.

"It's all right, you're okay, we'll find out who did this, don't cry."

Right about then Sherlock decided that he was not at this time about to admit three things:

1) He had fallen asleep inside the mortuary refrigerator. 2) That he was *in* the mortuary refrigerator as part of an experiment. 3) That the man from whom he 'borrowed' the keys to the mortuary was technically no longer working at the Royal

London hospital and, therefore, Sherlock had basically broken-and-entered.

Judging by the previous violent swearing of the man peering down at him, Sherlock smartly deduced that admitting to any of these things was not going to end well for him.

So instead of saying, "I'm light-blinded not weeping," Sherlock Holmes acted his naked arse off. So to speak.

"Where am I?" he all but mewed, staring so unblinking at the lights overhead that his eyes positively streamed.

John plucked his pen off the not-dead man's sheet-shrouded body, as if this were the thing currently offering him the greatest discomfort.

"You're in the Royal London hospital mmm—" John's never had to discuss with a corpse its unfortunate locale so he choked briefly, then ploughed on. "—mortuary. In the fridge."

For a long second Sherlock did nothing much, then realised he should not be blasé about this intel. "The mortuary?" he squealed. "With the dead bodies?" (Excellent use of rising inflection.)

"Can you move? We should get you out of there."

Now that he was awake, Sherlock was a lot colder than he'd been asleep. He indeed wished to remove himself from the chilly mortuary tray. Sherlock attempted to rise from the mortuary tray.

This was the point where Sherlock realised he sort of couldn't, as the whole falling-asleep-inside-a-morgue-fridge-during-an-experiment thing had apparently left him as stiff as a day-old corpse. With a few grunts of effort and a doctorly hand on his elbow he at last managed but, in his distraction, he forgot to bring his sheet with him.

Then he belatedly did, covering most of his nakedness with a dramatic drape of cloth. But the damage was done. When he looked back at the doctor his skin washed cold with adrenaline and his heart ramped high.

He sees me.

Sherlock Holmes knows better than most that there are all kinds of seeing. Few have the time or inclination to see all the things that flash-flick by their eyes day-to-day. People walk past buildings, crowds, dancing dogs and if their mind is elsewhere they won't notice, they might as well be blind. So Sherlock's grown used to seeing—and being one of the things to which so many are blind.

"There is," said John Watson, his voice low, his gaze fixed at the tall man's solar plexus, "a lot of you."

Sherlock grunted against the feel of something pressing there, right there, at the bone in the middle of his chest, as if the doctor's gaze had weight, as if his words created pressure.

"But there's not *enough* of you," the good doctor finished, finally looking fierce and unblinking into Sherlock's eyes.

Sherlock's got big feet, long arms and legs, he's been taller than most for most of his life. But he knew that wasn't what the doctor was talking about, he knew that those sharp eyes—which still looked right into his—were talking about shadows too deep at rib and collarbone and jaw.

I'm fine, Sherlock was about to say, but oh yes, Sherlock *sees* and so he saw, by the tilt of a head, the clench of a fist, the bunching muscles in a jaw, that to counteract a doctor's eye that sometimes sees too much, this doctor had tricky, tricky ears that would go deaf when convenient.

So Sherlock's six-letter lie died in his throat, and six words came from John's. "You're not taking care of yourself."

Sherlock Holmes was good at lying to strangers. Most of the time he didn't bother because he'd learned long ago not to care what people thought of him. But Sherlock's not shy about lying and when he wishes, he can do so exceedingly well. He didn't do it now because he knew this wasn't a question. Half-healed chemical burns on the backs of his hands and arms, the depth of boney shadows on his body, these spoke clearly, so Sherlock spoke the truth. "No."

And *that* was when the manhandling started. And really, honest to god, cross his heart, Sherlock was so stunned to be suddenly prodded, then herded, then nearly lifted up onto a dusty scale shoved in the corner behind the doctor's desk, that he *let himself* be prodded, herded, and nearly lifted. He might have made a small mewling sound out of sheer surprise, but about *that* he *will* lie, so don't even ask.

"No," barked the doctor, after looking at what the scale said. "No, nope, no."

Look, John Watson doesn't belong in a mortuary. He was a surgeon once, very good at what he did and it wasn't just because of a steady hand and steadier nerves. It was because he cared a little more than he should, it was because he didn't stay quite distant enough from those for whom he cared. Though a war and a wound had ended his surgeon's career, they hadn't taken from him that too-much, that need to get close to people who *needed.*

So that was why John Watson stepped back from Sherlock Holmes and said, "You're going to eat lunch with me now, yes?" What was left off that deceptively soft-voiced sentence was a whole string of expletives, blasphemies, and obscenities that sort of said *or else.*

It has already been said that Sherlock was used to seeing, but not quite to being seen. And though the good detective will boss with the best of them when on the scent of a case or a clue, he right here and now learned that he was capable of being bossed by more than his brother, because he heard himself reply, "All right."

*

A dozen minutes later introductions had been made, Sherlock was back in his own clothes, and John was back with some surprisingly good cafeteria falafel, salad, and banoffee pie.

"Good carbs, healthy fats, protein," John intoned, starting on the pie first. When Sherlock, still working the chill from his bones with entirely too much coffee from a pot brewing over-thick on John's desk, said something about the pie providing none of the above, John took umbrage and with quite a few expletives declaimed on the importance of indulging small pleasures where possible.

This got Sherlock off on a tangent about the surprising contents in the stomach of a corpse he'd recently seen over at, ironically enough, Coffinswell in Devon. *This* intel led John to exclaim, "Oh yeah, well..." and it was two hours and twenty-one minutes on a slow day in the Royal's mortuary before Sherlock—who was now not only extremely coffee-hyper but full of most of John's falafel and some of his pie—left the morgue, having made an appointment with John to see a flat over on Baker Street.

It wasn't until three years later, nearly four dozen cases, as many stories written about their adventures, and a solid stone put on Sherlock's reedy frame, that John finally, at last, and hallelujah realised he'd never asked his flatmate just how he'd got into that mortuary fridge.

John's not sure what puzzle piece shifted all those years later but, standing in front of their open refrigerator, staring at its astounding lack of anything interesting, the good doctor's gaze skewed left, then right, then John tilted his head and started shouting at the top of his lungs.

"You little, little liar! 'Where am I? Where am I?' You knew Sherlock, you *knew* where you were because you put *yourself* in that mortuary fridge. Sherlock? Oi! Sherlock? Where are you?"

From the very first little in 'little liar' Sherlock had known this would not end well for him. Which was why he was halfway to Regent's Park, his shoes scuffed half on, his coat clutched in his fist, fumbling his phone off.

And yet *still* he could hear the expletives loud and clear. Sherlock fled faster.

SH

Terry the Terror

Mayfair, near Berkeley Square, London — 1882

"And what do you think of our delightful tour guide Mr. Holmes?"

Sherlock Holmes clasped his hands behind his back and looked from his dowager tour mate to the well-groomed man heading this summer stroll through London's richest neighbourhood. "I think that Mr. Shere has a clandestine business in rare orchids, is not yet sure if he'll propose to the lady he loves or the one with the inheritance, and enjoys sweet white wine."

The dowager lady laughed into her hand and said, "Mr. Holmes, you say such incorrigible things."

Holmes was not alone in this.

Stopping his dozen-strong group, the tour guide leaned intimately forward, and with an arched brow said, "And this was the home of Duchess Leikola, whom I'm sure needs no introduction to such well-informed people as yourselves."

Titillated murmurs of 'scandalous business' and 'twenty-three husbands!' rippled through most of the small crowd. Less interested in tepid scandal and more keen on the simple diversions of walking and talking, Sherlock Holmes fell into step beside the benign-looking fellow at the back of the group, said conversationally, "This house is also where the French upholsterer, Guilleret, invented the straitjacket."

John Watson looked at the mansard-roofed home. "You know, I once worked with an attending who gave his wife a straitjacket for her birthday. She seemed rather taken with it."

"You two at the back, do please keep up!" The tour guide pointed at a white-brick house with stone wreath embellishments. "This is Walhill House, where the horse feed magnate—"

Sotto voce Holmes said to Watson, "Did you know a reclusive pasha lived in Walhill House during the Great Persian Famine? It was only discovered he was a she upon her death. They never did figure out how she died, though some think her Persian lover poisoned her. I know what happened, but Lestrade won't let me at the police records to confirm my theory. He looks positively spooked if I ask."

"I visited Persia once," replied Watson, "they have the most lovely mosques and a marvelous pomegranate tea."

Three tour attendees turned and frowned at the chattery men. Both nodded an apology and fell further back.

"Are you," said Holmes, "that exceedingly rare Englishman who'll deign to drink something other than black tea?"

"I am indeed sir." Watson slowed, held out his hand. "John Watson, at your service."

"Sherlock Holmes, delighted."

Watson released Holmes' hand with a start, gestured at the red-brick mansion beside them, its blue doors framed by a broad arch of massive white stones. "My god, I once helped deliver twins here!"

Holmes looked the house over, then made an inquisitive noise and stepped close to its doors.

"Well, more honestly, I stood by whilst a senior doctor delivered the babies. He thought bringing me along might turn my mind from surgery to obstetrics. It didn't, but that experience is still the most precious memory of my student days."

Sherlock Holmes dug a thumb nail into a shallow crater in one of the home's white bricks. "How poetic."

Watson smiled. "Do you think so? I sometimes fancy I have a way with words."

Holmes took out a small magnifying glass and peered closely at another crater in the brickwork. "What? Oh, no, I meant the circle of life is rather poetic."

Holmes pocketed his magnifier and fell into step again with his tourmate—though neither yet realised they'd completely misplaced the tour. "You attended the birth of twins in a home that, not twenty years previous, saw a brutal double murder."

As if paid to do so, plane trees suddenly cast ominous shadows across both men and Watson exclaimed, "The hell you say! What happened?"

The men strolled down a busy mews. "The place was home to a country squire, his wife, and their daughter Teraza, back about 1861 I believe; I'd need to check my records to be sure."

Holmes and Watson stepped aside so that a landau drawn by two Windsor greys could pass. "Teraza was an amazing young woman and happily spent her days devising clever mechanical machines, little devices that could do mathematical sums, or walk unaided, like small insects. Alas, when she turned eighteen her parents forbid these 'infant entertainments' and insisted she marry some old country count."

Watson made annoyed mouth noises. "Treating young women like chattel to trade, it's barbaric."

"Humans are nature's most barbaric animal, don't you find? Well, needless to say the young lady resisted, but her parents wouldn't relent and hounded her unmercifully. After two years of this awful pressure Teraza created her final mechanical machine: A homemade gun."

"No!"

"Those cratered marks I was looking at on the house? They were from two of the bullets she fired from that gun, unerringly killing both her parents. The final bullet was found in her bedroom, along with her body and a great many of her machines, most destroyed beyond repair. The only one that survived unharmed was a tuner now integral to every telegraph, boosting the quality of its signal. A terrible waste of potential."

"Bullets," murmured Watson, "are rather good at destroying that."

Sherlock Holmes is no fool. He understands there are times when a stream of deductions will lead a stranger to delighted gasps of 'incorrigible,' and other times when they only open half-healed wounds. So Holmes didn't talk about a bullet and a war that had cut a surgeon's career short, nor of a poor bright girl the yellow press had dubbed Terry the Terror and forgot as soon as another scandal arose. Instead Holmes said, "If I'm not mistaken we've walked ourselves right into Hyde Park."

Watson shook off his brief melancholia. "So we have! I think this calls for tea and cake from my favourite merchant over by the Serpentine, what do you say?"

"You know," said Holmes, following, "there was an interesting case, oh I think it was 1803, where the Marchioness de Aiken submerged her family's jewels—a five hundred carat moonstone being the most notable—into the Serpentine. Attached, if I might be indelicate, to her dead husband's family jewels."

Watson bellowed a laugh that startled the geese. Holmes joined him.

SH

Sucker

Bodleian Library, Oxford — 2011

"You need to tell your girlfriend to suck a little softer," whispered John Watson. "Or your boyfriend. Or…never mind, not my business."

Sherlock Holmes, minding his own business, continued to peer at the document in the distance. From what he could barely see of King Somebody's seventeenth century proclamation about a Magna Carta proclamation, there was nothing helpful concerning where to find an heiress' vanished heir.

"Except the bit about sucking softer, she—he?—they really need to do that because those aren't love bites. That's a feeding frenzy."

Tucked away in this dim, tiny room dedicated to the Magna Carta, was the clue to finding his millionaire client's son, a museum curator six months missing. In this dim, tiny room currently crowded with four *thousand* tiny people. Four thousand wee six-year-olds, squirming everywhere, like maggots on a corpse. They seethed up between him and the display cases, between the display cases and the plaques, between the plaques and the dark-painted walls. They buzzed and crawled and accidentally elbowed him in the kidneys approximately every twenty-eight seconds and Sherlock could barely get within a fathom of anything.

"Except, you know, love bites like that can get infected if you're not careful."

Sherlock Holmes looked up, finally aware that the only other person in the room over five foot tall was talking to him.

Sherlock nodded, gestured vaguely toward something Magna Carta-esque and said the first thing that occurred. "Yes it's very nice." Sherlock then went back to wading through the maggots—the *children*—in an attempt to get closer to anything, absolutely anything at all.

For his part John had long since turned away from the one of Britain's most famous documents, entirely involved in the more pressing considerations of a stranger's hickey-riddled neck.

"But seriously, I know it doesn't seem like much, just a little blood blushing the surface of your skin, but contusions like that can keep bleeding. It's an actual wound. People don't tend to realise that."

Sherlock looked up from a distant display case.

"Sorry, just saying."

Sherlock looked back down.

Buffeted by the roiling children, all Sherlock saw at this point were the partings on eight thousand heads. As the children swarmed against displays, stroked little hands over plaques, jabbed kidneys and stepped on feet, Sherlock was driven inexorably away from everything, until finally he was flush against the wall, the unforgiving jut of a humidity sensor digging into his back.

Because it hurt, and because he had absolutely nothing else to do, Sherlock turned around and scowled at the sensor. Its nickel-plated face shined dully up at him. The gauge on the sensor told him that the humidity in the really very tiny room full of all the very tiny people, was a moderate thirty-two percent. A small sticker told him that the sensor had been

168

serviced in July. A tiny gold badge said it had been made in Solea, Italy.

"Good god, how did she…he…how did your partner find the *leverage* for *that* one? Must be very tall or you're very—"

Sherlock looked over.

"—never mind. Sorry, just, well, the mark up behind your ear is even more livid than the ones on your neck."

Something behind the chattery man winked at Sherlock. Sherlock appeared to wink back at it, though it was just a squint. The something appeared to be a thermostat. Sherlock pointed. The chattery man turned.

"What does that say?"

There were maybe nine thousand children between the man and Sherlock, but as the room was no more than ten foot on a side, this did not actually amount to a great deal of distance and so John heard him just fine.

In turn Sherlock heard John's report. "Twenty degrees."

"And?"

John's eyes flicked over Sherlock's neck, then back to the thermostat. "Uh, it was serviced in September and made in Solea, Italy."

As if there weren't twelve thousand children under the age of six to hear every word, John said, "Contusions are caused by internal bleeding, you know. Clotted blood. If you think about it, blood, in *clots,* isn't exactly sexy. Maybe unless you're a vampire."

John smiled. Sherlock smiled back. Except Sherlock wasn't smiling at John, he was grinning at the big plaque behind John's head.

"That," he said, pointing, "where was it made?"

169

"Uh, it—" John accidentally stepped on a pair of small feet. "So sorry. Um, Solea, Italy."

Sherlock's grin grew. Even though there were about fifteen *thousand* children hemming him in, Sherlock twisted around and patiently pushed his way toward a display case. After about three hours he was reading small etched script on a small plaque attached to the case's side: *Made in Solea, Italy.*

"Holy mother of—what the hell were they trying to do, eat you?"

Sherlock looked to his left. The man had waded through thirty thousand children in order to get right beside him and peer down the collar of Sherlock's shirt. He appeared angry, disbelieving, and moderately scandalised. When Sherlock peered back at him, the man looked away, muttering, "Sorry."

On something of a roll, Sherlock checked out every dark-wood cabinet, every plaque, each fitting, gauge, and bauble inside the dim little room: *Solea, Italy.*

Sherlock now believed that the missing curator—who was responsible not only for this room's collection, but all its fittings—might have vanished to a town in Italy.

Sherlock nodded at the man and proceeded to wade through fifty *thousand* children who, frankly, seemed to consist of nothing more than squeals, elbows, and hair partings. When he gained the foyer he pulled up stats on his phone.

Solea, Italy: Founded in 1792. Well-known producer of high-spec fittings for museums, military, and hospitals.

Population 21,800.

And there it was. Somewhere on the Achilles heel of the Italian boot, a town so very small, and so very far from millionaire mummy's madding crowd—and expectations.

Sherlock sent an email. He sighed in serene accomplishment. He gazed about himself. He spotted the helpful man. The man spotted him and awkwardly tried veering away.

"Thank you."

John stopped veering.

"In there," Sherlock tilted his head toward the tiny room. "Thanks."

John grinned, came close. "You're welcome. I just, well I'm a doctor and you've just got to think of your *health.*"

"What? No. No, the plaques, the thermostat. Impossible to see anything over the heads of seventy thousand children."

"Oh. You're welcome. But really, you've got to talk to your girlfriend or your boyfriend or your—"

"Octopus."

"—your octo—what?"

"It was an octopus."

John stepped back, to make room for his incredulity. "What?"

"I deduced an octopus. For a case in the biology department. I'm a consulting detective."

As if this were a completely normal explanation for the presence of twenty-three hickeys and one actual semi-bite scattered livid across pale English flesh, John Watson said, "Oh. I see."

John chuffed out a breath. Sherlock scratched at one of the suck marks.

"I'm at a conference here, staying with a friend at the edge of town. She can prescribe a cream for the itch if you like."

Sherlock started scratching up his left sleeve. "Okay."

John started scratching in unconscious sympathy.

171

"How about now?"

"What?"

"Now. For the cream."

"Oh, sure. Her practice is on Cornmarket Street. It's not far."

They started toward the exit.

"So the octopus told you to come look at the Magna Carta did she?"

"He," corrected Sherlock, "Actually, what he did was…"

By the time they got to John's friend's practice, the good doctor must have said, "Really? You're kidding me. No way." eighty thousand times. *At least.*

SH

Paper Mites

The Grenville Library, British Museum, London — 1888

The *Times Atlas of the World Vol. 3* was big and black and, unlike so many of the other books, resolutely unflaky.

The atlas had the air of a thing with too much will-power, too much *will*. As if it would show you what for, whether you wished to be shown or not. The book was abstemious and clean, without crack or fade. A dark blue spine with gold letters and a serif font, it was the book's excessive height and leanness that first caught Sherlock Holmes' eye. He picked the atlas up, looked disinterestedly inside, expecting nothing and receiving the same.

Carelessly placing the over-large book on a nearby table, Holmes proceeded to do what he'd been doing for the last hour: haunting the edges of the library, his mind its usual welter of impression-shadow-fact-bit of dust here-stained shirt cuff there, but as yet none of the jumble of clues clarifying into a single, simple *solution.*

It hinged on the victim's note, he knew, the only thing she'd had time to leave behind. *The key is hidden where York Watergate is touched by the tides.*

Except the Thames hadn't washed up against that lonely gateway since the embankment was built more than twenty-five years ago. The clue was simplicity itself, but Holmes knew it was the very simplest of things that could make a case complex.

Damn it!

This was what happened when the skein was too deeply tangled, when too many voices had too many conflicting tales, when evidence was lost, when lies were more common than truths. When his mind got tangled in that snarl, Holmes could be staring right at the solution and not see it. That's when he'd have to throw down his shag, get out of his chair, and *move*.

It never mattered where because wherever it was he wasn't actually *there*. All he needed was a roof to keep out the chill and the rain, a place where with pacing and some peace he could worry the problem, nibble and gnaw on clues, natter to himself, eventually sorting the skein to order.

Though sometimes, just very rarely sometimes, the past would interrupt him, bleeding in at the edges.

Holmes stopped, smiling at the flaking creases in a regiment of Berry Encyclopaedia Heraldica and their oxblood spines. Oh, he'd loved this colour when he was a little boy, and never did know if it was for the hue or its name. He ran long fingers over the books' edges. They were tired and worn, as if they'd hoped for much and been too long disappointed. In the end they let the years bow them into weariness. Holmes plucked one encyclopaedia up, glanced inside. Nothing.

As negligent with this tome as the other, the moody detective placed it willy-nilly on the shelf, laughing without mirth.

A scientist, a logician with a machine-like mind, Holmes could see what everyone saw, then look deeper and see everything they missed—and yet *this* was what his great mind would do when frustrated: Deduce the leather and ink of old books. If he wasn't careful he'd probably start analysing pencils, rulers, or the book mites he was sure were clogging his nose and gumming up his eyes.

At the thought of mites Holmes reflexively sniffed, but it wasn't those imagined mites that caused him to scrub his eyes. It was the nearby shelves of Italian Monografie e Musicas and the German history books, the whole lot of them bound in sensational shades of gold, cadmium, and lemon. Frowning, Holmes wondered who would decide to bind centuries of knowledge in colours that would cause even the most devoted eye to tire. He didn't touch these bright spines, somehow knew they wouldn't cut through the knot of his problem.

Just around the corner the capricious detective washed up near shelf upon shelf of navy and azure and electric blue books, they crashed and roared and churned with variations on a theme: Victoria County History: Cumberland... Gloucestershire... Kent... Northumberland... Sussex... Dozens of names on blue spine after blue spine until he felt like he was drowning.

He wheeled round another corner and onto the quiet shore of French manuscripts bound in soothing leathers of chocolate and caramel, burnt butter, black coffee, thick cream. It was in this aisle that Holmes stood still awhile though he didn't give one whit about what was behind the bindings of the books. Their ridged spines and foxed leather, their tiny gold type and most of all their satiating colour calmed him, made him feel as if his hands were wrapped warm around a piping cup of tea, two biscuits on the plate, and the answer was there, on a scrap of paper resting beside the saucer. If he simply breathed in the steam of the imagined tea, let it fill his chest with heat and his mind with clarity, if he didn't move too much or think too hard, if he barely glanced at that mental scrap of paper with a half-lidded gaze he'd see—

Crash!

—he'd see an avalanche of books spilling across the long library aisle, a librarian stumbling under a heavy load of books that were senselessly over-large and unwieldy.

Holmes hissed in remembered frustration. When he was a boy he'd become cranky with really big books, the ones that, like the *Times Atlas of the World,* were almost as tall as he. His four year old self couldn't pick up such books, that young self wasn't yet tall or strong or so very smart. No, that wee child was still bound in a chrysalis and he had *felt* that, felt it in his small bones and baby brain. He was trapped inside but shifting, turning, *changing,* eager to be done with his metamorphosis and *get out.*

Holmes sniffed again, scrubbed at his eyes, irked with the invisible paper mite plague, and the useless memories of the past. Holmes decided to work his frustrations out on his feet. He'd brave the London rain and walk his way to revelation.

Fate, however, had him figured. And gave him purple.

Oxblood was fine, chocolates, caramels, and creams were well and good, but Holmes had a quiet fondness for that rich, royal hue. Maybe it began that long-ago autumn at the London Exhibition, when his eight-year-old self had giddily consumed a cloud of pale purple candy floss nearly as big as his brainy little head.

Well, just so. Whatever the reason, in a forest of book spines of hunter green and oxblood, in a room submerged in sea blues and frothy whites, it was a princely brace of purple spines with silver-stamped titles that slowed him just moments before he fled somewhere else.

These purple-backed books stood straight. They wouldn't bend with time, no. Or, if they did, Holmes suspected that they'd slouch, insouciant, they wouldn't bow, broken. The silver glittering on their covers would fail to fade, instead it would gently hush, as if drawing a curtain, retiring like a moody grand dame from the worldly bustle.

Holmes grinned, insouciant, stood tall, unbroken. No one knew this side of him, this imaginative, flight-of-fancy man. People persisted in thinking a scientist could only be reasoned, an artist just a dreamer, but the great strength of humanity was that we are none of us just one thing.

One thing, one thing...*one thing?*

"Oh!"

Holmes snatched up *Eboracum of the History and Antiquities of the City of York.* There it was, the one thing Holmes needed, on that bold, purple spine: *The city of York.*

The answer was indeed simple. As simple as initial caps. Recalling that the victim was a persnickety professor of English and had a family estate in Brighton, Holmes realised that her note didn't refer to London's York watergate, but to her family's seaside croft *named* York Watergate.

Holmes hooted, got a *shoosh* for his troubles. Oh the missing key was as good as found!

Not so Holmes' umbrella.

As he dashed up the library steps toward the great museum's doors he realised *that* item was now either in a long-gone hansom cab, a Mayfair cafe, or at the Met. Where that umbrella was not, was with Holmes.

About to bolt out library doors Holmes was stayed not by a downpour but by a man.

"You'll get drenched if you go out now," said the man standing calmly just inside, tapping his own umbrella on the museum's marble floor.

Holmes looked at him. The man was clearly ex-military, a doctor, enjoying his day off. An affable sort, he was the type of man who would make small talk, who would ask—

"Good day inside, at least?"

Holmes grinned. His body was warm, as if filled with tea; his muscles steam-loose. He felt very good indeed. He knew the feeling would last hours yet, the feeling of knowing, knowing he had knowledge that would be of *use*. The lot at Scotland Yard didn't always like it when he solved their cases for them, and they usually pocketed the credit, but that bitter pill was for later. Now he simply felt…happy.

"If you call solving a twelve year old murder case by perusing the spines of books a good day, then yes."

Holmes' eyebrows marched right up his forehead. He'd no idea he was going to say that.

The man with the umbrella tapped the floor again, faster. "The deuce you say!"

For a moment Holmes frowned. Words like that were for later, from the mouths of annoyed Yarders who still demanded he prove himself with each case—and then resented him when he did. Now was for steam and warmth and—

"Well don't keep a man in suspense, how'd you do it?"

—and a man Holmes looked at again and…*saw*. Grinning beneath a fine moustache, his eyes as bright as the title on a freshly-stamped book, the man tilted his head, curious, and without thinking Sherlock Holmes said to John Watson something he'd never once said to anyone and never would again.

"I got angry with paper mites."

John Watson's grin grew. He introduced himself. Sherlock Holmes replied in kind. And as they waited out the rain—and that would be awhile—one man talked of mites and gates and deductions, the other questioned, exclaimed, and admired.

In future flights-of-fancy Sherlock Holmes would sometimes think of John Watson as a solid, straight-backed book. And though it was true he'd always be easy to read, Holmes would find he'd never grow tired of this sturdy, medium-sized tome, and that if he looked carefully, he'd always find something inside he'd never read before.

SH

A Curious Man

Her Majesty's Prison Wandsworth — 2012

John Watson hadn't seen his first day at 221B Baker Street going exactly this way.

John hadn't really seen himself moving out of his grotty Finsbury flat any time soon either, much less finding a finer place to live for less than he'd been paying. So, if John was going to sit on a cold bench, taking stock, well he had best take stock of everything.

Everything started not quite two days ago and it started with an email. No, that wasn't right. John had time right now, so John wanted to get this *right*. As a matter of fact, he was going to write a few notes, so he could remember all the *right* for later. Somehow it seemed important. For posterity or something.

So. Yeah. It started with a post on LondonLodgers. Why he'd still been checking that site for flatshares he didn't know, but after six weeks of emailing people, of *almost* finding—look, never mind, that didn't matter. What mattered was that checking the site had became a breakfast routine.

And then without warning, the routine changed.

A curious man seeks similarly-minded individual for flatshare. Excellent Baker Street location, 3.1 miles from New Scotland Yard, 4.0 miles from the Royal Courts of Justice, 7.2 miles from Catalyst Chemical Suppliers, and 4.0 miles from St. Bartholomew's Hospital. I am often tidy, quiet, and introspective except for those times when I am not. If interested email sherlock@holmes.co.uk.

John sat up straight. Interested? John was interested. Why? He wasn't sure why. This wasn't at all the type of advert he'd responded to previously.

John started typing.

*

Hi Sherlock,

My name's John Watson, I'm a doctor, Afghan vet, new to London. I do occasional shifts at Bart's, recommend Doyle Labs over Catalyst (the staff are more responsive, and they're less than three miles by foot from Baker Street). I'm quiet, steady, and tidy, though I can be partial to a bit of excitement, a dash of the unexpected, a modicum of mystery. Now I'm curious...to what are you partial? — John

Perfect, when can you move in? SH

Uh, what? — John

When. Can. You. Move. In. SH

You haven't asked me anything. Or answered my question. — John

Partial: Violins, chemistry, solving crimes.
Not partial: Almost everything else.

About you: You've written two emails after midnight, another at five a.m. You keep odd hours, which suits my habits perfectly. You're friendly enough to warrant good service from a multi-national chemicals supplier, but not so friendly that you recommended any salesperson in particular. This implies amiability without unctuousness. You work part-time at Bart's and gave me the walking distance from Doyle's instead of the much longer route necessary by car, which suggests you have spare time and know London. This could be of use to us both as sometimes I need help on a case. You insisted on an answer to your sole question which suggests curiosity and tenaciousness. Your final sentence did not end with a preposition. I prefer a grammatical flatmate.

So, when can you move in? SH

John Watson kind of grinned. His heart kind of raced. He kind of paused before replying.

Because John means it when he says he likes quiet and steady. No, he seriously thinks he means it, which is why he kept applying for flatshares with shut-ins and retired people.

John's eyes darted over the email again. *Solving crimes. Need help. Curious. Tenacious.* John typed.

When? Where?

Sherlock's reply was immediate.

221B Baker Street. Now.

*

182

The flat was a disappointment.

Wait, no. No, no, *no*.

John shifted on the cold bench, crossed that bit out. He was trying to write the facts *right,* which was harder than he expected. This would be important later. Somehow he knew this would be important later. John started again.

The flat was fine. It was more than fine, it was *great.* Comfortable without being small, lived-in without being shabby, John dropped his few possessions onto his new bed and it felt like he'd always been there, as if he was simply returning from a trip away.

So yes, the flat was great. The problem was his flatmate.

Wait, wait, wait. No, no, no *again.* His flatmate was fine.

No, the problem was that he was *missing.* John was surprised to find he was disappointed that the man who'd said *crimes* and *curious* and *help* wasn't there, because John had wanted to ask him: What crimes? How could he help? *When could he start?*

But the only person in the flat didn't even live there: a perfectly nice landlady. She'd given him a key, a smile, a lingering gaze, then left.

Then John saw the note. The nice note. The one beside which rested a less-nice photograph. One that looked a lot like a mug shot.

Hello John,

Make yourself at home. Sorry, I had to run out unexpectedly, tie up a few loose ends on a case. Should be back before midnight. Here's a fairly recent photo of me so you don't presume I'm a prowler and decide to give your service revolver an airing.

If you're up when I return, I have a few anatomy-related questions. There may be an interesting case regarding a woman whose entire skeleton is blue, a non compos mentis collector, and the feasibility of living without bones. As yet no laws have been broken but I feel it's just a matter of time. Hopefully.

P.S. No that's not a mug shot. SH

*

Blue bones? Crazy collector? 'Hopefully?' John wished Sherlock would get back. Or he could find Sherlock. Everything sounded so, so, so...*not* steady, and *not* quiet.

Well, be careful what you wish for.

Twenty minutes later, as John was wondering how Sherlock knew he had a service revolver, he got a text. And then John wondered how Sherlock knew his mobile number.

Then he forgot to wonder about all of that after reading the text.

JOHN I AM IN WANDSWORTH PRISON DUE TO THE ERRONEOUS PERCEPTION OF A POLICE OFFICER THAT I WAS BREAKING INTO AN INFORMANTS HOME TO ACCESS INFORMATION THE INFORMANT WAS HOLDING BACK AND DESPITE THE FACT THAT I WAS CORRECT ABOUT THAT I AM STILL BEING ARRESTED AND THEY ARE PROCESSING ME NOW 888 IF YOU COULD PLEASE POST BAIL MY BROTHER WILL REIMBURSE YOU AND I WILL PAY YOUR FIRST THREE MONTHS RENT 888 APOLOGIES FOR THE

CAPITALISATION AND MISSING PUNCTUATION I AM USING THE INFORMANTS MOBILE AND SOMETHING IS WRONG WITH IT 888 MUST GO THEY HAVE COME FOR THE PHONE

John grinned. John stopped grinning. He grinned again. And stopped again.

This wasn't exciting. No, absolutely not. He shouldn't find an arrested flatmate exciting. He wasn't going to scramble to find his cheque book and toss his new keys in the air and whistle. He wasn't going to wonder who what why where when and how he played a part. He wasn't going to think that breaking the law was intriguing or that posting bail for a man whose face he only knew via mug shot (oh yes it was) was fantastically mysterious.

No. No. No…yes, he was. He absolutely, positively was.

"Hello John."

John Watson stop writing. He stood up from a cold bench in a prison waiting room. He looked at his new flatmate.

And John Watson grinned, held out his hand to the tall man standing there, and said, only a bit breathlessly, only a dash intrigued, and just a touch excited…

"Hello Sherlock."

SH

185

Down to Earth

Berkeley Square Gardens, London — 1881

"May I have your shoe?"

John Watson doesn't often feed ducks in the park, so the good doctor doesn't usually dally long with daydreams. Which explains why he was so distracted by *what if* contemplations, that at first he frowned at the flock gathered round his feet, as if a duck had not only learned the art of speech, but used it to request one of his brogues.

Sitting straighter on his bench, he tossed his feathered companions more bread, then returned to fruitless reveries of the days before Afghanistan, days when he'd believed many things and hoped for more. Most of those dreams had centred on a surgical career, on a purposeful life, one where steady hands and a steadier temperament would assure a good living, perhaps companionship, a—

"Excuse me doctor, but I was wondering about your shoe."

John Watson shook his head, the movement so sudden after so long still that one duck complained, and two moved a duck-length distant. In apology Watson tossed them more bread, and finally looked to the true source of the short speech.

On the other end of the bench sat a bright-eyed man, eyes focused and wide. He had a determined chin; a broad, clear brow; and a thin-lipped smile curling one side of his mouth. He appeared intense, friendly, alert.

John Watson disliked him instantly.

No, no, no, that wasn't true. Watson *judged* him instantly. The stranger's deep-set eyes were blue-bruised beneath, bespeaking long nights of insomnia. His jaw was sharp, the bones of his wrists prominent. Having seen a great many bodies in a great many states, John Watson can recognise one that's thin more from abstinence than nature. And yet the man radiated nervous energy.

The doctor in Watson judged, and Watson's verdict? The stranger was wound up in a way that bespoke explosive release. With nothing more pressing than a day with ducks, Watson should have been curious, yet loneliness often instills in the lonely a tendency to withdraw, so instead his reply was vague and distant. "Sorry, no."

And that would have been the end of that, for Sherlock Holmes is a persistent man, but not an unsympathetic one. He knows when someone can be coaxed to engage and when they should be left to their own thoughts. Holmes tapped long fingers on his thighs and went back to staring at the softly murmuring ducks.

When he caught himself deducing the one with the black-streaked beak Holmes sighed. Maybe it was time he took that ridiculous rare rose case—before the bloom went off it, so to speak. At the very thought of the pending boredom Holmes grunted. A little duck grunted back and waddled away.

The problem was that Holmes already knew it was the florist's sister's gardener fiancé, intent on blossom blackmail. In exchange the gardener would honour the brother's request that he spurn his sister's affections, thereby keeping the family fortune *in* the family.

It was dull, desperately dull.

"Wait. My shoe?"

Even duller would be *explaining* the case to the Scotland Yard lot. Really, it mystified him that not one 'detective' there seemed to actually *detect.* None realised that attention to abstruse detail, like a thorn-pricked finger and the colour of a woman's gloves, were at the core of sound deduction. Anyone should be able to connect the shape of a heel print and the smallness of a stride with the obvious fact that—

"Why on earth would you want my shoe?"

Holmes stopped frowning himself into a dour mood. "What? Oh! Because in the last two hours you've been somewhere near Wandsworth."

John Watson should be a suspicious man. A doctor is very used to patients lying about what they have eaten, drunk, or done; a soldier is familiar with far worse from humanity than lies. Yet no one told Watson that he should always favour caution over curiosity. So, instead of collecting his coat and bread crusts and walking away, the good doctor looked at his shoe and said, "How could you possibly know that? And that I'm a doctor?"

"Your first question first: I want your shoe so I can get a scraping from it. The consistency and colour of the earth on it is new to me. It's heavy and thick, like the soil you'll find near Greenwich, but dark brown like mud more to the west. Yet there's a reddish tint when the light strikes, which makes me think north, perhaps as far as Kentish Town. However, there's that small smudge of yellow running through the whole lot which hints at Thames chalk. I've been writing up a bit of research on soil from different corners of our fair city. I don't yet have a sample from Wandsworth.

188

"As for how I knew it was from that location, well your clothes told me. You're smartly dressed, hat brushed, moustache trimmed, carrying a new satchel. Clearly you're a man seeking to make an impression. And yet look at the state of that shoe! Obviously you've been somewhere quite muddy quite recently. Where would a respectable man hoping to impress come across a good deal of shoe-riming muck? Perhaps near the building site of Wandsworth's new hospital.

"The rest was a bit of guess and guile. Because the muck sticks so closely I guessed it's still moist, therefore only a few hours old. I presumed doctor because I caught sight of your résumé which is peeking out of your satchel."

John Watson beamed. "My word that's exactly right! You should give lessons."

Sherlock Holmes beamed back. "Really?"

"Of course!"

Right here and now John Watson and Sherlock Holmes were about to set a pattern from which neither man would veer for years. Both would try, both would fail, and yet this pattern would be at the heart of their partnership. And their legend.

And that pattern was this: John Watson will always ask and Sherlock Holmes will always answer. *In detail.* In detailed detail. With embellishments. These'll take the form of graphs, formulae, and samples if necessary.

In turn Watson will tease from this the drama, the romance, and the adventure in what Holmes does. In *his* turn Holmes will mutter corrections, oaths, and promises that *next time* he'll keep the details to himself—a promise he will never, ever, not one time *ever* keep, each time Watson simply says, "How on earth did you know that?"

As if to prove the future point, Holmes said, "If you'd consent to being my first student I know a quiet, uh, 'lecture hall' over on Marylebone. They have an good selection of whiskies and serve a fine roast duck."

Holmes paused, remembering the company they kept. As if understanding the insult, a few disgruntled ducks turned their backs. No matter, the two new friends turned toward the city.

"When it's done, you should publish your soil research."

Holmes had had every intention of creating a monograph. With graphs. And formulae.

"You could study the muck from the parks around the palace right on through to the alleys near opium dens."

Holmes' brows crept up his broad forehead. He'd never thought of classifying his studies quite so melodramatically. His was a more systematic—

"I know what you could call the article: *Down to Earth!*" Watson hooted, gleeful.

Holmes' brows crept higher. He'd thought more along the lines of *Practical Studies in Soil, with Observations upon Its Relevance to Detection of Crime.* Or even—

"No, I've got it!" Watson crowed, "You can call the articles—surely there should be a series of them—*The Game Is a Foot.*"

Holmes' brows could go no higher. As a matter of fact it felt as if they were lodged somewhere up in his hairline.

His mouth, however, was free-moving.

"Now see here doctor, it's not a game at all..." Holmes began, but it was too late, Watson was busy half-shouting a dozen more titles—some of which he later stole for his own

190

writing—and was still going strong after they sat down to their whiskies.

It wasn't until much later that Holmes realised he never did collect that mud sample.

SH

Make Love, Not...

Paddington Train Station, West London — 2011

Christa said he should get drunk and stay drunk the whole week before.

Bobby said he should do all the touristy things the city had to offer.

Ashraf said he damn well shouldn't go, Diane was surprised he hadn't gone sooner, and Levison said he'd follow him over (he didn't).

In the end John Watson got a lot of advice, a bit of attitude, and a raft of good wishes before packing up for what would turn into his first and only Afghan tour of duty.

What John didn't think he'd get was a kiss goodbye.

He and Ashraf had long since parted ways but she was still a good friend. And though he hadn't asked her to see him off, he'd hoped she'd offer. She didn't.

So at 8:14 pm on a chilly London Tuesday and three hours too early for his train, John Watson paces a Paddington platform and frowns. It's darker than he thinks it should be. Afghanistan won't be dark, even at night. The stars'll spangle the desert sky like spatters of milk, something the light pollution in London makes impossible.

Suddenly John wants the city to fix that. Pacing the empty platform he wants London to pull out all the stops...see him off. Dazzle him. Make him want to stay.

He's a fool he tells himself, an absolute fool.

*

Sherlock Holmes could get up from his slouch and move to another bench in the station, but he doesn't feel like moving. What Sherlock feels like doing is telling the platform-pacing *fool* to go somewhere else so he can *think*.

Yet Sherlock doesn't say the words. He's said them before, to other bothersome idiots, but the man's pulled-back shoulders, serious eyes, the bad buzz cut he's given himself, tell Sherlock where the man's soon headed, and that keeps Sherlock's mouth shut though he doesn't realise it.

Because Sherlock thinks he doesn't respect the concept of self-sacrifice, that only the gullible give without expecting something in return. The good detective never lies better than when he lies to himself. Sherlock understands, of course he does. The only thing he doesn't yet comprehend is that it's he himself who hasn't yet had a reason to give selflessly, and that that's what makes all the difference.

Sherlock looks at his watch and sighs in long-suffering. The pacing man's early; the next train to Manchester doesn't leave for nearly three hours. Sherlock had hoped to have most of that time to sit on the vacant platform and watch nearby pigeons and distant people. He'd sit and talk to himself and somehow it'd help him figure out how D connected to X connected to A. Of course D was always a dead body, X and A could be anything from a larcenous sister to a car battery to a factory in Crouch End.

But the infernal pacing.

"Sit down," he says and means it to sound sharp but it sounds…genial. Sherlock's so surprised at the tone of his own voice he sits up straight. This automatically makes room for the man, who distractedly perches on the bench edge. His fists are clenched on his knees.

Without even questioning why he wants to, Sherlock tries to ease the man's tension.

"Afghanistan?"

John doesn't hear the man and then he hears him and frown-smiles, "How'd you know?"

Sherlock says, "I didn't know, I noticed," and tells the man how. By the time he's done, John's grinning and his hands are resting open and easy on his thighs.

By the time John's finished talking about why he's going, Sherlock thinks maybe he understands why *some* people are good at self-sacrifice. *Other* people.

By the time the train arrives they've talked for three hours and there have been obvious deductions Sherlock did not share. Because a lonely man can recognise a lonely man; he can also recognise another man who's trying, trying as hard as he knows how. Still, Sherlock is surprised by two things he himself does as the train comes to a stop.

The first is scrawling his email on the back of someone else's business card, then placing it in John's upturned palm.

The second thing Sherlock Holmes does is stare at his own shoes, look up, then lean forward and kiss John Watson on the cheek.

Afterward he takes one step back and clasps his hands.

The conductor calls. The train whistle sounds. John steps back and up into the rail car. The door closes between them.

*

They don't write to each other much. They do write to each other just enough.

The emails are sporadic but most of them are long. That first year of John's deployment they talk about John's adjustment to military life, what's happening in London, and Sherlock's cases (John helps on four).

The second year of John's deployment they use words like "what if," and "when you get back."

Near the middle of John's third year, four of Sherlock's emails go unanswered. Sherlock pesters his brother Mycroft until they know why. In hospital a few weeks later John gets four handwritten letters all at once. By the time he's done reading them he's laughing and typing an email that starts with *My god you have awful handwriting.*

When John's sent home six weeks later he doesn't tell anyone he's coming. He's gone from a stunned peace at having survived, to the black knowledge that he's got few prospects, god damn multiple disabilities, and nothing at all to offer anyone.

The train from Manchester pulls in at Paddington at 11:57 pm. John thinks very seriously about not getting off. He could go back to Manchester. Start somewhere new.

One of the train crew sees his sling-bound arm and thinks John needs help. She picks up his small suitcase and puts it on the platform for him, then reaches to help him down.

Because John Watson is a polite Englishman, he gets off the train he meant to stay on. The woman reboards and the doors close just as John hangs his head. He stands there a long time trying not to think about his arm, his pain, his gun.

Later he'll laugh about it, but you'd think a soldier so recently returned from war would have felt someone getting as close as Sherlock did just then, but John didn't.

What John *did* do was be a polite Englishman once he saw who stood beside him. When Sherlock looked uncertain John smiled. When Sherlock tentatively smiled, John laughed. When John said, "hello," and held out his hand, Sherlock hugged him and said...

"Welcome home, John."

SH

Chamber of Horrors

Hackney, London — 1880

> *Well, that's not quite right.*

John Watson leaned toward the thing that wasn't quite right. Sure enough, on closer inspection it was *still* not right. The raw-bleeding heart clutched in the killer's hand had only three chambers instead of the required four *and* the organ was a good fifty percent larger than even the largest man's heart.

Also, to be frank, the blood oozing through the madman's fingers? Well it was an awfully strange shade of—there was no other word for it—ginger.

A guide entered the quiet room full of wax work horrors. On his heels a tall man loomed. They bustled past Watson and to a shadowy corner. "That one, there," the tall man said pertly.

Watson peered at the heart closer still. Yes, the gore definitely should lean more toward a Titian tint. After all, if this strange-chambered heart was meant to be newly-plucked—and judging by the arterial spray all over the murderer, it certainly was—then the ichor ought to be entirely less *orange*.

In the near distance the tall man gestured again at a decapitated corpse, looked pointedly at the guide. "Certainly you see the error?"

Watson stood straight. To be sure, the mistakes with the heart and its vital fluids didn't even begin to address the lunacy of the victim standing upright, grasping his heart-empty chest as the killer grinned at him.

Now, presupposing a lunatic *could* rip a heart from a body—and John Watson was a surgeon who had used fine-grade tools in times both urgent and leisurely and he'd tell you it's no small achievement working through dermal and epidermal layers, muscle and bone, to get at the beating bits behind—anyway, barring *all that* there was just no way a human being could yank out by hand another human being's heart without the attendant veins and arteries coming along for the ride. So really, this wax work was—

"No, no, no! Did you *count* them?"

John Watson glanced at the two men by the diorama, then returned his gaze to the error-riddled tableau containing the Ogre of Augy.

—sheer folly. And never mind that the bloodthirsty ogre was never caught, or that no one understood exactly how he'd disemboweled his victims, it was just unforgivable that basic anatomy was being so callously treated.

"Yes he has five fingers on his left hand, *that* is the problem."

Again Watson looked over at the two men, but this time his gaze did not stray away. Because frankly, the good doctor was bored. He lived in the grandest city in the world, with more attractions per mile than any man could enjoy in one lifetime, but Watson attended each and every one of them alone. (Barring that one disastrous afternoon with Miss Arbica at the army fête where—*never mind,* Watson was still trying to remove the tea stains from his shirt and that's not the *point.)*

The point was that John Watson, lately of the Second Afghan War and currently unemployed, needed diversion, and whilst getting riled by anatomical inaccuracies in wax work figures was distracting, it wasn't half so engrossing as the mysterious conversation over by the guillotine. Watson drifted toward the shadowy corner.

"—the point is, sir, that the Butcher of Bath had only *three* fingers on his left hand. Would it have been so difficult to give his wax effigy the correct number of digits? Here, I have a jackknife with me, I can lop off—"

The guide didn't get paid enough for all the things he had to do day-to-day. At Madame Morbid's Weird Wax Works and Evil Effigies there were always women screaming at the entrails and men falling over in a dead faint, and *who* had to calm the women and drag the men out? Terrence Anarion Jr., that's who. And now there was this strange man insisting that he'd cut up the exhibits and frankly Terrence was tired of it.

"—no sir, you cannot cut fingers off the—"

"—and as we're counting, I'd like you to look at the number of rivets on the blade at the end of the guillotine's rope. Would you mind terribly?"

Terrence Anarion Jr. sighed. He felt feverish. He was probably getting another cold. Nettie was forever coming home with colds from the other children, and he was forever catching them. Terrence Anarion Jr. daubed his nose and did as bid. He looked at the guillotine's rivets. He flatly announced the result of the looking. "One. There's one rivet, sir."

Holmes seemed at that moment to reach the end of his own rope. "My good man, surely you at least see the error in *this?*"

"The blade could rock on its mount," said Watson behind them. "If it did it'd be more of a butchery than a beheading."

Sherlock Holmes spun smartly on his heels, gesturing toward John Watson before he'd even set eyes on him.

"Exactly!" Holmes announced. "Surely you weren't short of bolts the day you put this monstrosity of a monstrous contraption together?"

The guide rubbed at his nose and sniffed hard. His head ached. Yes, this was definitely another one of Nettie's colds.

John Watson leaned conspiratorially toward the tall man. "You should see how they've mishandled the organs over by the Augy Ogre. Just shocking."

Sherlock Holmes looked at John Watson, shocked. "It's pernicious carelessness, that's what it is! Sherlock Holmes!"

A long-fingered hand was thrust out. Watson took it, shook it. "Doctor John Watson." Watson cocked a brow. "Frankly I'm beginning to suspect a group of children fresh from the nursery put this chamber of horrors together."

At this point the guide was out of handkerchiefs and patience.

"Did you see the Tragedy of Tyburn in the next room? As a doctor I'm sure you were outraged."

The guide sidled sideways.

Watson stood tall. "Of course I was! Drowned bodies rosy as new babes when they should be pale as milk?"

"Slim as a water reeds when they should be—"

"—grossly swollen!"

The guide managed to flee the scene without either man noticing.

For all their picky pedantry about the exhibits, Dr. Watson and Mr. Holmes didn't notice many things that day, including the man who fainted in front of the Foulmire Felon or the woman who gazed rapt at the Greenwich Garrotter's victims and wrote copious shorthand notes.

And it wasn't until the weary guide, now so congested he'd completely lost the use of his consonants, rounded up Messrs. Holmes and Watson many hours later, that either realised night had long since fallen and they'd progressed from gleefully discussing murder to planning to see a flat to the quality of the Criterion's teas.

As he bolted the door behind the still-talking gentlemen Terrence Anarion Jr. did not know they would go on to not only take lodgings together and become legends in their own time, but that a quarter century hence he would himself be caring for Holmes' and Watson's own wax work effigies—and he'd be quite pedantically particular about how the gentlemen were represented.

SH

Criminal Class

Somewhere along the A102, London — 2010

Criminals are nearly always boring.

Crime is fascinating, because entropy is the rule rather than the exception, so in all but the rarest of felonies evidence goes missing, false clues arise, a well-meaning someone moves a vital something.

So crime? Crime's rose-coloured, vibrant, endlessly interesting. But criminals? They're...

Orange.

Or their high-vis bibs are.

"I am not a criminal." These are the words Sherlock Holmes has been muttering for the last sixty-two minutes. And for sixty-one of them John Watson's been replying, "I know."

Except John didn't *actually* know, because John Watson doesn't know Sherlock Holmes. They'd met sixty-two minutes previous, inside the probation service van but, after picking up rubbish on the side of the road with the cranky whiner for the last hour, it felt to John as if he'd known Sherlock for approximately eight thousand years.

There was surprising comfort in this.

Mostly because nothing quite takes a person out of their own misery like the miseries of another. John knows this for absolute fact because John's a professional misery-remover. Or was. As a surgeon he'd helped dancers keep dancing, writers keep writing, and in one memorable instance, a snake milker keep milking.

Not content with helping just a few people however, the good doctor Watson decided to be of greater use and went to war. In Afghanistan he sublimated any and every desire or dissatisfaction under the daily—often dangerous—onslaught of everyone else's.

Until he couldn't.

The bullet that brought John Watson back to England brought him back to something he'd very long avoided: A focus on his *own* needs and wants.

And that pretty much sucked.

So John sublimated some more but, since he was no longer a surgeon he took up another calling, drinking too much, over too many nights, in too many cheap pubs. And here's a fact about that: If you're a mostly-quiet man who tends to be mostly-alone when you drink, you will eventually—it's almost a rule—run across an idiot or two who see you as easy pickings.

The "altercation" (that's what John called it) lasted thirty seconds and because he was the one holding the broken-edged bottle in second thirty-one—when the police arrived—he was the one who ended up with the anti-social behaviour order and the community service.

Of course no one believed the twelve-stone man had disarmed one five-stone heavier no matter how many times John offered to show exactly how that was done. As a matter of fact, it was his insistent insistence that he would *show them how he did it* that got him his community service sentence.

And Sherlock Holmes.

Who was not only still insisting he wasn't a criminal, now he also maintained he was a *detective* and on a case of *national* importance. As they still had five hours left of picking

203

up rubbish roadside, John just kept playing along, and was about to ask Sherlock if he also had a licence to kill, but suddenly the man was stridently whispering in John's ear, "When I say run, run. The direction doesn't matter, just make noise and *go.*"

John was about to laugh in Sherlock's face, one of those irritating—"Oh ha ha ha!"—laughs, the kind that nearly got him a jagged-edged bottle in the face three weeks ago, but suddenly Sherlock was screaming like a banshee, brandishing what was, to John's limbic system, a gun (later it turned out to be a wildly-waved stick), and John didn't have to think about whether to run, he just *ran.*

Ran up into the tree line and out of Sherlock's sight—and then out of the tree line and toward Sherlock Holmes' back, a high-speed, cranky, Watson missile.

Within twenty seconds every *other* man doing community service with them was up in the tree line too (one had actually got a good few miles along the A102 when they found him).

In that twenty seconds of confusion a great deal happened. Some of it was good, some bad, one bit led to a medal, another to a bruised jaw and fractured finger, and what happened to lead to all *that* was all *this:*

Missile Watson disarmed Get Off Me This Is For a Case! Holmes with extreme prejudice. Sherlock did not make that disarmament easy because nothing, absolutely nothing motivates the world's only consulting detective like the taste of a nearly-concluded case.

And so when John employed three of the near-lethal fighting techniques Major Sara McCombs taught him one particularly eventful weekend, Sherlock responded by applying the tips of his steel-toed Armanis—polished to a sheen even after an hour of bagging rubbish—to John's more delicate anatomy.

The end result would have been bad for them both if it hadn't been for the betting that broke out up in the trees—and the fact that the 'Russian' who had been grunting monosyllabically all day was actually now shouting in a Scottish so broad no one understood him until he was waving a fistful of money, the flashy pink-red of fifty pound notes doing all the clear speaking necessary.

It was those notes and that strange voice that at last confirmed for Sherlock exactly who the state secret-selling spy was, and it was only because Sherlock stopped fighting back that John stopped fighting at all.

"Thank you John," Sherlock said pleasantly as John heaved in confusion on top of him. From some place on his person Sherlock produced a mobile—as they weren't allowed to have one John refused then and forever to contemplate from *where* the mobile came—pressed a few numbers and said crisply, "I've found her. Yes, her." Sherlock paused long enough to be gratified by a response, hung up. And there was the medal.

And that's when most of *It* happened because, before John could say you're welcome in the form of "What the fu—" hands were lifting them both, the service supervisor was putting handcuffs on Sherlock, John was fussing loudly about that, and then a cranky bet-loser was shoving Sherlock so hard he tripped backward, falling gracelessly into the road. That's when Missile Watson became Incendiary Watson and he blew up. And there was the bruised jaw, the fractured finger, and *another* anti-social behaviour order on his record.

In the long run it didn't matter, because in the short run a helicopter was thrumming lazily overhead, a Russian-Scottish-actually-Norwegian secrets-stealing spy was soon taken away for questioning, and John was pocketing two hundred quid.

"What?" he replied in the face of Sherlock's indignation. "You were such a little piss-pot right from the start that I bet Clive you'd cause trouble inside the hour."

It did not matter then and wouldn't matter every single time Sherlock mentioned it in the future, but that didn't stop him from insisting regularly that "it wasn't *trouble,* John, it was *heroism,* I even have the *medal* around here somewhere to prove it. And besides, it was a full four minutes after the hour when I noticed that the suspect had—John? John Watson get back here I'm arguing with you!"

SH

Stop. Over.

Kabul, Afghanistan — 1879

Stop, stop, stop.

Dr. John Watson says it softly, a mantra muttered through pressed-thin lips, but it does not stop his pain.

Clutching his trousers with sweaty hands, sitting alone at the dock, and seven hours early for the first part of a journey that'll finally take him back to England, John Watson rocks in his creaking wooden chair and whispers *stop, stop, stop.* But there is only one thing that'll stop the fire in his shoulder, and it sounds much like an Afghan viper when he turns the bottle slowly in his hands, the tablets inside whispering with that snake's soft *shhhh.*

Watson tugs the morphine from his pocket and though he's not due for another tablet for six hours he thinks maybe he could break one in half, maybe just—

"No," he says to no one. Another tablet this early will just overburden his system. He's seen soldiers get addicted by taking the drug too early, addicted snake-quick.

As John Watson rolls the bottle round in his trembling hands, he stops saying *stop* and he listens closely to the soft, soft *shhhh* of the tablets.

*

Over.

Sherlock Holmes stands at a dusty window and stares out at grass pushing up through the slats of a badly-laid boardwalk, plants and planks both dry and faded in the Kabul sun.

Another case over before it had begun. Another missed chance to prove what he could do. Another failure to put words to invisible facts, to make people understand, to show them what he sees.

Over.

Sherlock Holmes is over this. He's tired of the *heat* of words and images bunched up in his head, fire trapped behind a door. He's tired of opening the door and watching everything *burn.* He doesn't know how to do this right, he doesn't know how to use the fire to make light, he desperately wants to illuminate, instead he turns everything to ash.

And he's over it.

Holmes slides a hand in his pocket and wraps long fingers around a bottle of cocaine and the needleless syringe nestled beside. All he has to do is *do it.* Put the lot in a vein, let the feel of its flowing prick his jaw bitter, and he'd be *done* doing. Done trying.

It'd be over.

Sherlock Holmes closes his eyes, bows his head to the dusty window, and he turns the bottle round and round in his pocket, it rubs against the syringe there with a sweet, soft little *shhhh.*

*

The man doesn't know he's banging his head against the window, John Watson's sure of that. Watson's less sure of

208

himself as he comes alongside the stranger and says in what he hopes is a pleasant voice, "Bad day?"

Holmes stops. Turns. Sees. *Soldier. Wounded. Alone. Distraction.*

"I have," Holmes says softly, "not often had worse."

*

Over the next seven hours Watson buys them both coffees. Then sweet chai. Then naan.

Holmes buys them sandwiches which contain a filling neither can identify but it tastes of fish and smells like dates.

Watson asks after his favourite English rugby team, about the latest Gilbert & Sullivan opera, if city hall is still ugly.

Holmes asks about Afghan food, Watson's shoulder, if it's true tongue prints are unique as fingerprints, and when human bones cease fusing.

When Watson asks why Holmes is asking they spend part of those seven hours talking about the cases Holmes has had (there have only been three, but he neglects to mention that), the deductions he's made, the experiments he's done.

By the time they're ready to board the ship John Watson is nearly one hour past his next pain tablet and Sherlock Holmes has dumped his cocaine out in the gents.

They have a two day-long stop over in Jerusalem, then another in Istanbul before they make berth in London, and by that time they have talked without pause for most of the waking hours of most of the days of their journey.

Even so, when they arrive in London and neither is met at the dock, they are sure this is over.

With silent nods and tight smiles they begin walking in separate directions. Within two strides both stop. Turn.

And both start over.

Holmes winks. Watson smiles.

They leave the docks together. They talk in the cab all the way into the city.

SH

Flying Saucer Men

New Row, West End, London — 2014

"That's an urban myth."

Sherlock Holmes ignores the man behind the sweetshop counter and frowns down at the colourful box in his hand.

"About the thing they say those things'll do."

Sherlock continues to ignore the assistant behind the counter and frowns harder at the box of sweets.

"I mean I know what you're thinking about those popping things because that's what all the adults who come in here think about those popping things."

Sherlock stops ignoring the man behind the counter and stares hard at him. The man blushes a fine shade of scarlet beneath his dark skin.

"I haven't tried the popping thing myself. I mean, you know, I've heard."

Sherlock narrows his eyes at the assistant. *Gay. Lonely. Sort of likes his job.*

Sherlock Holmes looks at the box of strange sweets in his hand, then again at the assistant. Not for the first time he wonders how far he'd go for a case. Sherlock appraises the man behind the counter. The man steps back a little, as if toward safety.

Answering his own question with action, Sherlock steps toward the counter. The man, slightly alarmed, steps back again.

Sherlock debates. He's done many things in the name of a case.

He's attended an embassy fête dressed as an eighty-year-old dowager from a country his brother Mycroft insisted *does* exist, despite its shocking lack of vowels. He's consumed an energy drink containing four raw eggs, cooked liver, and half a cup of god-forsaken *soy*.

Sherlock Holmes has even allowed six women, one man, and a Dachshund to French kiss him in a dance club. That one was *completely* worth it when he eventually pick-pocketed the right pocket (and yes, it was in the Dachshund's little coat) stealing the keycard back from the thief and successfully closing the case.

Anyway, Sherlock's pretty sure he's pretty willing to progress beyond a dog's tongue in his mouth if it would help him close this week-long case, so despite the fact that the assistant is now half-hiding behind the stockroom door, Sherlock steps up to the counter, opens his mouth—

—and trills.

Actually no he doesn't. The door behind him does as a straight-backed man walks in.

Sherlock's gaze darts over him. *Strong for his size. Ex-soldier. Keen on excitement. And danger.*

Sherlock smiles down at the popping candies in his hand, nods at them as if in agreement, then looks back to the soldier. *Yes. Perfect.*

Clutching the sweets, Sherlock coasts over to packets of humbugs. He touches their cello wrappers until the crackling has enough disturbed the quiet that the straight-backed man looks at him.

Sherlock grins and murmurs, "Sorry."

Dr. John Watson nods a half-smile at the tall man, and looks again at the plump packet of flying saucers in his own hand. John loved these things as a kid. The summers he was five and six and seven grandma would sometimes sneak a dozen of the feather-light things into his pocket. Hours later he'd be digging round her back garden and find them. Immediately he'd lie on the grass, and one-by-one he'd hold each translucent sweet up so that it blocked the sun. Their thin rice-paper shells had glowed in a way that had made John think of adventure.

Then young John would eat his little dream machines carefully, always the yellow first, then the orange, the blue, the green, and finally the pink.

John looks up. "What?"

The tall man is no longer over by the humbugs. With bright, alert eyes that maybe have a touch of the crazy to them—John's a working physician who often deals with hyperactive children, he *knows* what crazy looks like—the tall man's now close, smiling down at the package in John's hand.

"—I said, the orange first of course, then the yellow, blue, green, and the pink last." What Sherlock does not add is that this was the precise order he learned to eat flying saucers by watching his brother that summer they spent in Brighton with the beekeeper.

John looks at the sweets in his hand, then back up at the tall guy. He leans away from the man and his own delighted surprise. "Yes. Exactly. Well nearly. Almost. The yellow first though. I mean that's obvious. Any five year old'll tell you that."

Sherlock Holmes knows a great many things. That he's smarter than everyone he's ever met except Mycroft. That he'll solve this case today so help him. And that he has been compared to a three year old, a four year old, a five year old, and a ferret on speed, times past counting. Whilst Sherlock's never quite got the logic of these comparisons—which are usually being shouted at him by a Scotland Yard detective, a client, or his brother—Sherlock acknowledges he has perhaps a certain *passionate* manner when on a case, but frankly he sees this as a strength and not the weakness implied by most.

So Sherlock nods at this familiar juxtaposition and plows on, regardless, going full-speed-ahead with the unfamiliar business of trying to seduce a stranger so that he can close a case by verifying that a packet of popping sweets applied to a man's p—

The man who likes flying saucers is suddenly laughing and pointing.

Sherlock looks at where the man is pointing. The man stops pointing at the box in Sherlock's hand but doesn't stop laughing.

As has been said, Sherlock Holmes knows a great many things, including the fact that honeybees can recognise human faces and blue urine may signal drug abuse. What Sherlock also knows is that this war veteran and working physician knows something he wants to know. So Sherlock lets him laugh, even if that laughter is being directed at him.

(Later Sherlock will be annoyed for having presumed for even a moment that John Watson was in this way like everyone else.)

"I shouldn't laugh," John says, plucking the popping rock candy from Sherlock's hand. "Though to be honest, even my patient was giggling at the time."

Sherlock Holmes begins to hover. There is a case-closing

clue on its way and he has a tendency to loom when they do.

"It's just, I had a couple into the surgery last year. He was all shy and embarrassed and she, well she was *blue* with—" John reads off the colourful box in his hand. "—E132 food colour. She and her boyfriend had been applying the rocks—did you know it's carbon dioxide that makes them pop?—yeah, well, anyway they'd heard that story about how if you put them on a man's, well, right, anyway, they'd been putting them there and she'd been removing them as you'd expect, but in the end all he got was sticky and all *she* got was a very blue mouth and the new knowledge that she was really allergic to E132."

John hands the box back to Sherlock. "Skin inside the wrist's more sensitive though. They should have just, you know, sucked them from there."

At this intel Sherlock nearly leaps in the air. He almost does a *'that's* another *case closed ha ha I told you so Lestrade!'* dance. He does not do either of these things however, what he does do is say,

"I'mSherlockHolmescomealongwe'regoingtoScotlandYardthank swhyareyouwaiting?"

It takes John Watson probably five seconds to parse not only what's just happened but what's been said.

After he's done this he thinks about whether he really needs to go back to the surgery to finish paperwork precisely *now.* He decides that he can do it tomorrow. Or this weekend. Because John's never been to Scotland Yard. He thinks it could be an adventure to go to Scotland Yard. John has always liked adventures.

"I'm John," John says, shaking Sherlock's hand. "Let's—
"

John doesn't get to finish because Sherlock dashes toward the sweetshop assistant—who's still half-hiding behind the stockroom door—tosses five pounds at him, grabs up two plump packets of flying saucers, shoves one in John's hand and, with a shout of "The game is...it's...let's go!"—is out the door.

As the door trills merrily John looks at the assistant. The assistant shrugs.

Then John Watson turns and, for the first time, follows Sherlock Holmes. It will very much not be the last.

SH

A Close Shave

Jeremy James & Daughter, The Strand, London — 1882

"How fast would I bleed out if you cut my throat right now Mr. James?"

Straight razor gently skimming his client's Adam's apple, Jeremy James, nee Jerchandra Jayaramanium, did not so much as flinch. James has shaved potentates and politicians—once during a continents-spanning treaty negotiation—and so has heard (or more importantly, *not* heard) nearly everything.

Still, Mr. James always plays along with Mr. Holmes, if for no other reason than the man is truly asking. "I don't usually time the bleeding, sir, I like to let it simply flow."

The barber smiled serenely, Sherlock Holmes talked to himself, and from beneath the swaddle of a moist towel, the customer two chairs over said, "It would depend on the width of the cut, how far into the epidermal layer it went, the person's cardiac health, and their diet."

Sherlock Holmes sat up so suddenly Jeremy James nearly answered the detective's question through direct action.

"Diet?"

The customer two chairs over nodded beneath his towel. "Well yes. Certain foods help thin the blood. Thin blood of course flows faster."

Sherlock Holmes frowned at his barber, as if the man should have known this. Then he began struggling out of the plush embrace of his fully-reclined chair. Jeremy James placed a staying hand on the man's lean shoulder.

"Your midnight killer will still be there in ten minutes Mr. Holmes. Hastening off half-covered in shaving foam could be dangerous."

The towel-shrouded man two chairs over unshrouded himself, struggled to sit upright in *his* chair. "Midnight killer? Dangerous? Beg pardon?"

Prone once more, the razor flicking fast along his jugular not the slightest impediment, Sherlock Holmes rattled off fast as fire: "Good heavens, the woman's an assassin, a hired *assassin,* which is entirely different from the 'midnight killer' the press insists on so luridly painting."

Two chairs over and with gentle hands, Isabelle James encouraged her favourite client horizontal again, reshrouded him carefully. Living on a small army pension, Dr. John Watson was hardly ever in, only treated himself to a proper shave and trim a half dozen times a year, if that. So today she'd do it. She'd ask the doctor if he would take tea with her. Yes, that's what she'd do. That was, if Mr. Holmes and her father would ever just *be quiet,* why was it they could never just—

"Tell me more about the effects of diet."

A man habituated to both command *and* obedience, John Watson responded immediately. "Nutrients found in various nuts and rice, as well as those in many vegetables such as cabbage, are natural blood thinners."

"Fantastic!" Holmes said gleefully, then fell silent in rumination. Soon the only sound was the gentle scrape-scrape of keen metal over Holmes' pale skin, and the shush-shush of a · buffer over Watson's thumbnail.

One breath, then two, three for luck and Isabelle James cleared her throat, said softly, "Doctor...uh...John, yes, you said last time that I should call you John. Well then, doctor, uh—"

"Of course!" shouted Holmes, "She knew the victim! She *must* have or else how could she know about his eccentric diet? The man would barely eat anything not pulled directly from the earth, turned his prodigious nose up at eggs and dairy, steak, even tea. Oh this changes everything."

Isabelle James waited one heartbeat, two, three for *luckier* luck, opened her mouth to begin again and—

"Wait." This time John Watson didn't bother removing his towel shroud or sitting up. He simply uncovered one eye and looked two chairs to the left. "Are you serious about a midnight kil—uh, about an assassin? We're not truly talking about a woman who goes around shooting people are we?"

Holmes waved a thin hand, narrowly avoided his barber's straight-razor. Isabelle James frowned, clutched the nail buffer tightly, and a little bit wished *she* was shaving Mr. Holmes.

"Oh the killer is neither here nor there, doctor...?"

Though his charms were quite legendary and his knowledge of women continents-spanning, the good doctor failed to register the low growl of his lady barber. "Watson," replied John, "And I thought you said she wasn't a kill—"

Another limb-threatening wave, this time in the doctor's direction. "Delighted Dr. Watson, delighted. My name is Sherlock Holmes and I am a consulting detective, the only one in the world. Now how long can you be away from your practice today? For mark my words, Watson, there's the dark shadow of crime here, and it goes far deeper than a governess trained in the black art of contract killings, oh yes."

Beneath his now-cool towel John Watson calculated how long he could be away from his patron's practice. In the future he would wonder at his quick acceptance that he had both the time *and* inclination to follow this stranger, but history would show that the legendary partnership of Dr. John Watson and Mr. Sherlock Holmes had indeed begun one temperate London day, at a respectable barber's shop not very far north of the Strand.

The last of the shaving foam wiped from his throat, Holmes bolted energetically from his chair, clapped his hands. "I could use an assistant skilled in medicine and combat. What do you say?"

Watson unswathed his face at last, sat up in his chair. "I'm your man."

It wasn't until much later that the good doctor realised he'd meant to have that very nice Miss James shave off his moustache. Ah well, no doubt that could wait for the month after next, when surely he and Holmes would have finished with the Sumatra case, and that one with the lovely heiress. Those treaty papers, however, that was a tricky business...

SH

My Brother's Keeper

Trafalgar Square, London — 2009

We teach our children many cruel things.
Big boys don't cry.
Children should be seen and not heard.
There's nothing to be afraid of.
Of each of these barbarities that last is the most savage untruth. There is always something to hive up the hair on the back of your neck, hammer your heart to triple time. Life is full of things to fear, of things that *should* be feared, it's fit to bursting with so much terrible wrong that the best thing, the very best and kindest thing we can do for our children is to tell them this truth: There is everything in the world to fear, but what you can learn to do is…

…hide.

*

Mycroft Holmes knows of no man brighter than himself. He wishes that he did. Being the only of something, singular, unique has, he will assure you, nothing at all to recommend it.

Rare has many synonyms and Mycroft knows them all. Take a moment, look them up. Read the list of words that mean *only*. That cold catalogue includes *odd* and *unusual* and the one Mycroft hates most: *isolated*.

Being unique in a world of people who are not is, Mycroft Holmes will tell you, should you be asking, the most frightening thing in the world.

Why, he's pretty sure it'll drive you mad.

Of all the things that Mycroft's afraid of, and he's afraid of more things than he has time to tell you, should you ask, Mycroft is afraid that he's crazy.

After all, look at Sherlock.

Sherlock's *almost* rare. He's *nearly* unique. He's mostly everything Mycroft is—though not quite—and sometimes Mycroft's sure his brother is stark raving.

He twitches about like a puppet with cut strings. He dashes like a demented bird. He wants and doesn't want, needs and doesn't need, yells and whispers, runs and stills, he seems one day to the next to try on a new trait, a new belief, a new voice or gesture or...

...sometimes Mycroft looks at Sherlock, who is emphatically *not him,* and he thinks: He's bloody barking. He's insane.

And so what does that make me?

It makes you, should Mycroft Holmes actually be asking, one simple thing: Your own worst enemy.

*

John Watson's pretty sure mundanity will make you crazy.

The day-in-day-out certainty that today will look-smell-sound like yesterday, that it is nothing more and nothing less than a shining preview of tomorrow, well, it'll sometimes make you sure you're going a bit mad.

The thing to do about that is the thing John's doing now: Anything. Because he knows it is only in the trying that answers are found. Yet, though he tries a treat does John, today he's found little more than Trafalgar Square pigeons who like the same pasties he does.

That's okay, because John likes pigeons and the sound of Big Ben and just wandering the square and wondering if he'll get a call back for that St. Bart's job or if Mary will answer his email. It's on his third go around the square, thinking a bit too much about this bit too little, that John realises he's gone by the same man each time and that that man has not moved at all.

That in itself is almost de rigueur for Trafalgar Square, busy as it is with busking men and women who instead of singing, play at being costumed statues, the better to entice tourists close for a photo—and then a quid dropped in a nearby hat.

But this man isn't painted statue bronze from head to toe, he's in a business suit and sitting so close to the wind-blasted spray of one of the fountains that he's half drenched, and—this is what stopped John in his tracks—the man isn't blinking.

"Hey," he says, stopping in front of the man, whose eyes are tearing badly from exposure. "Are you all right?"

John knows the man's not all right. He's seen catatonic stupor before and suspects that this is that. He needs to move him, get him dry, and somewhere safe.

Touching, getting involved, John doesn't have half the hesitancy in these that most do, and he's not sure if that's because of the army or if he entered the army because of these.

Doesn't matter, he got involved, he *touched,* and he told the man he was touching what he was doing. "I'm just looking for your phone," he said, reaching into the left breast pocket of an impeccable suit coat. "I'm just going to call your family or a friend, okay?"

The mobile was there against the man's heart, and quickly John flicked through its electronic phone book and found what he wanted.

ICE

Later John would come to know that a man as thorough as Mycroft Holmes of course has an *In Case of Emergency* phone number programmed into his mobile. Later still John would understand why Mycroft actually had *three*.

On instinct John chose not the first, nor the second, but the one marked ICES and why he did that he'd never know but when the call was answered—

"Mycroft! Have they found the third eyeball yet? I can't move ahead with this case until I have the blue one, too."

—John for a moment had no clue what to say.

The man on the other end knew something was wrong anyway.

"It's okay My. Breathe, breathe. Where are you?"

John opened his mouth but didn't get further than letting the thing hang open because the man on the other end told him where he was.

"Big Ben's going six and I hear water and that awful violinist disgracing Vivaldi again. Which fountain are you near? Never mind I'll find you. Five minutes, My. Breathe, *breathe.*"

And then the man hung up.

It took John about eight seconds to realise his mouth was still open. He closed it.

The man took six minutes. John knew it was the same man because he spoke just as quickly, only this time it was to grouse about traffic and taxis as he approached the catatonic man. It took him eight seconds to register John and don't you even think John didn't tease him about that later, at random times, and just to see him bluster.

"Eight seconds, Sherlock, you didn't notice me *standing right there* in front of your brother for eight seconds. You seeee but you do not obseeeerve."

The jokes were for later however, now the tall man standing there was registering John's presence and he was flick-flick-flicking a gaze from the crown of John's head to the Converse on his feet and he was saying, "He doesn't need a doctor, thank you, he's...this is...he's fine."

John didn't ask how the man knew he was a doctor or why he was now body-blocking him, preventing him from seeing the catatonic man, because John's not a fool. This was a secret, what was happening here, this was something other eyes—blue or otherwise—were not supposed to see.

But instead of walking away, letting one man care for the other, John said the exact right thing at the exact right time. And changed three lives.

"Between the two of us we can get him behind the National Gallery. I know of a tiny library back there, very private, hardly anyone goes."

Sherlock Holmes blinked at John Watson. For maybe eight seconds more he saw and saw, observed and observed, and then he simply nodded and turned to his brother and then he and the stranger, as if of one mind, did on instinct the same thing.

They closed Mycroft's unblinking eyes.

Then John reached for one arm, Sherlock the other. They stood Mycroft on his feet and, eyes closed tight, a man who was afraid of far too many things and very good at understanding that those fears were justified, well he was guided to a quiet and safe place by his brother. And by the man who would eventually become his brother's quiet and safe place.

SH

Violin Concerto in Blue

Near St. Thomas' Hospital, London — 1884

The beggar was playing Strauss.

John Watson let the song slow his fast stride along the river path, let it stop him in front of the ragged violinist sitting cross-legged on the pavement, and he let the song start his toe tapping with each bright strike of the bow.

Though the air blowing from the river was chill, and the morning sky still winter-dark, Watson lingered, appreciating each invigorating note. As soon as one song ended, the violinist began another, and it wasn't until the fourth tune that Watson checked his watch and realised he'd lingered too long. Tossing a half-crown into the beggar's case, the good doctor hurried off, making it to St. Thomas' just in time for his dawn shift.

The day there went as most days did: Quickly. Hospital corridors bustled with people getting well or getting worse, with doctors happy to help or too tired to care, and by the time Watson checked his watch again, it was well past four and a frigid December dusk was tinting London's sky icy blue.

Even so, Watson could still hear the violin's mournful notes—Chopin this time—as he hurried along the slick embankment toward the station. And despite a wind still whipping sharp from the river Watson slowed, grinning under gas light, perfectly content to brave the cold, because good doctor Watson knows what he likes.

He likes Strauss waltzes, music that taps his toes, and songs that remind him of lovely Miss Phynn on the maternity ward. A wonderfully competent nurse, Sabrina had a roguish glint in eyes of bright blue, and often hummed Chopin as she worked. One of these days, when he wasn't still 'that new doctor,' Watson would formally introduce himself.

Tossing another half-crown into the violinist's case, John Watson tipped his hat and smiled at the man, who tipped his flat-cap as if it were a top hat of finest rabbit. "Evenin' doctor," the man said, beginning another waltz.

*

Some mornings called for Mendelssohn.

Or so Sherlock Holmes said each time a business man paused long enough to drop him a shilling. As the dawn crowd thinned, Holmes stretched out long legs in their beggar's rags, and began entertaining himself by composing his deductions. For the pugnacious trio walking mute along the river path he concocted something faintly martial. For the two old men with their heads together, he orchestrated a twittering, gossipy tune.

And all the while Holmes waited for the coming and the going of Mr. Vladimir Artemis Griffin, thief.

Each time the man appeared—and he had done so twice yesterday—Holmes took note of his newspaper. Yesterday at dawn it had been the Coburger Zeitung, late that evening the Heidelberger Zeitung. As the suspect did not speak one word of German, Holmes knew this implicated Lady Von Sutton as his embezzling accomplice, not that bumbler Fitch, as Athelney Jones insisted.

All Holmes needed now was to spot Von Sutton and his case was made. After clapping eyes on her, he'd dispatch a message to Jones, wash these blasted rags, and spend the evening in front of a fire, leeching the chill from his cold, cold bones.

"It should still be warm."

Holmes had just finished a raucous little tune to accompany a brace of noisy boys running by, when the doctor from yesterday appeared, the one who loved Strauss and got giddy over Chopin.

"Just some roast on bread, with horseradish. If nothing else that bit'll warm you." The doctor placed the wax paper packet next to the violin case.

Holmes grinned. *Smart fellow, doesn't want to smudge the fusty old velvet with grease.*

In thanks Holmes began the stately opening of *The Blue Danube,* because Sherlock Holmes knows what people like.

The footsore nurse who'd come by an hour ago? The fleur de lis on her well-loved scarf, a careful chignon, and the heavy scent of her Fantasia de Fleurs perfume hinted at a fondness for things French, so Holmes played Saint-Saëns' *Danse Macabre,* low, as if in secret, and the woman grinned, her stride perking as she passed.

The skinny hospital secretary who fiddled with a ring box in his pocket, mumbling a speech as he went to work? For him Holmes' nimble fingers danced over Wagner's *Bridal Chorus,* winking when the nervous young man looked up, mystified and smiling.

And then there was this proud, moustachioed doctor. Like the raucous boys or the straight-backed trio of before, he was an open-book to Holmes' all-seeing eyes. Clearly a medical type, he had the strong will that went with such a profession, but was also easy-going enough to talk with beggars. His was a soldier's past, with all the adventure that implied and much of the darkness, too. Ultimately, however, here was a straight-forward and spirited man, so Holmes played for him the cheering comforts of *The Blue Danube*.

And it's likely Watson would have stood there on the busy river walk for the song's entire eleven minutes but for a sudden silence that brought him out of chill-defying reveries five minutes later. When he opened his eyes, the beggar was tapping the watch pocket of his own tattered waistcoat. Cottoning on quickly, Watson tugged out his timepiece, said, "Oh!" and with a quickly dropped crown, was on his way.

*

The day was long for John Watson. It was even longer for Sherlock Holmes.

Afternoon snow kept one physician away and delayed another, so Watson worked well into a second shift. It was nine before he walked outside, tugging his collar closed, chafing his hands against the cold.

Scuffing wearily along the river path, he'd nearly forgotten about the violinist until there it was, drifting sweet in the after-snow quiet: Evocative music, so much like and yet not really like music he'd come to love nearly half a dozen years ago.

As he approached the violinist, Watson wondered how an instrument with such small and simple parts—a bridge and bow, pegs and strings and chinrest—could make such hauntingly big music. He would never ask really, because there are some thing about which Watson's content to remain blissfully ignorant.

And some thing he emphatically is not.

"What happened?" The words were something between a growl and a gasp, both gentle and furious.

Holmes ceased his playing, looked up with tired, triumphant eyes. "Ah, hello, doctor. It seems a young woman took umbrage when I helped to have her sister arrested."

Holmes continued plucking the tune he'd written as he waited for Von Sutton, the Lady having appeared not two hours previous. Holmes' telegram to Jones was dispatched soon after, whilst Von Sutton's sister—and her well-swung umbrella—had followed within the hour.

Watson squatted in front of Holmes. "You'll need ice for the swelling."

Holmes smiled, winced in pain, then pronounced in bald-faced lie, "It's perfectly fine."

"You're blue from cheekbone to brow, my man." It was another growl, with careful fingers taking hold of the beggar's chin, turning his face toward the gas light. "You're developing a most spectacular bruise. Any dizziness? Nausea? Can you stand? Come, I work at St. Thomas'."

Holmes tucked away his bow and violin. "Truly I'm fine, and besides, I have a better plan. I live across the river and by now my landlady ought to have a fine fire going. If you'd be so kind as to administer your first aid back on Baker Street—and let me get out of this miserably drafty disguise—I'll happily submit to doctoring as we warm our bones with brandy."

Watson narrowed his eyes. Whereas most would have scowled in suspicion—fire, Baker Street digs, disguise?—his frown was of a doctor loathe to brook argument. "We'll first fetch some laudanum from the hospital, you'll be in quite a bit of pain soon."

Joints creaky with cold, Holmes accepted Watson's hand and rose. "I'll take care of that with my preferred opiate."

Holmes said no more and Watson did not pursue the matter.

Not *then.*

Though Holmes can deduce much, he's no fortune teller. So on that first evening of their lifelong acquaintance the good detective had absolutely no idea how exceedingly annoying the good doctor would become as regarded preferred opiates.

That was an issue for another time. Now was for introductions, then revelation as Holmes said, "I wrote a tune this evening you might like, I was playing it as you approached. It's called *Afghan Waltz.*"

That was why the music had seemed so evocative, thought Watson. "What an amazing coincidence. I'm very partial to waltzes, and I happened to have served in Afghanistan not quite six years ago."

Holmes grinned and said pleasantly. "Oh really, you don't say?"

SH

Stiff Upper Lip

Court Chemists, Rotherhithe, South-East London — 2012

John Watson has never been an insomniac. Except lately. Once or twice a week. When his shoulder bothers him.

John Watson's never been much of a shopper. Except when he's got insomnia. And the only place open at two a.m. is the all-night chemist.

And John's also never been a security guard. Except he was about to pretend to be one in the all-night chemist. Because the real guard was a berk.

*

Sherlock Holmes knows the rules.

Thou shalt not crash a funeral in search of evidence.

Thou shalt not impersonate a mourner to gain access to the evidence.

And thou shalt not then take the evidence you find.

Yes, times yes, multiplied by yes, Sherlock Holmes knows exactly what's acceptable and what is not, and he knows because it's in knowing the rules that he knows how far he can go in *breaking* them.

The answer is: Pretty damn far.

So far that he *can* crash a funeral, *can* impersonate a mourner, and therefore can sidle up to a glossy coffin tastefully surrounded by flickering candles, and then surprise a hundred well-dressed mourners by mouth-kissing a sixty-year-old corpse.

*

"That's not done."

Sherlock Holmes stopped applying *Sienna Sunset* to his lower lip.

"Trying on the pricy lipsticks, you can't do that I'm afraid."

Sherlock looked around the empty chemist's as if prepared to implore a higher power. Then he looked back at John Watson. "There are one hundred and eight from this maker alone. How do you expect someone to choose the right flavour? Colour. The right colour?"

John likes Mrs. Marie, the assistant in the chemist. Every time he comes in they chat. John doesn't like the security guard, to whom John now glanced.

"Sorry, I don't actually work here. Mr. Brackenstall over there just asked me to ask you to stop trying everything on."

Sherlock Holmes looked directly at John Watson. He blinked slowly, said nothing. John's stared down angry four year olds with sharp-toed shoes, he cannot be phased.

"Why didn't Mr. Brackenstall do this himself?"

"Because he's a berk. Marie said you could try the Sassy Girl lipsticks, over there. She says this is the only shop that carries them and they're cheap. There are samples open."

For a long second Sherlock Holmes continued to look right at John Watson, as if he was reading fine print upon his brain. Then he grabbed John's shoulders and shouted. "You're a genius!"

One second later Sherlock was spinning a tottery plastic carousel from which the rear ends of three dozen lipsticks protruded. "She was old money, land scattered from Scotland down to Southend-on-Sea. I just assumed her lipstick would be one of those thirty pound things. *I'm* the berk."

His job done, John could have walked away. John didn't. "What're you doing?"

"Catching a woman's killer."

"Are you serious?"

"Very."

John glanced at Mr. Brackenstall, then leaned toward Sherlock. "Who're you?"

Sherlock stopped twirling the carousel. "I'm Sherlock Holmes, consulting detective. You?"

"Uh, John Watson, doctor at a children's clinic."

"Well you can add conductor of light to your CV, Dr. Watson. How would you like to conduct a little more?"

"I don't under—"

"I need to gather evidence. Do you want to help?"

It was two in the morning. John had to be at the clinic in six hours. John was not one tiny bit tired. Not *now*.

"Sure, what do you need?"

"Eccentric millionaire, dead of natural causes though previously a robust sixty. All suspects with alibis. I think she was poisoned. Through her lipstick."

"Right."

"She had a favourite kind, no one knew where she got it, or from whom, only that it was made especially for her. Her children were privy to everything else about the woman, her computer passwords, her safe combination, her shoe size. But not this. Which seemed…strange. One receipt no one was able to explain contained three charges: seven pounds, one pound fifty-nine, and thirty pounds. The generic listings for each were medication, cosmetic, cosmetic. The receipt bore the watermark of a south Rotherhithe paper manufacturer. So I've been visiting every compounding chemist in the SE16 postcode looking for an almond-flavoured lipstick the colour of blood two hours old."

"Blood? Almond?"

"It tasted of almonds, the lipstick. I should have realised the lipstick I was looking for would be inexpensive. Almond flavouring can be chemically manufactured for a tenth a penny per litre and its intensity masks off flavours, like sub-grade emollients."

"How on earth do you know what the lipstick tasted like?"

"Well no one could find an actual tube of the stuff after the funeral home finished with her—which was also suspect— so I got a sample by kissing the corpse."

"You…kissed a stiff?"

Sherlock's silence was all the answer the good doctor required. "Right. So what next?"

"We put the lipstick on, taste for almonds."

"We."

"This would go much faster if you'd help." John's silence was all the answer the great detective required. "We can do two at a time—what?"

"Isn't tasting for an almond flavour enough?"

"I need a colour match, too."

"Right. And when you find it?"

"This is a compounding chemist, meaning they personalise medication for their clients. Why stop at medication? If we find a colour match we've found the

236

pharmacist who made Lucia Fitzwilliam's one-of-a-kind lipstick. And poisoned her with it. Will you help me?"

Everyone has choices, every day, with every thing.

A man can ask a question to which he doesn't want the answer ("Because you bore me Johnny, I'm sorry.").

Do the thing someone else won't do ("Go over there and tell that pansy to leave those lipsticks alone, wouldja doc?").

And when almost every day is like the one before it, a man can decide, apropos of everything, to choose a more unusual path.

John twirled the carousel. "Well, if it was the colour of semi-fresh blood we can skip right past the *Tangerine Torture, Bodacious Bruise, Cream Pie Crime,* and *Pretty Pink Punishment.* We can also pause a minute and have these people sectioned. Uh, how about these?"

John handed Sherlock *Chokehold Cherry,* took *Very Venomous Vermillion* for himself. Both carefully applied the lipsticks to one lip, looked in the mirror.

"Well?"

Sherlock gazed at their reflections. He turned his head away from the bright lights, made a moue. John did the same. Without realising it, both men appeared to be blowing kisses at Mr. Brackenstall.

"Yours is close but not quite. How does it taste?"

John licked his lip. "Almonds! Yours?"

"Same." Sherlock grinned.

"So this is the chemist's. This is the brand."

Sherlock kissed the lipstick tube. "Oh yes."

Already officially down the Holmesian rabbit hole, John went on to metaphorically converse with a hookah-smoking

237

caterpillar by saying, "Well *Mostly Mad Merlot* sounds promising. I'll try the *Rabid Rose Wreck.*"

They did.

"Well?"

"No."

They scrubbed their lips bare with nearby tissues. John plucked up *Murderous Maroon,* handed Sherlock *Scarlet Scare,* noticed something. "Why are you wearing nail varnish?"

Sherlock painted his upper lip. "At another chemist the assistant kept looking at me—no."

Autumn Amputation in Auburn, and *Carmine Cadaver* were next.

"—so I had to pretend to sample the nail varnish—no."

Bloody Brown Betty and *Dismembered Mahogany* followed.

"—until he went on a break and I could try the lipstick. No."

This made mad sense to John, much like a disappearing cat and a Cheshire grin made sense to Alice. "I see." The good doctor held up a pair of tubes. "Last two."

Sherlock put on *Serial Killer Crimson,* looked in the mirror. "No." John put on the final lipstick.

"That's it! That's the colour! What is it?"

John scowled. *"Sort of Red, Three Hours Ded.* No really, these people need psychiatric care."

Sherlock scowled. "Three hours? *Three?* Blood that colour would be not one minute over two hours old. Clearly they—"

"Focus."

"Right. Scotland Yard next. Let's go."

"You want *me* to come?"

When two men try on lipstick together at two in the morning, something happens. Friendship, partnership, bonding...*something.*

"Would you?"

John blotted his lips. Wondered if a Mad Hatter or a King of Hearts was next along the Wonderland path.

"Let's go."

As they left John mumbled "Berk" at Mr. Brackenstall.

Sherlock blew him a kiss.

SH

The Elegance of Triage

Alexandra Cemetery — 1883

John Watson does not walk through graveyards. It's too damn much like work.

As a doctor and a soldier both, John Watson's seen too much dying to be enamoured of the trappings of death. Graceful a monument may be, necessary a cemetery certainly is, but Watson doesn't while away time in one, no matter how shaded its lanes or how pretty its tombstone angels.

Yet right now, on an autumn morning both rainy and grey, this cemetery stood between Dr. John Watson and hope.

Hope was called the Royal Albert Hospital, hope specialised in caring for men returned from whatever war in which Her Majesty was currently embroiled. And hope might, oh my yes, hope might, for the first time since he came back from Afghanistan, allow the good doctor to use his gifts to the full.

Except. Well. There was a half mile long city of the dead between Watson and hope. Mind you, Watson had consulted a map. He'd planned his route around this place. He'd also forgot his map. Which was fine really, just fine, because the hospital was simply on the other side of one, long, tree-shaded lane. On the other side of this cemetery. The one he did not want to walk through.

Watson checked his watch. Briefly closed his eyes. Time for triage.

Triage: The assigning of degrees of urgency to a thing. The concept can be applied to battlefield wounded, the ill, to your own conflicting desires. Through the lens of triage, priorities become clear.

In the end Watson knew it was more urgent he get this job than avoid the discomforts of memory, so he stepped through the cemetery's tall iron gates.

It was raining hard under the trees. Of course it was, for trees both bar the rain and collect it, but that was fine. Watson once worried about snakes in his bed and sand in his bullet wound, he was fairly sure he could ignore a bit of wet.

Unfurling his umbrella, he could also fix his gaze straight ahead, ignoring how long a half mile could seem.

If he walked fast, if he didn't turn, if he didn't *look,* Watson could also ignore the well-dressed man sitting on a bench just to his right. He could pretend he didn't notice that the man was soaked to the skin, that he had his face turned skyward, mouth open, as if the steady downpour might fill him up, wash him away.

And if Watson walked faster didn't turn his head didn't look didn't look didn't look, he could pretend he didn't see the gun beneath the man's hands.

So Watson didn't look. And Watson walked by.

Sherlock Holmes didn't notice. It wasn't important to see a shadow in a cemetery, a cemetery is full of flitting shadows.

Yet distracting shadows weren't the reason Sherlock Holmes had come to dislike cemeteries. No, Sherlock Holmes disliked them because nothing *happened* in them. No one spoke. No one *needed.*

Sometimes Sherlock Holmes came to such places

241

anyway, because once in very great while the quiet buzzed his mind active, tripped him into a deduction, recalled a clue half-seen. And so he would come to these places of shadow and silence because in the end it didn't matter how a puzzle solved itself, it never mattered. Oh but *having* a puzzle to solve, seeing touching tasting smelling hearing clues evidence victims suspects leaves on trees distant shouts insomnia-bruised eyes? All of it, everything, every *little* thing was a glory to be picked up, held close, dissected with tongue and touch and sight and sound and it was wonderful every time, it was perfect except...

...except it didn't happen enough. Not *enough.* All over London there were lives riven by cruelty, crimes committed, there were people who needed resolution, closure, *proof.* He could help them but only if he could *find* them. Yes, Scotland Yard came calling when they needed him, they let him solve their most convoluted cases then took the credit. That just left all the between time, the silence of the moving air, the shout of an empty room.

And the knowledge that if he didn't do something it would no doubt be that way tomorrow and tomorrow.

Sherlock Holmes was in Alexandra Cemetery to do something. Something that would change everything.

As Sherlock Holmes looked down at the gun beneath his hands, a man sat beside him.

For a moment the second most observant man in the world did not see him.

Then he felt him, a shadow amidst tombstone shadows, right there, close at his side.

"Dreadful day, isn't it?"

Sherlock Holmes is a contradictory man. He shouts in

churches, whispers in crowds, ignores a straight-forward question because he understands that the question's asking something else entirely.

Sherlock Holmes didn't want to hear the question beneath that question, so he didn't.

That was fine.

John Watson could talk for two if necessary. He was good at performing many tasks at the same time. He could talk for a man not talking, could plan on what he'd say next, and he could watch that man's hands stay tight around a gun, and whilst he did all that, he could think of four ways to get the gun, one probably safe, two dangerous, the last likely fatal.

John Watson was a soldier. He is a doctor. And so Watson's learned the art of triage on two entirely different battlefields. He has always been good at it. Always been good at saving lives. Just not always his own.

Watson was drenched now too. It happened when he paused out of sight of this man, when he stood next to a mausoleum and tried to talk himself into not caring more about a stranger than he did about himself.

He stood there long enough to get rain-soaked, breathless dizzy, to grunt against the ramping beat of his heart. To realise hope could be anywhere, everywhere, hope could look like a well-dressed man bereft of it.

"Everything changed after Afghanistan. Everything that was, went away and now I walk everywhere, and write down in a small notebook how high the river is, or whether it rained, and I can't get back *in*."

If you'd asked John Watson what he'd say to this stranger sitting on a bench with a gun beneath big hands, he'd have said something like, "I will tell him it gets better. I will tell him to be brave, that he can do it, that I've seen it done."

John Watson would never have imagined he'd sit down in the rain and *ask for help.*

As soon as he realised that was what he was doing, Watson shut up, but it was too late because Watson had had the wonderful misfortune to sit beside the world's only consulting detective.

Holmes heard all the unsaid words between the words spoken.

I'm at the end of my tether. I need to make a difference. I need to be of use.

Here's the thing. Holmes was in that cemetery not because he was at the frayed end of a rope, he was there for quid pro quo.

Inspector Tobias Gregson wanted a gun. Holmes had a gun. The irony was that *Gregson* had had the gun, so to speak, but he'd overlooked the evidence in favour of something simpler, something easy. "We've got the case sewn up proper and the gun had nothing to do with it Mr. Holmes, you can keep it," the inspector had said, after Holmes found the weapon and laid out the particulars of a particularly grisly crime.

Of course Gregson had been wrong about how complete his case was. He found that out soon enough and came to call. He wanted the gun back. Of course Holmes would give it back, but this time he wasn't ready to simply be *part* of the investigation, his services used, his contribution ignored. This time he wanted quid pro quo: Access to all the new cases, complete inclusion.

Gregson had reluctantly agreed, extracting his own quid

pro quo: They had to meet somewhere far from the prying eyes of Inspector Lestrade, who would be delighted to know how far off-course Gregson's investigation had gone.

So.

One gun, in exchange for *more*. More access to crime scenes, to files, to evidence. For the mental exultation of facts, closures, proofs. Holmes would be part of the analysis, from now on he would be there at the *start*. And all he had to do was hand a gun over to a moderately capable inspector from Scotland Yard.

Holmes handed the gun to the man beside him.

Because the world's only consulting detective understands triage. He understands that right now, here, in the too-quiet battlefield of a rain-drenched cemetery, he must sort the casualties so that as many survive as possible.

Gregson will come to Holmes again. Holmes knows this. Yes, Holmes will have to start the struggle for access all over, but they do need him. They'll come. In the meantime Sherlock Holmes will continue to dart around crime scene edges, pocket evidence they miss, he'll continue to survive on crumbs whilst going doggedly after the feast.

But this man beside him was starving. Bereft of purpose, of power, he had precious little strength left. He needed a scrap, a crumb. He needed to make a difference.

So Holmes handed him the gun and that day, tomorrow, the next, and for all the years they would know one another, Holmes would let Watson believe that he'd saved him, saved him from doing something terrible.

Watson took the gun and that day, tomorrow, the next, and for all the years they would know one another, Watson

245

would never tell Holmes he'd been heading toward hope, that in stopping to help he'd lost a job. No, Watson would never tell his friend that.

By the time Gregson showed up, Holmes, Watson, and a case-closing gun were long gone.

Four weeks later there was a three-city spate of bank robberies with no pattern and no suspects. After some foot dragging Gregson came to Holmes, keen on having his help on the case before Lestrade did.

Besides, he'd heard the detective had moved to a place on Baker Street, got himself an interesting new flatmate. Gregson should call around anyway, size things up. That's what any good detective worth his salt would do. Gregson laughed. Lestrade probably didn't even know where Baker Street was. Gregson laughed again, he laughed himself absolutely stupid.

SH

An Inspector Stalls

Storey's Gate Medical Clinic, London — 2010

Inspector Lestrade gets drunk about once every never. As in not today, not tomorrow, not next week, not a little bit, not ever.

Well, he was rat-arsed *now*.

"Sorry I'm breathing gin fumes all over you."

Dr. John Watson continued iodine-swabbing the inspector's palm. "It's fine."

"It's just that I'm a little bit stressed."

John continued swabbing. "That guy you were just talking about?"

Lestrade nodded. "Yeah. Ouch."

John looked up. "Sorry, did that hurt?"

Lestrade shifted restlessly on the examination bench, blinked at the doctor, then both men looked back down to Lestrade's palm, through which a rusty fishhook was pierced. "Actually no. Just when you did that thing with that silver thing it seemed like it should hurt."

John grinned, "Well then, small mercies."

Lestrade watched the doctor work and continued to breathe gin fumes at him. "I'm not jealous of Sherlock, mind, I'm proud of him. I mean it's a fact, I'm a…a…a pocket watch compared to his Big Ben."

Nearby, the great clock of which the inspector spoke, underscored this profundity by striking the quarter hour. G. Lestrade, of New Scotland Yard, nodded as if his point had been soundly made. "There's no way I can do what Sherlock does. No one can."

"Stay still now, I'm going to snip the hook as close to your palm as I can."

Lestrade swiped at his nose with his free hand, peered close at the other, not in the least squeamish at the sight of rusty metal stuck straight through his fleshy bits. John reflected that he'd probably seen worse.

"I've seen worse," muttered Lestrade. "You wouldn't believe what we found in the neck of a headless nun who—ouch!"

John Watson murmured, "Sorry, we...ah, there you go." He dropped the two pieces of fishhook into a small metal tray. Both men blinked down at it. Lestrade murmured, "Sherlock found the headless nun, too. Because she liked peppermint tea."

John cleaned Lestrade's palm. "He sounds like quite a man. Is he the reason you got drunk?"

Lestrade sighed. "I'm drunk because I got what I asked for."

The inspector poked at the rusty fishhook like a six year old. John took the metal tray away.

"They want to promote me. At work. They keep asking. I keep stalling."

John finished wrapping the inspector's hand then, with a polite pat to the bandage, went still. Somehow he knew this was where listening would matter. So he listened.

"I thought I wanted to be on my own. Go off and be a detective inspector, lead my own team, make a real difference. But you know what?"

John knew what, but he let the nice drunk man say it

248

himself.

"I already do make a difference. I mean, I'm not Sherlock Holmes no, but I don't want to be. That day we found the nun? He knew where to look because I'd spent a really long day whinging about tea. 'I need tea,' I said, and from that he put together the nun's chronic nausea with the community garden, with the herbs she grew, and we found the poor thing three feet under her peppermint plants. Peppermint grows like a weed, did you know? It'd already covered over the spot where that nasty bishop had buried her."

"No way."

"Way." Lestrade looked wistful. "But you see? I helped. I know it doesn't seem like much, but what I did counts for something because I helped. I don't want to stop helping. I don't want to stop helping *him.* Not everyone can. He's not always easy to be around."

The examination room door slammed open. A tall man stepped in, glanced around, murmured, "Knew it."

Lestrade smiled at the stranger, as if understanding perfectly. He then smiled at John, as if John understood perfectly.

John was pretty sure he partially understood, so he squinted in a fashion both wary and amused, "The man of the hour, I presume?"

The tall man extended his hand. "Sherlock Holmes."

John Watson reached back. "John Watson."

Big Ben began chiming the hour, portentous.

Lestrade was the only one who noticed. He'd mention it a couple years from now. John would include the detail in one of his little stories. Sherlock would roll his eyes.

That would be then. Right now Lestrade slurred pleasantly, "Sssso, how'd you find me?"

Sherlock Holmes started roaming around the tiny examination room. "Your newspaper was missing."

The inspector nodded, as if all was suddenly clear. "What?"

Sherlock stopped roaming, looked at John. "His Sunday Times. It wasn't on his desk."

John looked at the inspector. "What?"

The inspector grinned at John in a very *see what I mean?* way.

Sherlock wandered over, looked into the fishhook-containing metal tray, poked at the bits with his finger.

"I went to find the inspector at the Yard but his paper was missing. He only takes his paper when he wants to think. He generally does *that* at either the Horse & Pear Pub, or Hunter dock. He wasn't at the pub, so I went to the dock. Saw size ten shoe prints in the sand by the ladder, then a little further up, two smudged handprints. Hunter pier used to be a popular place for recreational fishing, the rocks there are still littered with old line and even older hooks. Lestrade doesn't drink but the bartender told me that in twenty minutes he'd downed two gins, neat. Clearly the inspector was drunk, had fallen, and no doubt inadvertently collected a souvenir to mark the occasion. It was then just a matter of searching for an after-hours clinic near New Scotland Yard."

John Watson fast-blinked for about a year. Lestrade looked at him and beamed.

Then John said, "You got all that from a newspaper. From the *absence* of a newspaper. You found something by not finding anything."

John blinked some more. John grinned. This time Sherlock beamed.

This went on for about a year. Then Sherlock stopped smiling. "Wait. Say that again."

John looked at Lestrade. Lestrade looked at John. They both looked at Sherlock. Then John repeated, "You found something by not finding—"

"That's it! She couldn't find her watch! She said she couldn't find her *watch.* The professor's alibi is a lie!"

The examination room door slammed closed. Sherlock Holmes was gone.

John fast-blinked at the door. Eventually he turned to Lestrade. No one said anything for awhile, then John whispered, "Don't."

Lestrade leaned forward and whispered back, "What now?"

"Don't take the promotion."

"Oh. I never even thought of that."

*

That evening Inspector G. Lestrade turned down his promotion.

The day after that the inspector and the doctor got a pint at the Horse & Pear. The consulting detective found them, stood around, listened to them chat. After awhile he squinted at John, said, "Say that again?" John said that again. Sherlock yelled something gleeful and dashed off.

A few days later he did the same thing, in a different pub, only he came back after.

One week later, John found Sherlock in St. Thomas' morgue and said, "I hear you're looking for a flat mate."

Sherlock grinned.

Not very far away, Big Ben began chiming the hour.

SH

The Child is Father to the Man

Marylebone Road, near Baker Street — 1886

John Watson was a steady child, faithful and true.

On his fifth birthday an oft-absent aunt had not only bumptiously appeared in the middle of his party, but had proved herself keen on purchasing John's childish affections.

Auntie Annie had not only presented him with a wooden Palomino horse and a tin whistle, but secreted half a pound of coconut gems and wine gums into his tiny pockets.

The small Mr. Watson had thanked her gravely for the toy treasures and went on to allot himself exactly one sweet per day. This proved problematic when the winter coat in which he'd stored his horde was washed. The laundry was quite sticky that day.

Not as sticky as it would have been had John Watson been a different child.

Because every day little John shared his bounty with two other children. Every day he brought Timothy Benjamin Theorclair and Fiorinda Margaret Jones a single treat each. Together the three best friends consumed their coconut gems layer by layer, discussing the various colours and the relative merits of the liquorice over the coconut, the brown layers in comparison to the white, spending up to ten entire minutes in serious contemplation.

When, one afternoon, Timothy's mum came upon her son and her son's friends, on their bellies and examining their dissected treats, she chastened her youngest for going against house rules and eating sweets just before tea time.

It was right then, and for the first time, that John Watson did something wrong in favour of protecting a person that needed protecting. He lied. "That's mine Mrs. Theorclair."

Sara Theorclair looked at John Watson. She knew he was not telling the truth, but right then Mrs. Theorclair decided it was more important that her child—who was still far too small for his age—know another child who was steady and true and willing to be faithful to him, than it was for every truth to be told.

She didn't know it, but Sara Theorclair taught five-year-old John Watson a vital lesson that day.

*

Some children are easy to hate.

They are too short or too tall, too thin or too fat. They're dark-skinned or light, or maybe, just maybe, they are Sherlock Holmes. Sometimes that's really quite more than enough.

Because the problem with little Sherlock was that he was too many hateful things all at once.

He was slim and so looked frail, he was tall and so smacked of authority, he was smart and so he made others feel stupid, and the worst thing, the oh-so-very worst thing: Five-year-old Sherlock Holmes noticed *everything*.

He saw it when Marie Louise found Mary Jo's pretty new hair ribbon and put it in her own pocket instead of giving it back. He saw when the maths teacher Mrs. Madron brushed shoulders with the violin teacher Mr. Shannon and both of them smiled. And worst of all, that wee child asked questions about what he saw, the very moment those questions popped into his curious little head.

This rarely ended well for Sherlock Holmes, and so the tall, reedy child was oft bullied by other children, and admonished for failing to 'mind his own business' by quite a number of adults.

So yes, some children are easy to hate, and for a long time Sherlock Holmes was one of those children. It was a gift in its own way, for soon Sherlock learned how to pick out the children who would hurt him, how to notice the things that hurt them, and how to tuck that information snug away in his little brain attic—that's what mummy called it, and he liked that very much because it helped him learn how to put memories in very specific places. So he could find them again later.

What Sherlock Holmes remembered most of all, however, was how to *see*.

*

London was often beset with a fog so thick and so yellow, a thief could go about her thieving business and, once her prey was taken, she could vanish like a tiger in the jungle, disappear into dense and perfect cover.

Yes, that's how Marilee Smith liked to think of herself, a tiger prowling, though she knows such beasts don't have crinoline or lace gloves, they don't have a lovely smile or the latest in ladies' fashions. She has all those things and what she also has is great daring, an allergy to the idea of being dependent on anyone, and a sharp-bladed knife.

"Please give me your receipts for the day, madam."

Mrs. Una Merrick enjoys *The Strand* magazine quite a lot. Probably she most likes Zig Zags At The Zoo for its humour and its rather remarkable illustrations, though she does enjoy the serials, too. When the shop isn't busy she'll take her time with each new issue and, until this young lady walked into her grocery, it had been a somewhat quiet half hour indeed, all the city workers dashed through on their way home for the evening.

"I'm sorry miss, I'm a bit deaf, what did you say?"

Sherlock Holmes looked up. Mrs. Merrick often lets him come by and test the newest tobaccos in the little office tucked away right next to her till. Though a lung complaint meant she no longer partook herself, she found it 'a comfort to smell the smoke.' So, in exchange for access to the ever-changing array of tobaccos that came through Merrick's Grocery & Incidentals, Holmes performed some of his initial experiments—which primarily involved smoking—at Mrs. Merrick's small desk.

Which was why, when the lady, all of four foot eight and built of a hummingbird's bones but a buzzard's fierce and territorial heart, claimed a deafness she did not have, Holmes looked up and looked out the small gap in the curtain separating the office from the shop.

Sherlock Holmes doesn't notice pretty ladies, not in the way that others might. He notices instead the slight cant in a pretty lady's hat, sees the inelegant weight of their unmatched bag, and—like anyone would—Sherlock sees the slim-bladed, six-inch knife she steadily pointed as she threatened his friend.

Sherlock Holmes stepped from Mrs. Merrick's office and said very low and simply, "Give me your knife."

Marilee Smith widened her eyes and slid her blade into the sleeve of her dress, as if no one saw her do it. "Excuse me?"

256

Holmes stepped from behind the grocer's counter and toward the young woman. "Kindly give me your blade."

"I don't know what you mean. I'm afraid you don't seem to sell what I was looking for, I'll be on my way."

"Ah sir," said Holmes to a whiskered man who had just entered the shop, "if you have a moment, Mrs. Merrick here and myself could use your assistance."

Marilee Smith did not startle, but her bright smile faded as she turned. A man with moustache and brown hat stood behind her.

"This lady has threatened Mrs. Merrick, the owner of this shop. She has used the knife inside her left sleeve to do so. Just as she used it to steal the two billfolds she carries. She's not taken the time to empty and discard those as she's been in quite a hurry tonight. The weather has been unusually fine and clear in London for weeks now and the coffers must be quite empty..."

Holmes glanced at the indignant woman's shoes, which just peeked from under her fancy frock, noted a yellowish mud on both heels and soot on one toe. "...in a little flat somewhere quite near the Brush Electric Light factory."

Sherlock Holmes knows that if he talks fast enough, long enough, *personally* enough, his deductions can seem like black magic, unsettling even a strong mind. This is, at times, of great use. Marilee Smith stood rooted to the spot.

"The young lady wears the latest ensemble, almost identical to the one visible in the shop window just across the street. Cream-coloured gloves, hat, and dress, but the lady's purse is unlike the delicate little beaded thing shown across the way, instead it's a rather ungainly black bag that, it so happens, will fit far more than theatre tickets and a few coins.

"It will fit a man's billfold." Holmes tilted his head. "Unfortunately the weight of the first drew the purse strings too tight, so you couldn't quickly get the second billfold into it as you ran into the fog after your second theft, so you pushed it under your hat, which now sits askew.

"Sir," here Holmes looked at the man in the brown hat, "If you'd be so kind?"

John Watson nodded to the tall stranger and without a word stepped up to Marilee Smith.

"If you touch me I will scream."

"I'm not going to touch you," replied Watson. "You're going to hand to me all the items that Mr...."

"Sherlock Holmes."

"...Mr. Holmes has named. My name is John Watson, in case you wanted to know. Please?" Watson held out his hand.

Smith was usually much better at picking her marks. And on the rare occasion she erred, she was even better at bluffing her way through. Not this time. *Taking* her time, Smith handed Watson the two wallets and her knife.

Straightening her hat and closing her bag, Smith then took control. "I'm leaving now and you'll not follow me. You have no reason to, no proof of anything. Goodbye." With that the young woman turned and disappeared into the fog.

Watson looked to Mrs. Merrick. "Are you all right Una?" At the grocer's nod, Watson turned to Holmes, "Would you like me to follow her?"

"You know, the young lady would be very good at her chosen profession with a little more shrewdness and a bit more time, but she's not going to get that time."

"What do you mean?"

"She'll be back."

John Watson was a soldier and he'll tell you war is the most senseless business he knows, but there is a bit of dark logic to its madness. Similarly he expects that a thief who has managed to escape justice is not soon going to return to the scene of her most recent crime. In less than three minutes he learned he was wrong.

"It was that man officer," said Smith. "That's the man who took my husband's wallet."

The police officer looked at the man to whom Smith pointed. He frowned and rested a hand on his night stick. Then he reached behind him, stepped up to John Watson and, pulling out his own billfold said, "Johnny! I was hoping to hold onto this crown until next week's game, you old card sharp. Shoulda paid you last week I guess. See you Thursday?"

John Watson smiled, pocketed his winnings. The police constable looked at Mrs. Merrick. "Can I get a pint of milk for the baby and something nice for the missus please, Una?"

Mrs. Merrick grinned and bustled off.

"So Mr. Holmes, do I deduce that this young lady has done something wrong?"

Marilee Smith's great misfortune that night was picking the one shop in all of London that contained a tiny woman fierce, a tall man who could see, and a gentleman-soldier who would be ever steady, ever faithful, and ever true, for all the long years the three would know one another.

SH

If Convenient

Shoreditch, London — 2010

> *Come at once, if convenient.*

That was Stamford's latest text. John Watson scowled at it.

Come if convenient? *If convenient?* Yeah, well no, going to St. Bart's wasn't one bit convenient right now, okay? John tossed his mobile onto the stained pub table, sat up straight, looked around.

Hell yeah, John had a lot going on and heading to Bart's in the hope he'd *this time* find a flatmate to share a naff place over in Hackney was going to cut right into his busy schedule.

John looked out the dust-clouded pub window. Yep, he was damn well snowed under right now. Had a cold cup of coffee to finish, yesterday's crossword only half done, and he had to get on with the massive pity party he'd started six months ago after coming back from Afghanistan, a party that was, quite frankly, a real goer. So John saw no reason to change his plans for a *maybe.* A *could be.* He saw no reason to damn well *keep trying,* okay?

John picked up his phone. He deleted Stamford's message. He dropped the phone again with a clatter.

And then immediately picked it up again and sent a text. Because if John didn't do something he'd go mad.

Madder. Because John was pretty sure he'd gone stir-crazy already, staring out his own dirty window every night, loath to sleep because unconsciousness felt like the final insult on a day of quiet insults, and so he'd pace until his shoulder ached, until finally the oblivion of sleep seemed a refuge instead of a failure.

Come at once, if convenient.

This was the third or fourth time Stamford was trying to introduce him to a potential flatmate. Stamford had admired John's commitment in going to Afghanistan, so when the good doctor came home, shot in the shoulder but worse-hurt in the soul... well Stamford tried to help. First it was drinks down at the pub then, after John's brief email—*know anyone looking for a cheap flatshare?*—he'd tried helping there, too.

Problem was, John wasn't helping him help. The radiographer was annoying because she smiled with clenched teeth, the audiologist talked too loud, and by the time Stamford texted—*My friend's looking to share in central London, great price*—John just ignored it.

Then Stamford sent—*We'll be at Bart's at 2, what d'you say?* John had uttered a string of curses. *That* was what he had to say. By the time he'd got *come at once, if convenient,* John was in a right royal snit and wasn't going anywhere for anyone.

Except...

Tell your friend I'll be there at 2.

*

"Damn it."

John looked at his watch. 2:21 pm. He was on the slowest bus in London. The damned thing seemed to stop for butterflies going over zebra crossings and it had already taken an hour to get from far east London to slightly-less-east London.

"Damn, damn, *god* damn."

261

John checked his watch again. He swore again. He did not want to get off the bus. He could not afford another, perhaps-faster bus. He should have taken the tube. But the tube cost more. Ah! John knew exactly what he could do.

Suck it up and shut up.

When he checked his watch five minutes—and one hundred traveled feet—after the last time, John swore again and damn well got off the bus.

Yes, he was still two miles short of his destination but even a man with very little to do all day has limits, and public transportation that failed to actually *transport* was, John discovered—

"Oh shit."

—John discovered why the bus hadn't moved.

Bodies were in the way. Bodies were in the way *on* Old Street. And so nothing could move.

John ran to the nearest human stretched prone in the road. The man was ringed by half a dozen people, he was talking, which was good, and he was asking about his daughter, his seven-year-old daughter who was…there, over there, bleeding from her head and crying but calling out for her father in increasingly strident tones.

Then there…a woman a couple dozen metres from the man. She lay curled up in the middle of the road, also ringed by Samaritans. She was missing a trainer and clenching her hands under her chin, whispering, "I'm sorry."

John turned, and turned and…there. One other body in the road, just one more.

A tall, pale man lying a couple body lengths from a wrecked motorcycle. Only one person knelt beside this one and immediately John knew why. Because this one wasn't alive.

John's seen it happen before: To the living being freshly dead is catchy. Few people outside of doctors, carers, or police, will go unresisting toward the newly dead.

John himself stopped a half dozen feet from the dead man, turned to walk away. He should go back to the little girl, her father, he should help the living. He should…he should…

…help the *living*.

John turned back not to the dead man, but to the living one kneeling beside him.

The dead man and the one beside him had been strangers, John knew, because John knows what that looks like, when family or friends see the corpse of someone for whom they cared. It did not look like this.

And *this* was a man knelt beside a lean, pale corpse, holding his hand, lightly, carefully. No, not quite. John squinted. No he was pattering fingertips across the dead man's palm, the back of his hand, as if Brailling for information. John stepped near, put his hand on the kneeling man's shoulder, knelt too.

"I'm John. I'm a doctor. I can take care of him if you like."

The kneeling man looked at John, briefly frowned. Then he did a strange thing: He handed John the dead man's hand. And the strange thing John did after he took it was to think, *oh, he's kept it warm.*

"Thank you…"

The man rose then, and John thought he was going to go away. "Sherlock. Sherlock Holmes."

263

"…thank you Sherlock, I'll—"

But Sherlock wasn't going. He was kneeling on the other side of the body, looking at feet, fingers, then leaning over, sniffing the dead man's mouth and nose and then—

"What're you doing?"

—*tasting* his face.

Sherlock sat back on his heels, gaze sharp. "He was high. Cocaine. Probably to keep him awake. He had chronic insomnia due to chronic pain. Left leg. He was asleep when he veered in front of the jogger, who in a panic ran in front of the car, which turned to miss her."

John Watson sat back on his heels, blinked fast. Then he made a swirly gesture with his hand. "Explain. That. All that you just said."

A smile flickered over Sherlock's face. His explanation took less than a minute and included, "…taste it when I licked his face…the heel of his left boot barely used…broken blood vessels under his eyes…easy enough if you look."

Though the explanation was eye-opening, none of it was as surprising to John as the final few things Sherlock Holmes said, and those were: "Well, it's not murder," and "Bye." Then he rose and walked away.

He got two paces before a soldier of the Fifth Northumberland Fusiliers barked out, "Stop."

To his great surprise, Sherlock Holmes did as he was told. To his greater surprise he patiently waited as John Watson rose, came over, and read him a somewhat profane riot act. To his everlasting surprise Sherlock Holmes obeyed John Watson, following him to the recently arrived police cruiser.

264

Two hours later John and Sherlock finished giving statements and left Shoreditch police station.

Three hours later they were eating cake and drinking coffee in a miserable dive John liked.

Five hours after that Sherlock was talking about a flat over on Baker Street. Less than one minute later John sent Stamford a text.

Sorry. Couldn't make it. Met a man. Found a flat. Thanks anyway.

Stamford texted back immediately.

Congratulations! Wondered where you'd got lost to. Shame though, Dr. Parmadil's mighty pretty and her flat's a rather grand affair in Mayfair. Pint on Friday?

John felt a brief pang of regret. Flash Mayfair digs and a fetching flatmate? John started a text that said something about pints on Friday and bringing Parmadil along, but Sherlock said something just then, John asked a question, Sherlock replied, John laughed, and somehow the text to Stamford was never written and so never sent.

A week after John Watson met Sherlock Holmes, doctors Stamford and Parmadil went on a date. Six months later they were engaged. A year after that John Watson stood as Stamford's best man.

Sherlock gave the newlyweds Oyster cards in John's name. *Good for a year of bus travel,* the gift card said, *if convenient.* Neither Stamford nor Parmadil understood. John, however, laughed.

SH

Loser Takes All

The Criterion Bar, Piccadilly Circus — 1885

"Do you mind?"

Sherlock Holmes inclined a dark-haired head toward the seat beside him. He did not mind.

John Watson nodded a moustachioed smile, settled onto the bar's plush stool.

Each man sat awhile, drinking his drink, thinking his thoughts.

After a time the bartender placed a bowl of nuts between them and both reached out together, then both pulled back.

"After you."

"After *you.*"

"Thank you Mr...."

"Watson. John Watson."

"Sherlock Holmes." The men shook hands and then silence fell as silence does. Holmes proceeded to amuse himself deducing the contretemps of minor German royalty at a far back table, Watson enjoyed the silky to-and-fro of pretty ladies lunching.

After awhile these diversions were replaced with others, including a young couple breaking up at the end of the bar. "He's been unfaithful," said Holmes sotto voce and apropos of nothing.

"I've met Mr. Watts," groused Watson, clearly made no better by the meeting, "and happen to know that's true. Well-done you."

"Thank you."

A shift change brought more divertissement.

"Don't order from the one with the crooked bow-tie, he pours with a miserly hand."

"Abstemious, but still craves drink."

"Oh good job, well-noticed."

"The young hostess will have twins in the autumn."

"Pretty Miss Violet? Oh, she and her lad'll be pleased."

Eventually late afternoon turned to early evening and a second drink sat beading cool on the bar before each man. Naturally disinclined toward extended silence, Watson lifted his beverage toward Holmes. "Very good these, have you tried one? It's called a Criterion Safari and has in it—"

"Wait," Holmes said. "Indulge me. Let *me* tell *you.*"

John Watson turned a sly-smiling gaze on his seatmate. "You're not a bartender are you?"

Holmes grinned right back. "I've got the keen ear of one, but lack any of the social graces."

Watson placed his chilly beverage on the bar and slid it toward his companion. "Go ahead then, deduce my drink."

Holmes inclined his head, "What an interesting turn of phrase." With the curl of one dexterous finger—Watson noticed a spattering of half-healed burns along the back of Holmes' pale hand—Holmes brought the Safari in front of him.

Before he could so much as gaze into its cloudy depths Watson put a hand over it. "Are you a betting man?"

Holmes was not a betting man. Betting relied too much on chance. The flick of a wrist, the waft of a breeze, anything could change the outcome of just about anything. No, Holmes didn't gamble, instead he took note of the breeze, observed the

267

wrist, he took into account *variables* and from there he found his way toward certainty, poor odds need not apply.

So no, Holmes wasn't a betting man, but Holmes *was* a liar, if the lie got him what he wanted and was mostly kind (in that order). And what the good detective wanted right now was the simplest of things, and yet a thing somehow so difficult to find: Distraction.

"Yes, I am a betting man," Holmes grinned. "What're your terms?"

A new river of silk-clad ladies began flowing past for early dinners, but Watson didn't notice. "I'm not a man of means so we'll keep the terms simple. There are only five ingredients in this drink, two of which you see at the bottom of the glass. Get the other three right—and fair warning, one is unusual—and I'll buy you a shot of that lovely glittery stuff over there."

Holmes looked behind the bar, eyed the bottle perched on its own stand, lifted above dozens of other spirits. The gin inside sparked with fat flakes of gold leaf, more a publicity stunt for the firm producing it than a particularly flavourful drink, yet a shot of it was still twice as expensive as any other.

Holmes pushed aside his gone-warm cider, brought the Safari directly in front of himself and said, "And if I get it wrong, I offer the same."

Both men shook again, and Holmes leaned over and sniffed deep.

"The blackberries and raspberries are only slightly crushed yet the drink is very evocative of their perfume."

Another dramatic sniff, a third with closed eyes, and Holmes announced, "Passion fruit nectar." He then sat up straight and smiled as if entirely pleased with himself, which he entirely was.

"Excellent!" beamed Watson.

"Thank you," demurred Holmes, who this time lifted the beverage to his undemure nose. He breathed deep. He glowered impressively and sniffed again. He glared imposingly and inhaled a third time. At last he waved at the air in front of him, huffed heartily and pronounced, "Lychee syrup."

"Superb!" Watson hooted, patting Holmes on the back, clearly not at all interested in winning the bet. "It's a rare Englishman familiar with lychees."

Holmes deigned to look shy and retiring, "I recently performed a series of small experiments concerning whether lychee syrup contained enough acid to eat away the cornea of a human eye."

As a battlefield surgeon John Watson's heard a wide array of strange things from an extensive sampling of humanity. This particular nugget of not-right wasn't even up there in the top ten. "Well, was it?"

Holmes shook his head, "Alas no, and so a man was jailed for killing his rich Grand'Mere."

"Why on earth do you say 'alas'?"

"He was a rather repellent creature but he was also a philanthropist, having spent nearly a quarter million pounds on London's poor. He'd have gone on to build a children's hospital with the aid of his grandmother's dusty fortune."

John Watson thought a moment then placed *this* nugget of strange right behind number three in his top ten list of not-quite-right. After his mental housekeeping was done, Watson said, "One more ingredient now."

Again Holmes paused dramatically. He knew that Watson knew that he'd more or less given away the prime ingredient of the drink by what he'd offered in the terms of their bet, so Holmes couldn't conceivably get that final ingredient wrong.

Holmes wanted to get that final ingredient wrong.

"I'll tell you what," he said, "let's double the wager. If I can't guess exactly *which* gin—and yes, it's gin—is in this drink, I'll owe you *three* shots of anything you like."

John Watson's a betting man, oh yes, but this had never been about a wager, had it? This had been about time and the expanse of it, the *spending* of it, and the wishing to make that spending a little less lonely.

"I like your terms, Mr. Holmes. Now, do please stun and amaze."

Laughing, Holmes lifted the glass, made another production of peering and sniffing and even listening, then finally said, "If you'll allow, I'll need to take a taste."

A man who more than once has got another man's blood in his mouth, clenching between his teeth tools he had no hope of keeping sanitary on a dusty battlefield, Watson was far from finicky. "Taste away."

Holmes did.

As all gins are, this one was piquant with green juniper, yet there was more. A hint of coriander, a whisper of black pepper, the combination of these botanicals giving the alcohol a faint and pleasant taste of gunpowder. This made it clear to Holmes that the distiller was Plymouth and that the spirit was their famous Navy Strength.

Holmes took another sip for show, swished it around his mouth, frowned in thought, then took a third, larger drink.

"There's the obvious juniper, a hint of heat, a bit of something pungent. I'm going to say...Jubilee Blue?"

Watson's face wore an odd expression just then, part disbelief, part relief. It was clear he'd believed Holmes quite capable of tasting the subtlety of a gin overwhelmed by a brace of berries and swimming in syrup, but it was just as clear he was grateful the man hadn't.

Holmes looked rueful. "I got it wrong, didn't I?"

Watson smiled slowly, "Close, very close, Mr. Holmes. Let's call it even and go with our original terms."

Holmes lifted a pointed chin and deigned to look put out. "Mr. Watson, I'm put out. I have every intention of keeping to my half of the bargain."

The air was for the barest instant chilly with potential misunderstanding...then warm with shared laughter.

"Whatever you say, who am I to second-guess the great Sherlock Holmes?"

Neither of them had any clue why Watson phrased himself just that way, but neither did either question it. It sounded damn good to *both* of them.

"I owe you not only three shots but another Safari for the half I've drunk of this."

"Well the night's young in the great wilderness of London, why don't we finish these, then I know a place in Leicester Square where the lad pours with a heavy hand. What do you say?"

Holmes finished his lukewarm cider in two swallows, Watson his watery Safari. Each stood and gestured to the other.

271

"After you."

"After you."

"Thank you Mr. Holmes."

"You're welcome Mr. Watson."

"So," said the good doctor as they headed for the door, "I have two questions: How did you know about that fool Watts? And who took care of those acid burns on the back of your hand because that's just criminal."

Both men slotted themselves companionably into the Circus' bustle. "I cared for those wounds myself, but you're right, maybe you could have a look at them later? About Watts, it wasn't knowing, it was noticing. You see, when I saw his left thumb…"

SH

Starting From Scratch

Allsop Place, Central London— 2014

The only reason John Watson met Sherlock Holmes, was because John had a crap pencil. Or maybe it was because Sherlock had been flat-hunting by making holes in other people's walls. Either or.

Suffice to say, the day began as many of John's days did lately, with the classified adverts spread out over his desk at the clinic. Armed with a pencil and a bit of invective, John perused the paper between patients, looking for flatshares.

Convenient Hampstead Road bedsit...

"Absolutely not."

He'd had his first job out of med school on Hampstead Road. It had lasted two weeks and John still didn't think you could legally be fired for confessing a disinterest in opera, but apparently yes, yes you could.

John struck through the advert with a bold slash.

Lovely Acton Town studio...

"Nope, nope, nope."

A few years back some good friends had called him with 'a bit of a personal emergency.' The memory of what he saw when he arrived at their Acton Town flat—and of how long it took him to get those things out—still haunts him.

Another bold strike.

Several hours of diverting consults interrupted John's fruitless flow, but by afternoon he was again pencil poised and ready.

Airy flat in Angel...

"Oh hell no."

The worst date he'd ever had had happened in Angel. It had led to a great deal of unexpected bleeding. John looked at the fleshy bit between index finger and thumb. Yes, he still had the scar.

And so it went, until evening. London is large, its newspaper classifieds are similarly so. It took the good doctor most of the day to make it half through. As he did, he struck out each offer not suitable.

Sure it would make more sense to circle the flats in which he was interested, but that's not how John Watson works. John strips things until only the obvious remains. He does it at the surgery, weeding through a patient's words until he gets to what they *mean;* he did it in the army, literally taking a gun down to its component parts.

So, stripping and striking.

Beautiful Battersea...

"I would rather eat bugs."

John pressed hard to strike through the advert but his pencil tip, already much tried, surrendered and broke off. The pencil itself followed, snapping in two.

John snapped with it.

"Damn stupid damn *pencil."* John threw the shattered implement into his coffee mug, remembered too late that there was still coffee in it, and swore some more.

Fine. He was done. He'd just give up and stay in his crappy flatshare in Elephant & Castle and—

The broken pencil lead rolled around drunkenly, catching John's eye. It rested over an advert on the other side of the paper and…

Hmm. Central. Affordable. Surprisingly cheap. And John had absolutely no negative memories associated with Allsop Place.

*

Sherlock Holmes tapped his chin with a dart, squinted at the newspaper tacked to Lestrade's office wall, then closed his eyes and threw the dart. It stuck into the binding of a book three feet to the left.

Sherlock picked up another dart from Lestrade's desk and turned sideways. He held the dart against his cheek, squinted one eye, then threw. The dart stuck in an apple on Lestrade's window sill.

Sherlock picked up the final dart and stared at it, thinking deep, deductive thoughts about darts. Finally he turned his back, tossed it over his shoulder, heard it strike deep. Grinning, Sherlock turned—

"Oi, that's my wall! And my book! What did you do to my apple?"

Lestrade grumbled, tugged his newspaper off the wall, and stuffed it in the bin. The small bit through which the dart had stuck remained pinned in place.

"Would you kindly stop making holes in my walls every time I leave you in my office for two seconds? Now go away, I have a mountain of paperwork thanks to you."

Sherlock grumbled back, skirted Lestrade's desk, plucked the small bit of paper from the wall.

Hand on the door Sherlock paused, turned to make a small confession of a rather large omission, but the inspector spoke first. "I mean it, Sherlock. Thanks to you we closed the Holborn Hijacking case." Lestrade grinned. "I'll call if we get anything. Good luck flat hunting."

Sherlock decided to leave the inspector in a good and benevolent mood. After all, he could always tell him another day about the harpoon holes hidden behind his wall calendar, legacy of a theory he'd resoundingly proved for last month's so-called Black Peter case.

Yes, that confession was for later. Right now Sherlock said, "You're welcome," then looked at the scrap of paper in his hand.

Allsop Place.

Central. Affordable. And there'd been a very interesting triple robbery he'd solved there a few years ago.

*

All right, when it really comes down to it, John Watson did not meet Sherlock Holmes because of a crap pencil, and Sherlock didn't meet John because he recklessly puts holes in other people's walls.

They met because 44M Allsop Place had fleas. And only one step leading from the flat down to street level.

That single step was where John collapsed, right after walking out of the building. He began scratching at his flea-bitten ankles so fervently that it took him a good ten seconds to notice he shared the space with a lanky guy, also scratching. The lanky guy looked up. John recoiled.

"Oh mate, did you actually *lie* on that carpet?"

Sherlock can deduce many things. Right then he deduced that he and this man had recently viewed the same flat. He further deduced that neither of them had any intention of taking the flat. Finally—and most importantly—Sherlock deduced that the man beside him was a doctor and could get him drugs.

"I have just learned I'm allergic to fleath. I think I have hiveth on my tongue. I need drugth for my tongue." Sherlock punctuated this statement by scratching his tongue.

This revelation stilled them both for long itch-free seconds. Then John dug into his left ankle with both hands, leaned conspiratorially close to the lanky man. "I know where we can get some."

Sherlock scratched at the hives on his neck. "Exthellent."

Due to much pausing and self-manhandling, it took them five minutes to walk around the corner to the chemist on Baker Street. Then another five arguing about what creams to buy. They settled on an oral antihistamine for Sherlock and a half dozen topical creams to share. Then, after perfunctory introductions, John Watson and Sherlock Holmes left the shop, sat on the nearest step, and shared drugs.

Giddy with relief and possibly a bit drunk on lidocaine ten minutes later, they had progressed to using their least favourite cream to write out on the pavement the longest chemical formulas they knew. Recognising he was hopelessly outclassed, John was about to cheat when the door behind them opened.

"I thought I heard voices." A woman of moderately-advanced years looked down as they looked up. "Are you here to see the flat?"

Sherlock looked at John. John at Sherlock. They looked at the woman.

"Yeth."

"Yes."

The woman smiled. She liked it when friends flat-hunted together. She always found better tenants that way.

"Well come in, gentlemen. My name is Mrs. Hudson and the arrangements are simple. I live in 221A just there, and I'm letting 221B, the two-bedroom suite right up here. Now, if you'll follow me, I'll tell you a bit about the place."

They did.

She did.

And the rest is history.

SH

At First Sight

Harley Street, Central London — 1884

"Please stay still Mr. Holmes."

Mr. Holmes tries. He doesn't succeed, but he *tries*.

"I think I'll refer you to a collea—"

Holmes turns away, frowning.

Dr. John Watson patiently waits for his patient to stop acting like an over-large child. When he does, the good doctor again pulls up a lid, shines ophthalmoscopic light into an inflamed eye. He huffs softly against his patient's face and murmurs, "I appreciate this was an emergency, Mr. Holmes, but you'll get better care from a special—"

Instead of turning away this time, Holmes frowns so darkly his brows half-eclipse iris and pupil.

Watson huffs again. He is not aware he does this. "You were worried enough to come to the surgery Mr. Holmes, it'd be sensible..."

There is no frowning or turning away to hush Watson this time, there are just those eyes, up-close, looking, looking, *looking* right at him. They are not still and calm those eyes, they are not normal. They sweep and dart, they flick-blink, they seem to count, collate, conclude. Watson can see them *seeing* him.

He huffs softly and his breath is warm against Holmes' face.

For a long moment John Watson wonders what this man sees and of course Holmes sees that wonder.

"A scratch on the back of a hand, candle wax on the mantel, dust that isn't still."

Watson nods and he doesn't know why.

"I see them all. As if stage-lit. As if they *wish* to be seen."

Yes, Watson thinks but doesn't say…and he still doesn't know why.

A scratch, wax, dust…sometimes Holmes murmurs the words. He ticks clues off in his head by speaking aloud, staring into space at a world only he sees, one that looks like what's in front of every one else but which contains the scratch that shouldn't be there, the daub of wax, and with what he sees he finds the thread that leads from the dust to the wax to the man who took a life and thought he'd done it so well no one would see.

"I need to see," Holmes says softly, and though it's only four words Watson hears the pleading, and yes, certainly, everyone needs to see but… but…Watson thinks flick-blink quick that maybe, just maybe, for this man, seeing is all he has.

Watson's long since stopped peering with his ophthalmoscope. No, now it's just the two of them, eye to eye, and Watson slides his stool back, says gently, "It looks mostly fine. There's fluid under the conjunctiva which is a normal response to an irritation like excessive rubbing. Still, I want you to go see my friend, just to be sure. Please."

Now is when one man should turn from the other, but neither does. No, what they do is maintain eye contact for what feels a long and suspended time. Then John Watson says something he doesn't have to say but does anyway. "After you've seen Dr. Cross, come back to see me. For a check-up, since I was your first physician with this. I'll take a look at your eye. Yes?"

Now Holmes huffs a quiet breath. Watson smiles because he knows that's a yes, though he doesn't know why.

Smart as they both are in their own ways, there's a world of other things neither man knows. They don't know that prolonged eye contact can lead strangers to a sense of intimacy with one another. That such eye contact in close proximity can bypass the need for small talk, for tiny social negotiations, that it can be the first, second, and third step in a journey toward friendship.

No, neither John Watson nor Sherlock Holmes knows this simple fact about human beings, but then again that doesn't stop them from experiencing the reality of it and of that reality changing everything.

As Dr. Watson writes a prescription for his patient— which he suspects his patient will not fill—Watson asks Holmes just what it is he did to his eye.

Twenty minutes later, after the words blood spatter, lethal croissant, and biocatalystic yeast cloud have been uttered not once but twice, John Watson realises he's elbows to knees, chin in hands, and has just said, "That's extraordinary!" for the third time.

After another few minutes, when Watson notices Holmes hasn't rubbed his eye once—as a matter of fact that conjunctiva is looking quite bright—the good doctor understands that perhaps the prescription most suitable for this particular patient comes in liquid form.

"You're my last patient for the day and I was off to nothing more pressing than an evening pint. I'll buy if you'll tell me if they ever found that short tonne of chocolate and how you could have *possibly* known the Croissant Queen was allergic to caterpillars."

They aren't even halfway to the Criterion restaurant before they're discussing the temperament of peacocks as compared to ostriches, the services of the Metropolitan Railway, and possible shared lodgings in the city.

They speak with the intimacy of old friends. As if they've known one another a long time.

SH

A Likely Story

Holland Park, West London — 2008

Poems. The first therapist suggested he write poems.

So John Watson tried. He pencil-scrawled words on the back of Tesco receipts, wrote about the Charing Cross clock and the girl he saw with pink braids, and John threw out as many poems as he finished. Then he threw them *all* out when he realised each was ten percent swear words and half of those were adjectives preceding *therapist*. John got a new therapist.

The second therapist recommended he write war stories.

Write about what you know she'd said, get it out on paper. "Tell us something true." So John Watson tried. He even splurged and bought a Moleskine. By the time he'd filled three pages he was smiling. By the time he filled three more he was excited. By the time he'd covered a dozen pages he knew an awful truth: He missed…he missed…John threw the pad in the Thames. And got another therapist.

The third one suggested he keep a blog.

The therapist wanted John to write about what happened to him day-to-day, said it would help him fit back into civilian life. Tired of trying, John tried anyway. Every evening he put the computer on, and every evening he typed a sentence then deleted a sentence. Because John was a single man with a war wound, a small army pension, and a career he could no longer follow. And nothing ever happened to him.

Then something did.

John Watson found a dead body.

It was five-fifty on a Wednesday morning, he was skirting dew-damp shrubbery at the north corner of Holland Park's rugby field and there he was: A thirty-something Caucasian man half-hidden under the flowering bushes. The moment John touched him—and John did touch him because you'd be surprised how often a dead body doesn't look like one—he knew the man was gone.

John called the police. Then John did what John does: He waited.

The newspaper journalist arrived before the police. The TV news crew before the journalist. When the police arrived they cleared everyone away, including the tall, lean man who'd appeared out of nowhere.

"So, murder then?"

Standing a dozen metres from blue police tape, a microphone in his face, John Watson answered the questions of a persistent TV reporter.

"Well I didn't say that," he repeated. "because it's difficult to narrow down cause of death in a person so youn—"

"No, it's not."

John paused, looked at the tall, lean man suddenly standing close.

Instead of looking back at him, the tall, lean man looked right at the microphone held in front of John's face, clearly willing the thing to be held in front of *his* face. The reporter did not move her microphone. The tall man continued to *will* at it. John shrugged, continued addressing the reporter.

"And anyway, murder is rare, whilst unexpected death is—"

"No it's not."

284

This time John paused until the tall bloke looked at him. John glowered. The tall man glowered back. They did this for a long, wordless time. The reporter glanced behind her. Good, Jess was still filming.

"Well then, could you share any educated guesses as to cause of death, Dr. Watson?"

John's got sixteen hours of most days to fill. Physio, job searches, and failing to write poems, stories, or blog entries doesn't pass even half of it, so currently John busies himself watching police procedurals on the telly. As such, John damn well knew better than to give voice to anything that smacked of an opinion. It was time for subtlety.

"Well, the human body's a delicate system," he began, but never did finish because Sherlock Holmes had *had* it. Words, words, so many words—and none of them *his*.

"Enough with the prevarications! Either you know or you don't and it's clear you don't. Now if they'd let me into the crime scene for ninety seconds..." Sherlock lifted his chin, raised his voice, the very opposite of subtle, "...sixty! Sixty seconds with that body and I'll tell you if it's..." Here Sherlock dropped his voice, leaned toward the microphone, and insinuated a thousand dread things with one word: *"...murder."*

John Watson, ex-surgeon, ex-army officer, owner of both a gun and a cranky temper when pushed, glowered again on general principle. Because John's used to attention-seekers, bullshit, and problem children. As such he knew beside him stood all three.

John's got one way of dealing with attention seekers: Deny them the boon they seek.

He has two ways of managing bullshit: Ignore it or sling

it back.

He's got three ways of coping with problem children: Call their parents, give them a lolly, or act like a bigger baby himself.

Which is why John Watson turned his back on the microphone, the TV camera, and most of his own dignity and, jutting his chin at the lanky annoyance he said, *"What* the *hell* did you say mister...mister...?"

"Holmes," supplied the reporter, who'd actively ignored the man at half a dozen crime scenes in as many months. "Sherlock."

John nodded his thanks, took a step toward the man and hissed, "Listen Holmes Sherlock—"

"Sherlock Holmes," corrected Sherlock Holmes, stepping back.

"Look, I don't care if you're the damn Queen Mother damn it," John yelled, stomping forward. "I'll tell you what you are—"

The reporter glanced at her camerawoman, who was already trotting after the men as they traded invective. Though the reporter only heard, "painfully obvious," "brass-plated fool" and "sexually repressed" it turned out that not only did her mic pick up their entire argument, but all the audio after, when Sherlock Holmes, relentlessly herded backward by a cranky tank of a doctor, tripped across the police tape, landed beside the corpse—and discovered the murder weapon.

*

John sold "To Bee or Not to Bee," to *OK!* magazine whilst *Hello* snatched up "Bee-Ware." He wrote a peer-reviewed paper for the *Journal of Histometrics* called "On Recognition of Inconspicuous Inflammatory Response," and later was attributed with single-handedly reviving the magazine serial with a series of stories written for the *New Yorker,* called "The Beekeeper Murders."

John might well have made hay (or honey) for quite awhile from Sherlock Holmes' first successful case, but after ITV ran that lifestyle piece (using the reporter's park footage) where John explained how Sherlock had recognised the bee sting—

> "—an *applied* bee sting remember, to the allergic victim's earlobe. It looked like a slightly inflamed piercing and as Mr. Costa had eighteen other piercings it could have been easily overlooked. But of course Sherlock noticed—"

—they ended up working a case involving the MI5 (still classified), and one for the heiress of a prophylactic fortune.

But first they have to settle into the new flat on Baker Street, a process made endless by Sherlock's endless collection of macabre ephemera.

It's fine, in the meantime John's working on a promising little number for the "Brew Master" case that he's sold to *Fermenter's Monthly* and thinks he'll title "The Valley of Beer."

SH

Trial By Hudson

221B Baker Street — 1880

"Thank you madam," said Arthur Prosper, tipping his hat.

"You're welcome sir. As you'd expect, there have been a great many applicants for the suite. If you're selected, we will contact you later in the week. Good day."

Arthur Prosper tipped his hat again, smiled broadly, and bowed himself out of the flat.

Mrs. Hudson listened as Mr. Prosper descended the seventeen steps to the ground floor. She tilted her head until she heard the front door open, then latch closed. She walked to the window and watched Mr. Prosper cross Baker Street. When the gentleman with the broad smile, the quiet nature, and the fine suit turned and saw her standing sentinel, he tipped his hat again.

Mrs. Hudson nodded, watched Mr. Prosper hail and board a cab. When he twiddled his fingers in a friendly fashion she answered in kind. And only once the hansom had turned onto Marylebone Street, did Mrs. Hudson step over to the sitting room fire, carefully place Mr. Prosper's references into the flames, and watch them burn.

As the final slip of paper curled into pretty ash, Mrs. Hudson tutted to herself. She was going to have to sweep out the firebox before night's end. There was really quite a lot of ash in there now.

If you had asked Mrs. Hudson—she does have a Christian name, but everyone calls her Mrs. Hudson; even her long-gone husband called her Mrs. Hudson—why she didn't want a gentle-natured widower as her lodger, Mrs. Hudson could not have told you. If you pressed and asked again, she'd have murmured, "Like seeks like, I would imagine." If you'd insisted on clarification, Mrs. Hudson would have stood perfectly still and looked you in the eye until you withered like ash and blew away. So to speak.

That was neither here nor there. The next gentleman was due in ten minutes and so Mrs. Hudson bustled about, fanning guttering flames, and plumping sofa pillows until everything looked just so.

She then took a seat, and as she waited, Mrs. Hudson admired the comfortable space she had made. She was very fond of suite B. It was really rather her favourite, with its tall hurricane lamps, broad firebox, the sturdy mantel that played host to Christmas holly come December, and her own tulips in spring.

She'd lived with Mr. Hudson in these rooms when they were first married. When he'd gone she did not need so much space and now enjoyed the much snugger comforts of suite A.

The downstairs bell rang. Mrs. Hudson walked to the flat's window, opened it, spotted a man below. "Come on up."

It didn't take long for the gentleman to ascend, his step spritely, solid, yet not over-loud. That was good. She favoured a man who inhabited his space, who was *there,* so to speak, but wasn't keen on one who inhabited *her* space, who felt the need to trudge heavy on the stair, as if each and every time taking possession of the place.

There was a knock on the door, two taps that did not belabour the whole point of knocking. Mrs. Hudson has rented her rooms to many people over many years, has heard a symphony of knocks, from the rat-tat-tat of the nervous, to the impatient thud of the demanding. This knock matched the man's stride: Balanced. Steady. *Right.*

"Come in."

The gentleman entered, his hat already removed, his coat still buttoned, his smile friendly but not fawning.

"You can hang your coat and hat just there, it's chilly today so I've had the fire going all afternoon. That's lovely, do take a seat."

The man did all he was bid, alert eyes darting around.

"Tea?"

"Thank you. A dash of milk please."

Mrs. Hudson poured, handed the gentleman his cup. "First impressions?" she asked.

Though surprised at the question, the gentleman answered. "Several." He tilted his head. "You must favour tea over coffee for you make a perfect brew; I've only ever known tea lovers to get the strength exactly right." Another sip. "You or your lodger have been to Egypt. I recognise the style of rug and there are items on that far wall I've never seen west of Alexandria." Another sip, a demure pause.

"Speak freely."

A longer pause to be sure, and then, "You have the patience of a saint. Though the wallpaper is lovely, I haven't seen a design which includes a VR done in...bullet holes is it? And though I too tend to put my post on the mantel, I find my Gray's Anatomy serves a bit better to keep it there than a jackknife. And perhaps the less said about the acid stains on this fine rug the better."

The landlady of 221 Baker Street smiled. It was a slow smile, stealthy. It crept from lips to crinkled nose to plumped cheeks. Though she had made her mind up at John Watson's second knock, it was good to have more facts to support an initial conclusion.

"Are you interested then, Dr. Watson?"

"Oh very."

"Wonderful. Now it's just left for you to meet your fellow lodger, who should be home—"

"—at any minute?" The door swung wide, letting in a gust of cold air, a laugh, and a tall man. "Good evening!"

"Mr. Holmes, I've told you that you're to climb those stairs like a civilised human being, not sneak up like a cat."

Holmes bustled in, dumping a stack of papers willy-nilly across the dining table, draping his coat on a chair back. "At least you didn't say mouse." Holmes turned to Watson. "Mrs. Hudson is ever on about how much *cheese* I eat. I find that when the hours are crowded, the clues mounting, the solution very nearly near...well, nothing suits like a bit of cheese and bread, a pipe and some coffee. I could go for days on just that."

"A good pipe and a few periodicals are my addictions. I tend to be a lazy sort. John Watson, Mr. Holmes."

Holmes took Watson's hand, "Mrs. Hudson approves of you doctor, she served you tea in her best cups. I only rate second best."

"Fewer bullet holes or less spilled acid might give you the boon you seek."

"Oh then I'll take second best every day and leave you to be the responsible lodger. Would you mind?"

"Will I be well-compensated?"

"Very, if an occasional mystery and a bit of adventure suffice."

Mrs. Hudson plumped a pillow. She finger-dusted the mantel. She pretended to straighten the mirror. She caught her own grin in it and gave herself a pinch.

"Well gentlemen, I'll be on my way. Dr. Watson, rent is due the middle of each month, breakfast is at seven. I expect all of my lodgers to keep civil hours, never shoot the walls, and under no circumstances are the periodicals to grow into tottering stacks that collect dust and empty cups."

Mrs. Hudson picked an empty tea cup from an unstable pile of *Dr. Bell's Illustrated Guide to Autopsy* and winked at the good doctor.

As she closed the door behind her, Mrs. Hudson heard Sherlock Holmes say, "Speaking of mysteries, I've brought home a few fingers from a crime scene and it appears they have no fingerprints. Would you mind taking a look?"

Mrs. Hudson glided down an old flight of seventeen steps, knowing after long years where each squeak lived and how to avoid them, so she heard Watson's reply. "Good gracious, bring them here!"

Yes indeed, like finds like. Mrs. Hudson knows this. Mrs. Hudson knows a lot of things.

SH

The Moment Before I Am Powerful

* Brighton Beach, Sussex — 1864

or

* Brighton Beach, Sussex — 1984

For the longest time little things were enough.

When you are very smart but also very small, getting on your belly in the grass brings you up close with the wonder of ant regiments and caterpillar excursions. And there on your belly you learn that these smallest of creatures contain within their intrepid souls life and will and worlds, and when you're smart but still so very small, just such things can be enough to busy your whirring mind, fascinating you from a summer morning right on through to tea time.

Yes, for the longest time little things were enough for Sherlock Holmes, but little boys grow older, they always do, and so he turned seven, then eight, and by the time he was nine the conflagration of his own brilliance was already blazing bright behind curious eyes and for too many years that burning brilliance turned every possible friendship to ash.

*

For the longest time he watched the things that people do.

When you're young and a little bit empathetic and maybe sometimes a bit too serious in between the times you're not, you'll see the bad things that people do, the hurts they give with words, yes, but you'll discover that unlike other little boys, you also see the stranger hurts, the cigarette burns where such burns ought never to be, you see bruises blooming on delicate flesh, and once in a great while you hear shouts and you don't know what it is you know but you really wish you didn't know it.

Yes, for the longest time John Watson saw things his young mind couldn't understand and then when he was nine, and ten, and eleven he got it, all of it, knew exactly what those strange hurts signified and somewhere down deep he wanted to fix what needed mending but John didn't know how, not for too many years.

*

The day your life changes is usually a pretty regular day.

That's because such days tend to be bare of banners, quiet on the watch-this-space communiqués. You often only know your life has changed in the time after, when seeds take root and beg for water, and suddenly you realise you know more, want more, have, need, and see more.

The day John and Sherlock met, one was a little bit older than the other, though it was hard to tell which since one was tall and one was not. The autumn day John Watson met Sherlock Holmes, one was a teenager and one soon would be, and one was in a moody strop, and the other was crying.

Sat alone in a quiet beach cove Sherlock, already well on his way to disregarding everything the great unwashed *They* would teach him, rested his temple on raised up knees and wept for the pain in his arm. He didn't care if anyone saw and thought less of him because *They* already did anyway, and besides it hurt so much, his arm, but that wasn't the only place that hurt.

"Are you all right?"

Sherlock should have on instinct looked up but he didn't. Instead he watched the drip drip drip of his blood into the wet sand. At first the damp earth wouldn't take each fresh drop, already satiated with salt water, and then the gore eventually sank in and the low tide washed up, just tickling toes and bum and taking away evidence until the next drops.

Walking alone down the beach John had known something was wrong from a dozen metres distant, though he couldn't have told you how he knew except it was obvious…a boy alone on a beach, one arm wrapped around his legs, the tide soaking into his trousers, his shirt tails and yes, actually, John *could* tell you what told him: That shirt. The fact that before he could see the blood he could see one sleeve rolled up high and the other buttoned down tight.

When he was close enough to see why he wasn't surprised.

"That's too deep," he said, kneeling in front of Sherlock, looking into his eyes. "It's not going to stop bleeding unless you wrap it."

At this Sherlock finally raised his head and looked at the boy looking at him. He said, "Good," and lay his temple back down on his knees.

The cut bled fresh with every beat of Sherlock's heart and for long moments they both watched because blood is beautiful, there's no denying that, it's the richest gem-red, it moves fat and slow like syrup, and so they stared at it jaw-dropped, as people have done before uncommon and beautiful things ever since there were people.

"Did you do this to yourself?"

Sherlock blinked at the blood meandering pretty, thinking, honestly, for the love of god thinking for a moment that the blood had spoken to him, and that's probably why he just said the first word that came to him (actually he does that a lot, because even his well-considered words are usually the wrong ones so what was the point?), "Yes."

John had already seen cigarette burns and bruises and the other awful things people do to themselves and each other so he wasn't surprised by Sherlock's answer, and it would be another dozen or so years before he learned just how to talk to people so wounded within that the only way they could cope was to wear their wounds without.

"I'm going to wrap my shirt around it all right?"

Sherlock again looked at the boy in front of him, saw his straight-backed posture (pride), his unblinking attention (focus), his frown (worry), his wide eyes (hope), his hands hovering (to help), his reticence to touch until permission was granted (the rareness of grace and kindness and something more).

And Sherlock smiled and nodded and held out his arm.

John wrapped that thin arm up in his own shirt and never even flinched when the cold sea water splashed up on his now-bare back.

After a time Sherlock stopped bleeding. After a time John said, "All right." And after a time the boys went their separate ways.

Sherlock would go on to cut himself again though the frequency would soon lessen, legacy of the seed that took root that day when he finally saw how much he could see, and thought, "Maybe I can look, maybe I can tell people what they miss..." It was a seed of deduction planted, a seed of...detection.

They never did ask one another's names and it'd be more than twenty years before they would meet again—without knowing it *was* again—but that was fine.

In that time John would go on to find the whole damned world a confusing place, he'd see too many wounds that people wouldn't let him help heal, and he'd get annoyed and sad and frustrated. But that day on the beach a seed was planted, a seed to set things right, a seed...doctorly.

These were small seeds in young boys and they wouldn't flower for awhile so yes, overall, that life-changing day on a Brighton beach, that moment before they were powerful? It was a pretty regular day really.

Until the day it wasn't.

SH

Acknowledgements

Writers have more damn ideas than they know what to do with.

However.

Sometimes a writer strolls around their Holmesian brain attic, looks at all those fine ideas and thinks...*meh.*

It's not that the ideas aren't good, it's just that they're *your* ideas. They're your *style* of idea, they're the way you think. They're not surprising, they're not outside your mental box. When I feel *meh,* that's when I jump into the social media pond and splash around, calling plaintively, "Story prompts? Please? Anyone?" If I'm lucky, people reply.

I am *very* lucky.

Yes, a lot of these stories were prompted by Arthur Conan Doyle's flawless canon. Many more were prompted by my own idea about the characters. And many others, well they were prompted by friends and family and roaming Samaritans answering my call, responding with, "Well okay, what if they...?"

Here's where I give credit to those wonderful people and to all the people whose prompts I didn't have time to use...your encouragement and your 'what ifs' are like oxygen. Thank you for helping me breathe.

However.

First and foremost I want to take a moment to offer frankincense and myrrh and glittering dancing boys to my friends Isabelle and Verity. Each read every story here and, by sharing the gift of their patience and ideas, they made every story better. Forget the herbs, dear friends, you deserve unicorns, my eternal gratitude, and your heart's desire. And those dancing boys. Thank you.

Now, to thank the following people for their wonderful story prompts.

The Diogenes Diversion came about because my friend Sayaka really wanted Sherlock and Mycroft looking out the window of the Diogenes Club, deducing people, as they did in *The Greek Interpreter*. Of course you'd wonder then, what would they make of John Watson?

Blood Will Tell. In canon Watson falls ill with enteric fever—also known as typhoid fever—and becomes weak, emaciated, and, as is signature with such fever, a bit out of his mind. Take that, add SarahCat1717's suggestion that they meet in jail, and John Watson and I decided he was due to get all his bad luck done at once. Then find a bit of good luck, going by the unusual name of Sherlock Holmes.

Follow That Cab! was a must-have story. I can't tell you how many people have wanted them to meet in a cab, though I can mention that a few who prompted me with the idea included my brother Bobby, as well as Tellmemore90 and RoseGlass.

You and What Army? In the United States joining the military is often seen as a solution for problematic young adults. So after GWBear said, "What about Sherlock in the military?" I wondered what a problematic young Sherlock Holmes would think of that.

Shaggy Dog Story exists because my mum Diane loves cats and cockatiels and parrots and, lucky for me, she loves dogs too—I say lucky because I'm not sure what I would have done if she'd suggested Watson and Holmes meet due to a bird.

Fortunately she said dog and, of course, the good dog Toby had something to say about that.

The Bees'...Elbows was the result of my husband Tony sharing the idea of two men dancing a code, and of Sherlock Holmes deciphering that code. It was just a matter of moments to realise that that code would buzz with the wisdom of bees.

The Freaks, like the entire book, exists because of Amity Who. She wondered what would happen if Holmes and Watson "Met in danger?" What would happen was that each man would bring to the situation his own gifts—and they would paraphrase the judge-and-jury exchange from *The Adventure of the Abbey Grange.*

A Regular Day, Like Any Other Day, Only More So. Real life is full of momentous moments only recognised in hindsight, and I like the idea that it'd be that way for John Watson and Sherlock Holmes. What made this story far more lively was A-Cumberbatch-of-Cookies wondering if at some point the men might carry identical satchels—with decidedly different contents.

Expletive Blasphemy Obscenity is the extremely profane response to my wonderful beekeeping friend Britt, who wondered if John and Sherlock could meet in St. Bart's morgue. Thank you Britt.

Make Love, Not... Theorclair wondered if John and Sherlock could meet before the good doctor goes to Afghanistan. My first thought was, "I wonder how..." and then it was obvious.

Chamber of Horrors came about during a lunch date with Alexina Gannon who, after learning what I was writing, said very simply and quite brilliantly, "Well what if they met in a wax works?"

Criminal Class is the result of my friend, and jaw-droppingly prolific writer, Narrelle Harris, wanting to know what would happen if John and Sherlock met "in the paddy wagon." It's really a given that two men who so regularly take the law into their own hands would end up with jail time.

Stop. Over. Mithen was thinking deep thoughts as she endured a seven hour airport stop over. As we were conversing about the boredom of waiting, boredom naturally turned our minds to Holmes and those thoughts became Holmes and Watson, waiting…and having their own deep thoughts.

A Close Shave was the first story I wrote for this collection and Kimber was the inspiration for that, marvelously suggesting that our dear Holmes and Watson meet as each received a professional shave and trim.

Stiff Upper Lip came about because Verity Burns is a writer of fantastic Sherlock Holmes mystery stories. Apropos of absolutely nothing she one day said to me, "Sherlock has some case or other, involving lipstick. Off you go." And I did. Also, since I'm laying blame—uh, offering thanks—Verity is also the reason for *The Cold Shoulder,* in that she left the entirely wrong almost-empty latte cup on our cafe table, a trauma from which I still haven't recovered.

The Father is Child to the Man was the result of Ticopi wondering if I'd done a very young version of Watson and Holmes, and though I had just written *The Moment Before I Am Powerful,* it seemed there was more to tell about these men as boys.

If Convenient. Something most lovers of Arthur Conan Doyle's stories appreciate is their variety. Sometimes a case hinges on a murder, others times on misunderstandings. Or in the case of this story and PhoenixDragon's prompt, the day they met hinged on the surreal tragedy of a car accident.

Loser Takes All is the result of my friends Sayaka and Valerie believing Watson and Holmes needed to meet at the Criterion restaurant, where originally Stamford ran across Watson fresh home from the war. It is clear that Sayaka and Valerie were correct.

The Moment Before I Am Powerful was the title of a series of monologues staged by London's Trafalgar Studios, and the title still haunts me. It's so evocative of beginning, of that tenterhook-and-tiptoe moment before *becoming.* Take that, combine it with both my father Robert and Eternal Cat Moon wondering about John Watson and Sherlock Holmes meeting when they were children, and the result was this story.

Finally, at the end of these acknowledgements, I'd like to acknowledge a woman who never lived but who has changed my life in ways I couldn't imagine: Thank you, Atlin Merrick.

Also from MX Publishing

MX Publishing is the world's largest specialist Sherlock Holmes publisher, with over a hundred titles and fifty authors creating the latest in Sherlock Holmes fiction and non-fiction.

From traditional short stories and novels to travel guides and quiz books, MX Publishing cater for all Holmes fans.

The collection includes leading titles such as *Benedict Cumberbatch In Transition* and *The Norwood Author* which won the 2011 Howlett Award (Sherlock Holmes Book of the Year).

MX Publishing also has one of the largest communities of Holmes fans on Facebook with regular contributions from dozens of authors.

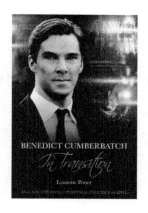

www.mxpublishing.com

Also from MX Publishing

Sherlock Holmes Short Story Collections

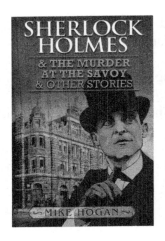 

Sherlock Holmes and the Murder at the Savoy

Sherlock Holmes and the Skull of Kohada Koheiji

Look out for the new novel from Mike Hogan
– *The Scottish Question.*

Also from MX Publishing

  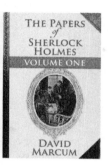

Our bestselling books are our short story collections;

'Lost Stories of Sherlock Holmes' , 'The Outstanding Mysteries of Sherlock Holmes', The Papers of Sherlock Holmes Volume 1 and 2, 'Untold Adventures of Sherlock Holmes' (and the sequel 'Studies in Legacy) and 'Sherlock Holmes in Pursuit', 'The Cotswold Werewolf and Other Stories of Sherlock Holmes' – and many more……

  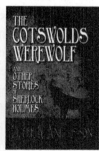

www.mxpublishing.com

Also from MX Publishing

"Phil Growick's, 'The Secret Journal of Dr Watson', is an adventure which takes place in the latter part of Holmes and Watson's lives. They are entrusted by HM Government (although not officially) and the King no less to undertake a rescue mission to save the Romanovs, Russia's Royal family from a grisly end at the hand of the Bolsheviks. There is a wealth of detail in the story but not so much as would detract us from the enjoyment of the story. Espionage, counter-espionage, the ace of spies himself, double-agents, double-crossers...all these flit across the pages in a realistic and exciting way. All the characters are extremely well-drawn and Mr Growick, most importantly, does not falter with a very good ear for Holmesian dialogue indeed. Highly recommended. A five-star effort."
The Baker Street Society

www.mxpublishing.com

Links

MX Publishing are proud to support the Save Undershaw campaign – the campaign to save and restore Sir Arthur Conan Doyle's former home. Undershaw is where he brought Sherlock Holmes back to life, and should be preserved for future generations of Holmes fans.

SaveUndershaw
www.saveundershaw.com

Sherlockology
www.sherlockology.com

MX Publishing
www.mxpublishing.com

You can read more about Sir Arthur Conan Doyle and Undershaw in Alistair Duncan's book (share of royalties to the Undershaw Preservation Trust) – *An Entirely New Country* and in the amazing compilations *Sherlock's Home – The Empty House* and the new book *Two, To One, Be* (all royalties to the Trust).

CPSIA information can be obtained at www.ICGtesting.com
Printed in the USA
BVOW06s0225051115

425636BV00008B/54/P